A Taste for Treason

ORA MENDELS

A Taste for Treason

A NOVEL

S.P.i. BOOKS

A division of Shapolsky Publishers, Inc.

A Taste for Treason

S.P.I. BOOKS
A division of Shapolsky Publishers, Inc.

Previously published in hardcover by Carol Publishing Group.

ISBN 1-56171-197-7

For any additional information, contact:

S.P.I. BOOKS/Shapolsky Publishers, Inc.
136 West 22nd Street
New York, NY 10011
212/633-2022 / FAX 212/633-2123

Manufactured in the United States of America

10 9 8 7 6 5 4 3 2 1

For Joe again, of course,
And for Gilla, Charles and David

Wrapped in a sheet, the body was suspended by rope from the curved arm of a cedar tree. The village mosque, its white paint pitted and peeled by wind and drifting sand, faced it across a small square. No mourners had watched in the grit-clogged air; only villagers and executioners had shared the moment, silent but for a hoarse communal cry as the head jerked forward and the sheet rippled with the final tremor. The only parts of the body left exposed were gnarled brown feet, with criss-crossed stripes from thonged sandals marked upon them like scars.

The crowd that had gathered to observe the hanging faded back into the scrub beyond the trees, sheltered from the piercing sun of early autumn. Once during the afternoon, two boys with a few sheep sauntered across the square. The boys averted their eyes from the body, but one of the sheep butted its head against the legs and for a long time afterward the corpse swayed gently, the rope creaking.

By nightfall the witnesses returned, but they did not tamper with the body, ripening like the carcass of a diseased donkey. It hung opposite the mosque for the full span of a day and night before anyone dared to cut it down. When the sheet was pulled away no one in the village recognized the swollen features of the corpse, but that was to be expected. The message was not intended for them.

ONE

The day after the execution the man who thought of himself as Gershom waited in a small house on a hill near Beirut, overlooking the sea. It was one of very few houses in the neighborhood that was not badly damaged. One wall was scarred by shells and a corner of the roof had been torn off and pinned back, but otherwise it stood oddly intact among the rubble and chalky dirt around it.

Gershom pulled a cot over to the window and lay on his side, propped on an elbow, staring down at the ocean through the slits between the shutters. Sunlight glinted across the surface of the sea, cutting beneath, shooting down. It was the same sea whose waves he'd jumped when he was growing up, the same glittering backdrop for community picnics upon the beach, the same tidal changes, the same seasonal variations, the same, the same. Except that now he was almost a hundred kilometers further north. Constant, like the ocean, he waited to learn if he had been discovered, exposed at last.

To contain his fear, he rehearsed the rituals that had helped him at the beginning, twenty years before. Then, hovering between sleep and waking, needing to identify himself, he had constructed billboards, keys to the mind as intimate as the

11

sensitive birthmark high on his left inner thigh. He recited the names of his brothers, the ones he barely knew, and then the names of his other brothers, whom he had never even seen. The place where he had learned his everyday language, and then the place where he now taught his own. The touch of the first girl he had loved, the names of the events between then and the woman who shared his life now.

Gershom hadn't needed the ritual signposts for a long time. He knew who he was. And why. He'd had a lot of practice. But now he needed them all again. He recognized his swollen terror as different from the fears he lived with always, the ones woven into him, ligaments laced through his body. Fear of loneliness, fear of lost contact, fear of torture, fear of annihilation. He needed these to live. They were his truest weapons.

Now, watching Akman walk slowly up the path from the sea toward him, he identified this fear as the same one he had begun with: terror that he would betray himself, that he would no longer be able to distinguish between what he was and what he had become. Back to the beginning, he thought, flexing long brown fingers as he went to open the door for Akman.

His two selves measured the implications of Akman's wide grin, slicing between curling black beard and mustache, quickly subdued.

"Well, Tewfik," he said, "you're the first here?"

Gershom nodded, swallowed.

"How did it go?" he asked.

"It went well," said Akman solemnly. He walked over to the window and peered between the slats. "I was right."

It was normal to be curious. Wasn't it? Wasn't it? But before Gershom could choose which question to ask, Akman had swung around from the window.

"Driving south every week. Unhindered. No one stopped him. No one—army, Syrians, Shiites, our boys, gangs, no one. Free passage south, driving Hanouri's Mercedes everywhere. No one dared to stop the millionaire's car. No one wanted to. This one had money for the whores on Hamra, gambling in Roache, drinking at the Alexandre, up and down the Corniche. It had to be him. I was right."

"Did you..." Gershom cleared his throat. "Did you...?"

"I got him, my friend. Yes, I took him out."

Akman whirled exuberantly and clapped Gershom on the shoulder.

"Tewfik," he bragged, "I stopped the leak. I was right. I took two boys from the training camp at Tripoli and followed him south. I was so certain, I didn't want to wait for him to get another message out, so I forced him off the road. I was right. The Israelis won't get this one." He slapped his chest. Paper crackled in the black denim pocket. "We get this one."

"What did you do with him?"

"I hung him from a tree near Sidon. Good training for the boys. I'm teaching the Israelis a lesson, too."

Gershom nodded

"Did you question him?"

"Yes, he knew nothing. A courier, that's all."

"How do you know?"

"Ah, Tewfik, I took him apart. I know. The message is going to show us the traitor. The boys will play some games with their computers while you're in Rome. When you come home we'll know."

"Yes, we will," said Gershom. He had never seen the courier, but he saw the message in his mind as clearly as when he wrote it.

"They know too much, the Israelis," Akman said slowly, the enthusiasm draining from his face, leaving it pasty above the beard. "All the time they keep catching our boys, one, then another, as soon as they get in there. The only way..." He stopped abruptly.

"Yes?" Gershom urged quietly.

But Akman wouldn't go on. His eyes shifted away from Gershom. He flopped down on the cot and stared out to sea. Gershom didn't press him. He understood that Akman suspected that the message might have been sent by one of the five

13

of them. It wasn't the kind of observation that could be made comfortably to a comrade of many years, a brother in arms. Gershom joined Akman at the window, waiting for the others. They would hear Akman's report together. When the message was decoded it would confirm that there was a traitor among them. They were the only five people on earth who knew that Tewfik Mahmoud and Walid Toucan were going to Rome to meet an American.

No message came from Beirut.

As soon as he learned about the hanging in the village north of Sidon, Dan Shemtov understood that Gershom had been sentenced to death. He calculated that it would take a week, two at most, to break the code; the message to him, whatever it was, could lead them to his man.

Standing near the window of the second-floor room high on a hill in Jerusalem, he slid a counter smoothly across the patterned table, nine spaces ahead, exposed on all sides. His index finger tapped it lightly. Early autumn light penetrated the jeweled mosaic chips, their colors glowing against the marble surface of the backgammon table. Even against a weak adversary, even against a novice, the mathematical odds weren't very good, but he left the counter where it was, moving closer to the window and the luminous hills beyond.

The odds that he could save Operation Gershom weren't very good either. Shemtov closed his eyes against the construction crews on the slopes opposite and reminded himself that he hadn't liked the odds at the outset, twenty years before, when he created Gershom in a desperate gamble by turning a brave, independent paratrooper into a Palestinian refugee. Eliahu Golan, outstanding cadet of his officers' class, transformed by Shemtov's ingenious wizardry, his surgical anticipation of priorities, into a homeless, destitute survivor, an outcast struggling to tug life from destruction and loss.

Who knew then, twenty years before, what Tewfik Mahmoud would become? Shemtov certainly didn't and neither did Eliahu, who went into the wilderness armed with nothing but patriotic idealism, abundant language skills, compulsive attention to detail. And his autonomy. Who expected that Tewfik Mahmoud would become a confidant of terrorists, a sage to revolutionaries, a counselor to bickering parties? Who knew that he would rise so high in the esteem of his people that he would be entrusted with the responsibilities of the Invasion Committee, one of only five to direct the infiltration of Palestinians back into Israel to prepare for power to change hands? Neither Shemtov nor Eliahu ever dreamed that Tewfik Mahmoud would accomplish all this. But because he had, Operation Gershom had produced a yield so dazzling that Shemtov had to devise a sleight of hand to try to protect it now. It seemed impossible.

In any case, whatever became of the operation that had for so long and so reliably delivered Palestinian plans to Israel's surreptitious inspection, Shemtov had to save Gershom, whom he had conjured from the conversion of Eliahu Golan into Tewfik Mahmoud. It went beyond Gershom's loyal and lonely years, the risks gallantly averted, the devious, secretive patterns of constant vigilance, the isolation at the core of his life. Shemtov had to extricate Gershom because he was his own creation, more than any son could ever be, riveted to him as indissolubly as his own bone and tissue.

By the time Uri arrived, summoned from Tel Aviv, Shemtov had defined a strategy. Although it was riddled with unpredictable holes, he couldn't risk delay. Spare, compact, contained, he sat behind his orderly desk, motioning Uri to an armchair at the side.

"What do you know about Operation Gershom?" he asked Uri, whose eyes widened at the name. He shrugged.

"Nothing. Except that it's so secret it's never mentioned. It's on the books as a title, followed by 'Shemtov only.' Not another word that I know of, even at H.Q."

Shemtov nodded and drummed his fingers on the desktop.

"Right. It's my case. I began it twenty years ago. When my predecessor retired from this office, I brought it with me. Even my support people don't know it all." He folded his hands together. "That hanging, north of Sidon. You heard about that?"

"Yes, of course."

"That wasn't the usual factional murder. That man was hung in public to send us a message."

"Who was he?"

"One of Gershom's messengers."

Uri leaned forward and stared at Shemtov.

"You mean—"

"Gershom is the code name of our agent as well as the name of the operation. 'I have been a stranger in a foreign land,' that's what it means, of course. I chose the name when he penetrated Fatah after the Six-Day War. Gershom has been in place for twenty years. He's grown in the job, you might say. He's on the Invasion Committee, right in the center of their operations."

"It's unbelievable. You—you're serious?" When Shemtov raised sparse gray eyebrows so high that his eyes bulged, Uri took a deep breath. "No one's ever lasted so long."

"He's not going to last much longer unless we do something very clever very quickly."

"He's in danger?"

"Very grave danger. He's within days of being exposed." Shemtov looked at Uri. "Imagine what they'll do to him if he is." He began to drum his fingertips on the desktop again.

"I'm going to stage a diversion. That's where you come in."

"How? My desk is Europe, anyway."

"To begin with, I need an agent, exactly the right one. The best man for this job is one of yours. Bring Benjamin Landau home."

"But you rejected the proposal."

"I know I did. That was before. Now, I don't care. I must have him. He's the man I need. Trade the terrorists for him. We'll catch up with them later."

"But Landau will hardly be in any kind of shape for an urgent—"

"He'll be in exactly the shape we need. Bring Landau in, if you please. I must have him at once."

Shemtov stood up, looking beyond Uri to the trucks delivering lumber to the crews on the slopes. How many people would be settled there in a few more weeks, another living fortress around the city?

"And, Uri, make sure the papers and television know when he's landing."

He turned away to look for some papers on a shelf, so he didn't see Uri's jaw tighten or his eyes widen. He didn't need to see Uri's disapproval. He knew all about it.

TWO

"I was expendable, wasn't I?" Benjamin Landau kicked the door closed behind him.

Uri was standing in front of his desk, hand outstretched. "Welcome home, Ben. It's good to have you back."

"Is it?" He hesitated, then shook hands briefly. He looked over Uri's head to the street below, deserted but for two soldiers leaning against a stone wall opposite, Uzi barrels glinting in the late-afternoon sunlight.

"I'm sorry I couldn't meet you at the airport. I asked your family not to go. It wouldn't have been good. Were there a lot of reporters?"

"Enough. There'll be more front-page photographs, in case everyone anywhere forgot about me."

Ben lowered his big frame into the only armchair in the room. Dark eyes angry under raised, heavy brows, he looked at Uri.

"Six months in a French prison."

"But we got you out."

"How kind, considering you put me there in the first place."

"Ben, that's not true. Naturally you're tired after the flight and—"

"What happened, then? Tell me." His voice was rough. His

chafed hands gripped the arms of the chair as he leaned forward. "I'm entitled to know. I went on a mission that turned out to be something else." His voice cracked, and he blinked several times, eyes narrowing.

"Ben, listen. We got the stuff. It was tough but worth it." Uri sat on the edge of the desk. "We substituted our men for the Iraqis and flew their plane out of Orly with all the launchers and discs for their Mirage missiles on board. We prevented France from supplying them. We stopped Iraq from getting them. And we have them for ourselves. It's a stupendous achievement. We couldn't have done it without you, Ben."

"I was a diversion. You made me the pawn."

He stood up stiffly. He was too big for the room, broad shoulders and heavy dark head looming over Uri on the edge of the battered desktop.

"How could you do this to me after all these years?"

"Look," Uri said quietly, moving into the shadows behind the desk, "we had to divert suspicion to get the stuff out."

Benjamin stepped forward again, filling the space in the little office with his sense of betrayal and his exhaustion.

"You sent me to Paris to look into the Iraqi order for the launchers. They were still being manufactured, you told me. I used a valuable local asset in the factory. We made inquiries, we poked about. I considered alternatives, hijacking, sabotage. The next thing I know, my man is dead from gunshot and I'm on trial for espionage, with my face on the front page of every newspaper in Europe and beyond."

"While they were chasing down your man and arresting you for spying, our boys grabbed a plane and millions of dollars' worth of equipment from Iraq and brought them home, Ben."

"You abandoned me. I was nothing to you. My cover was blown, my man killed. And then six months in a stinking prison before you could find something to trade for me."

"I understand how you feel."

"Like hell you understand. Did you ever try it? It's a jungle, swarming with wild animals, gnawing off bits of space. It's filthy. It's brutal. They'll cut a slice in your belly for a smoke. You sink so low you're crawling in slime. Diseased slime. Don't tell me you understand."

"I see you're very tired."

"I'm more than tired," Benjamin shouted. "I'm forty-five years old and I've served my country all my life. More than twenty years in this Service." He paused, blinking away images of the San Fernando district of Buenos Aires, the docks of Cherbourg, an exploding automobile in the streets of Beirut. Rubbing his damaged hands together, he stared at Uri.

"Now I'm blown. You've used me up, Uri. I've got no more left. I want to go home and see my family and blank out for a bit. Then I'm going to look for another way to live."

"Ben, I'm sorry to have to tell you that Kate's taken the children back to the United States." Uri spoke very quietly. Ben's eyes narrowed and he blinked again.

"You mean a visit? To her family?"

"I think...I think more than a visit. She took your arrest very hard. A couple of weeks ago she came to see me. She said she'd given Israel as much as she was going to and she wouldn't offer up her children."

"I see." He turned away, kicking out suddenly at a yellowing crack low on the wall; sickly plaster plopped onto the floor.

"I'm sorry."

"You're sorry? My life's ruined and you're sorry. I'd like to—"

"Ben, your parents will know the details."

"I suppose so."

"Why don't you go and see them, spend a couple of days? I'll have someone drive you up. And then come back, Ben. Sometime next week, please."

"To resign, Uri. Finish it off and all that."

"All that, yes."

The chicken coops smelled as foul as they always had. Even the latrines in the French prison had not inured him to this hot stench. He walked by quickly, waving at a familiar face checking thermometers behind glass. There were other places he wanted to see.

Benjamin's brief reunion with his parents the night before and then the comfort of the guest house, hot water and clean sheets hadn't yielded the tranquil sleep he'd missed since long before Paris; the night left him restless, angry, resentful. The subdued ache from the intestinal infection he'd endured in prison, the hot burning itch on his hands, pervasive stiffness and flawed joint articulation troubled him less than the bleakness of betrayal, his loss of trust.

It hadn't taken him long after his arrest to realize that he'd been a decoy, set up by his own people, after all his unswerving years, all his successful missions. He'd had six months to try to find reasons why they might have been justified; he hadn't found any. The more he looked for ways to excuse his masters, the more convincingly he proved their cynicism.

Now, here in the valley where he was born, he was determined to cut loose, somehow, from the constraints of his life. He had lost the secure precepts of his childhood. They had failed him. They had not prepared him for the change of rules in the middle of the game. As a child, Benjamin had automatically accepted that what was good for Israel was good for him personally, the way he took for granted his meals with the other settlement children in the communal dining room. Just as the value of physical labor and collective living were not abstract European theory but the bone and tissue of everyday life, so the nation's goals and his own were interchangeable, identical. Survival and security were paramount concerns; the question of how to achieve them was not open to debate. It simply didn't arise.

After the devastation of the Holocaust, followed by the desperate struggle for national existence, and in spite of the astonishing diversity of its citizens, the Israel in which Benjamin grew up in the forties and fifties was blessed with a unique consensus. A great deal had changed since then, of course, for Benjamin Landau and for his country, but until his Service had offered him to the French as a diversion for the hijacking of missile parts, it had never occurred to him to question his ingrained values. Now, after six bitter months in a French prison and a homecoming complicated by the absence, perhaps the abandonment, of his wife and children, he wondered if he had been brainwashed from birth, fed phony fantasies as routinely as apples and honey. They'd destroyed his idealism as well as his skills, he thought furiously, as he wandered past the settlers' cottages, neat, well-tended flowers brightly clustered near every door.

He rounded a curve in the path and saw the children's house, a little distance away. He paused, looked ahead through a screen of hazy sunlight, blinked and walked on slowly. It looked the same, it always looked the same, he never understood why it didn't change, although they'd added a big wing to the house, built a new playground, planted banks of lilies. It always looked exactly as it had twenty years before. He didn't want to stop there.

Blinking rapidly, he walked past the building, ignoring the babies in the sandbox, the young women supervising the play. He took long, jerky strides past the clubhouse, the dining room, the pool, walking through profuse, flamboyant gardens until he came to the factory. He couldn't go in, of course. Security was very strict around a settlement industry that made spare parts for the army. But Ben knew that if he hung around he might get a glimpse of Natan. He leaned against a cypress tree and waited.

The skin on his hands and forearms was itching again. He scratched, watching red spots rise angrily, then shoved his hands in his pockets, blinking against the sun and his burning skin. He saw a man walk round the side of the building, but it wasn't Natan. Ben badly wanted to see him. It had been more than a year. The boy was twenty-three now, strong, brave and serious. In a way he was the son Ben and his first wife never had time to have. Ben waited for Natan to come out of the factory like a man shot in the kneecaps waiting for a painkiller.

When the workers came out in two and threes, breaking for the afternoon meal, Natan was not among them. Ben was tired of waiting. He walked nearer to the fence and looked about for someone he knew.

"Yacov, *shalom*," he called, when the chief engineer walked out, stooping, much older than the boys who worked the machines. "Where is Natan?"

Yacov stopped for an instant and looked at Ben. Then he came through the gate toward him, clapping the security guard on the shoulder, eyes narrowed against the sun.

"How are you, Ben? I didn't know you were here. When did you get home?"

"Last night."

"How are you feeling? You must be happy to be back. Was it bad, over there?"

"Well..."

"I understand. I won't ask questions. I hope you'll stay for a while, have a holiday. We've all been worrying about you."

"I...haven't made plans yet. Can you tell me where to find Natan? I'd like to say hello."

Yacov looked down, rubbing his hand over his balding head. "Ben," he said.

Pinpricks of heat, dots of moisture, a peripheral tremor invaded Benjamin.

"What is it, Yacov? Where is he?"

"Nobody told you?"

"Nobody has told me anything yet. You tell me. Where is Natan?"

"He's dead, Ben. I'm sorry."

Ben took a step forward.

"No."

Yacov put his hand on Ben's arm. Ben looked at him and saw his own face reflected there, crumpled, fallen within itself, its outline blurred like a building after shelling. He took a step back.

"Tell me."

"Let's go and sit down and talk."

"No, just tell me, please."

"I'm sorry to be the one to tell you. I remember..."

"Tell me."

Yacov moved his feet, a small shuffle in the sand. Then he straightened his stooping shoulders and looked up, beyond Benjamin, to the heights above.

"Up there," he said, pointing to the eucalyptus groves. "Natan was on reserve duty. He'd been gone almost his full three months already. I know because of the factory shifts. Then they sent down some kaytushas. One of them hit a tourist bus below Metulla. You may have heard about it."

"I've heard nothing. What happened?"

"Seven killed, thirty-one injured. And another hit near Dafna. Burnt up the crop. So, a reprisal raid. Natan was on it."

"How did—"

"They were looking for bases. They had an idea one of their big shots had a training program started again. They went to destroy the base and try to find a leader. Maybe Walid Toucan, maybe even Tewfik Mahmoud."

"Hand to hand?"

Yacov looked up at the hills again.

"I believe that is what happened. We don't know any details."

"Did they bring him home?"

"Of course."

"Did you, did anyone...see him?"

Yacob looked at him.

"No, Ben."

"So you don't know exactly what they did to him? How long it took? What—"

"We don't know."

"When did it happen?"

"Less than a month ago."

They were both silent, staring up toward the heights. Then Benjamin glanced at Yacov.

"Excuse me."

He walked away as fast as he could and then broke into a run, wiping the sweat from his eyes, running back the way he had come, back to the children's house he had skirted painfully when he walked to the factory to find Natan. He'd visited his childhood home as infrequently as he could manage over the past twenty years, and when he did, he avoided the children's house. Now, it seemed the only place to go. His first wife, Miriam, had died there when she threw her body on top of a three-year-old orphan named Natan to protect him from a terrorist attack.

The spot where she died before any of them could get near was covered now with flowers blooming almost all year round. A little stake recorded her name and a tribute to her heroism. Now Natan was gone too, wasted in battle with the same enemy, all wasted, all for nothing, Natan and Miriam and the baby boy she had been carrying. Ben missed her still. He closed his eyes, but opened them quickly to escape the image of her shiny black hair, matted with blood, her arms holding Natan safe, her firm slim legs motionless on the sandy playground. It was a long time since he'd wondered what his life would have been like if she had lived; he'd spent the last twenty years in a personal struggle to wrest value from her death.

They had grown up together. The large group of youngsters on the kibbutz lived in the children's house, played together, went to school together, worked the fields together and, as they grew into adolescence, discovered socialist ideology, always together. They played volleyball in the evenings as the light faded, bumping and knocking into each other. They went to Kinneret to swim and loll on the sand, the smell of fish pungent on the air, the tourists easy targets for the arrows of their teenage contempt. They were complacent about their way of life, uncontaminated by exposure to any other. They were as unaware of their differences from each other as puppies tumbling in the same large litter. There weren't many differences anyway; they were all strong and energetic, competent and assured. The gilded product of their parents' struggle to summon security from nothing more substantial than swamp and radiant ideals, they were utterly certain of their righteousness. They all knew the difference between black and white and recognized nothing in between.

Benjamin hardly ever saw Miriam during the years of late adolescence they spent away in army service. He returned home first, ready to take his place in the community. He'd seen enough on border patrols to be sure that he didn't want to be a permanent soldier. He was home, ready to be a farmer on the land his parents had reclaimed when they settled it in the late thirties, building against the annihilation they'd left behind in Eastern Europe. Someday, his father suggested, he might seek permission to study, irrigation perhaps, or the new methods of citrus grafting, but that was for the future. Ben worked in the orchards, he swam five kilometers a day, feeling his big frame hold the hardness the army had taught it; he rode horseback in the valley in the evening, looking up at the hills and the tranquil sky draining into darkness. He enjoyed his shifts on guard duty at night, he felt strong and responsible, he had his place, he knew who he was and he liked what he did.

When Miriam came home, his confidence wavered. She seemed so composed, so much at ease with herself that he felt clumsy. He watched her across the dining hall, but looked away when she raised her eyes. He could always spot her in a crowd; with her shiny black hair tied back and spilling over her shoulders, her wide, gentle eyes and slow smile, she looked more inaccessible than any of the girls he'd known in the army. She wanted to work with children and was given a job helping to take care of preschoolers in the baby wing of the children's house. Ben made a point of walking by the house on his way to eat, looking for a glimpse of her and sometimes managing to walk over to the dining hall with her and some of the other girls. He wanted to know her, really know her. It was ridiculous not to know someone you'd grown up with, but he couldn't find any way to be alone with her.

They all went together to a party on a neighboring settlement, driving up the hill in an open truck, singing the songs they'd always sung; later, they all came home together, a few of them trying to remember the words of the new English songs they'd heard, one of the boys rotating his hips like the Beatles in their new movie, trying to catch the insinuating movement, the sweet confrontation in the sound. Ben looked away, embarrassed, and saw an old friend put his arm around one of the girls and hug her. He couldn't do that, he simply didn't know how. Miriam sat quietly, knees hunched up to her chin, smiling at the boy who tried to sing like John Lennon. Then a lot of them tried together, belting out "Lucy in the Sky with Diamonds," but they couldn't get it right, and as the truck rolled onto their own broad drive, they were singing "Tsena, Tsena" their own way, lustily, the way they always had. Before Ben knew it, Miriam had slipped away and gone to bed. It was like that for months.

One night in late spring, coming off guard duty, he walked back to his room behind the guest house, winding his way through abundant flower beds, past lushly blooming hibiscus bushes, whose flowers curved pale and perfect against dense arching branches, the air saturated by the mingled perfumes of blossoms and the spice of fresh-cut grass. He was thinking of Miriam, so that when he saw her, lying on her back, watching the stars, she echoed his fantasy. She smiled as if she'd been waiting there for him, as if it was the most natural time and place for them to be together. In a second he was next to her, one hand smoothing her shiny hair, the other gentle on the glowing skin of her cheek. She stared at him, smiling, until he bent and kissed her, holding all the length of her against him, watching the moon slant across her hair, gathering her softness to him. Neither Benjamin nor Miriam spoke for hours. Later, whenever they talked about that night, they remembered an enchantment, a magical light that had enclosed them, lifted them tenderly out of themselves, freed them to find each other.

27

The next day Ben told her that he wanted to get married at once.

"We don't even know each other," she said, moving her fingers lightly over the skin on the inside of his wrist.

"We've known each other all our lives." Ben's confidence had surged again.

"But it's different now."

"We've got the rest of our lives to enjoy the difference," he said.

But they only had a little less than two years. Leaning against the red brick wall of the children's house, hands shoved deep in his pockets, broad shoulders hunched against the memories he had tried to avoid, Benjamin stared at the spot where she had died.

The terrorists had come without warning in late afternoon, through the trees, across the deserted vegetable garden, up to the playground outside the children's house. Most of the children were visiting their parents at that hour. The playground was empty, except for Miriam and Natan. Miriam visited him there every day, because Natan was an orphan. His parents, hiking with a group of amateur archaeologists from the settlement, had been blown up by a Fatah mine. Miriam, six months pregnant, had Natan curled on her lap, examining a flower, when she looked up to see three men running across the playground toward her, waving rifles, red scarves like cords of blood across their throats. Miriam had screamed, shouted a warning, and thrown Natan to the ground, covering him with her own heavy body before they shot her. Three times, Ben remembered. A waste of ammunition. Once would have been enough.

Blinking rapidly, unable to move away from the wall, he saw that he'd come full circle. The new grief for Natan, the futile waste, his own betrayal by the manipulative ciphers who ran his service, had returned him to the empty despair he'd struggled against after Miriam was killed. There had been times since then when he'd thought he'd learned to fill some of the vacuum in himself with his work, and with Kate and the children. Tearing again at the burning rash on his hands, he thought that he'd lost all that, too, the work made worthless by betrayal, his wife and children gone, looking for shelter from the violence he'd brought them.

Hunched against the wall, Ben saw all the parts of his life strewn about like the limbs of a paratrooper blown off his body. He didn't think the pieces could be reassembled, and even if they could, he didn't want to bother.

He didn't want to discuss it all with his parents either. For a very long time, Ben had been isolated by his passports and codes, his radios and weapons, his secret and lonely travels, all the persistent, tangled skeins of deception. Between his furtive life and theirs, bounded by the predictable diurnal patterns of communal agriculture, there had opened a fissure so deep that even ordinary conversation seldom connected.

He had abandoned his childhood home; he had not lived there in the twenty years since Miriam's murder. Before that, he'd been raised as a child of the collective, bonded with his parents differently from families who lived together under the same roof, sharing thoughts and chores routinely. Raising his own urban children, even if only "part-time," as Kate often taunted, he had experienced the difference. But he cared about his parents. From the relatively uninvolved distance he had constructed when he chose that life most intensely separate, most demandingly removed, he cared, he wanted their well-being. He believed, he was certain, they wanted his.

Sitting with them on the grass at the end of the day, in front of the door of their low, one-story cement cottage, joined on both sides by other, identical ones, watching shadows overtake the ebbing light, Benjamin wanted them to feel that he was participating in the evening ritual, sharing the day, planning the next. But he could summon little interest in the storage of agricultural supplies, as little, he thought, as his father had in the gunshot that had killed his French agent.

"What's wrong with your hands, Benny?"

His mother peered at them through the last gray light. Her

cropped iron hair, still streaked with black, framed a face molded by the valley elements into soft and deeply creased chamois; her dark eyes glinted. Her sturdy, compact frame leaned closer to examine his rash. Ben, who awoke most days to an awareness of the fragility of his own mortality, was struck by her youthfulness, some vigorous, enduring energy, a consequence perhaps of her certainty in the value of her chosen way of life. Annie Yankelowitz had chosen Palestine when she was a bored, indulged and rebellious teenager in Poland, before she ever set eyes on Lazar Landau. When she found him digging holes for saplings on the training farm near Lvov, learning Hebrew and Zionist socialism along with a handful of other recruits, he fitted conveniently into her plans for the future.

As far as Benjamin knew, Annie never regretted either of her choices, Lazar or the land, not even during the hardships of their early days. She had made the right choice, she told him, and Annie always told the truth. At least, that had been Benjamin's experience.

"Ben, what's with your hands? I'm asking you?" She smacked his knee lightly to emphasize that she was waiting for him to answer.

"A reaction to prison, I suppose. I went to the clinic before supper. They gave me this thick yellow muck to put on it. It'll improve."

"All your troubles should improve so fast."

After completing this pronouncement, Benjamin's father shifted clumsily in his chair. He had gained so much weight since retiring from the orchards that it was difficult for him to find a comfortable position. He detested his new responsibilities of ordering and storing supplies even more than he had disliked the repetitive tasks of finding and directing water to the orange groves. Never admitting his resentment and boredom, Lazar had suppressed all his life his desire to pursue the abstractions of physics, in favor of reclaiming the Jewish homeland.

As a Polish teenager, inspired by youth leaders from Palestine, alarmed by frightful reports of German Jewish refugees looking for security and official protection in Warsaw, Lubin, Rovno and Lvov, Lazar was convinced that Jewish survival depended on the dignity of labor and the creation of a national home. Even before Austria and Czechoslovakia were seized, Lazar quarreled irrevocably with his parents. They wouldn't give permission, so he left without it, living near Lvov, at the *hachsharah*, the training farm, to prepare himself to go to Palestine and make the Galilee safe and productive. Lazar relinquished his passion for science as a Jesuit sacrifices fleshly pleasures. The break with his family was never to be repaired. They all perished in the ovens that Lazar escaped by emigrating. He had never intended, never even considered, a life utterly divorced from roots, family, intellectual pursuit, but that was what he settled for. The denial left dark smudges upon the skin beneath his eyes, deep creases along his neck, as if harsh self-righteousness had carved scars, an aloof distance from those around him, especially his wife and son, and an attitude that was dependably derogatory.

Benjamin saw nothing of himself in his father now. The resemblance of his childhood had disappeared under billowing tissue; even the disappointment, so meticulously repressed, at what Lazar judged the sacrifice of his mind was obscured by the settled thickness of the flesh around his mouth and eyes. Benjamin's height, his broad shoulders and strong heavy limbs were attributes of his own generation; the deep clefts from nose to mouth, the thick hair and bushy eyebrows were his own, sprung from a different source. His distance from his father had grown, along with his own disappointments.

"What troubles do you mean?"

Lazar shrugged slowly, looking away. Benjamin reminded himself he had done so often, that his father had been young once, had been bold and brave, filled with love for his mother and the socialist idealism that brought them, adolescents both, out of Europe just before all the gates crashed closed for eternity. They were barely in time, arriving just after the British White Paper, which limited Jewish immigration into Palestine, so that Lazar and Annie and their comrades were illegals everywhere, under fire in Europe from Poles, Nazis and Russians, under fire from British and Arabs as they landed illegally on the coastline north of Natanya. Lazar and Annie entered Palestine anyway, and built a fortress. They'd taught Benjamin to defend that fortress, one way or another. Still, it was very difficult to talk to Lazar. He could choose not to be inarticulate, and sometimes he did. But not now.

"What troubles, Lazar?" Ben tried to keep his voice neutral.

His father nodded slowly, then looked away, the folds of his neck shuddering.

"Ben, don't you want to hear about Kate?" his mother asked.

Ben blinked rapidly and clenched his hands together, clammy from the thick ointment. He'd made a career out of keeping the different blocks of his life separated, marked off, labeled and subject only to his own control. But he would have to learn about Kate from his mother.

"Yes."

"Oh, Ben." She established a pause. He would not look up from his hands, so she went on. "She came to see us before they left. We never suspected, never thought for one moment. We didn't know anything before."

"What did she say?"

"She said she'd been unhappy for a long time. Is that true?"

"I suppose so."

"And you?"

"Why don't you tell me what she said?"

"She said you two were having problems. When an American says 'problems' it can mean anything. You know, Ben?"

He would not look toward her.

"Was there another man?"

It hadn't even occurred to him. It didn't matter. One way or the other, she, too, had betrayed him.

"I don't think so," he said.

"She said she was taking the children and going home. 'Home,' she said. She still thinks her home is in America." She leaned forward again, waving her hands. "I couldn't believe it. I told her what does she think, doesn't she know they'll get you out of that French prison. You'll come home. No, she said, the rope had run out. You were sentenced to ten to fifteen years. She wouldn't remain and bring up Roni and Ruben alone here. It's not a life at all, she said, in an apartment on Jabotinsky Street, with the Tel Aviv drivers revving up their engines all day and night, waiting for a bomb in the launderette or the market, Ben in prison for spying."

Now Lazar put his palms flat upon the arms of his chair and stared across the dark toward Benjamin.

"We tried to persuade her to come and live here. The children should have the opportunity. They would all be safe. So. She laughed at us. Your American."

They'd never forgiven him, Ben thought. They regarded Miriam's murder by terrorists as more natural than his second marriage to an American. The hell with them, too. Before he could answer, a girl ran along the path in front of the cottages, calling his name.

"Yes, I am Benjamin Landau," he said. She stopped, short of breath.

"Phone call," she gasped. "It's urgent. In the library."

"Who is it?" His calves ached as he stood up.

"Your office. Hurry, please."

Ben followed, blinking, sensing the glances his parents exchanged in the dark behind him.

THREE

"Bring Laudau in for briefing tomorrow," said Shemtov, having pulled rank to force the duty officer in Tel Aviv to call Uri to the phone.

"That's impossible. I told him he could have a few days."

"It can't be helped, Uri. I must move quickly."

"He's not ready. He's not fit for anything."

"He will be."

"It's too soon. Besides..."

"Yes?"

"He as much as told me he's through. He's very bitter, Dan. He says he's all washed up. I don't think it's going to work."

"Bring him in."

"It's terribly risky."

Shemtov laughed. Gershom only had a few days to live. There were risks and risks.

"I'll be in Tel Aviv early tomorrow."

"Do you want to see him?" Uri's voice rose. He didn't take well to disrupting the chain of command.

"Oh, no. Of course not. I'll be upstairs. You go ahead as we discussed. Come and tell me about it after he leaves."

He laughed again as he replaced the receiver. Everyone needed to protect his territory. Everyone. Including himself.

Elbows propped on his orderly desktop, Shemtov rested his head on the tips of his fingers, feeling the ridges across his forehead rising all the way to the thinning hairline, gray eyes pulled dry and wide, muscles tight. The urgent concentration wasn't because of the power over life and death; Shemtov was long accustomed to that. It wasn't even the individual case, the threat to a large personal investment, the durable symbiotic relationship; these had always been counters in the tournament. Gershom had infiltrated the enemy's camp, established a convincing identity, risen high enough to have access to information more valuable than plutonium and as inaccessible. He had sent it home, a steady, reliable stream. Shemtov owed him a last shot at survival. He owed the nation a chance to keep their best agent in place, continuing the flow of vital intelligence. But more than all of that, he craved another massive strike against the enemy, another cornerstone in the edifice of his own legend, another bulwark against the manipulative tactics of his bureaucratic detractors.

There were a lot of reasons to run an operation to save Gershom; his own pride, the unfailing impulse of the defense of his own integrity, was not the least among them.

Shemtov's own place in history was not something he discussed with anyone at all, not even his wife. Berta had never had much tolerance for history and certainly didn't have any now; she wasn't around much either. She'd been spending longer and longer stretches of time in Bat Yam, ever since Shoshi, their daughter, married her dark-skinned semiliterate Iraqi and started having a baby every year and working full-time because all he could do was tack prefab boards together if he could find construction piecework. Berta took care of the five children in the stuffy apartment in Bat Yam, did the shopping and cleaning and often cooked the meals, so Shoshi could track down, counsel and guide wild runaway teenagers from Moroccan and Tunisian immigrant families in Yavneh and Lod.

Shemtov didn't really care that Berta was away from home so much. Things had never been the same between him and Berta since their furious fights ten years before, when their son Avi had wanted to marry a fanatic with a rag on her head and a missionary zeal for recovering all of Judea and Samaria on the Almighty's personal instructions. Hanna carried a pistol, quoted the Bible sanctimoniously and continuously and intended to live in a new and controversial orthodox settlement on a stretch of sandy hillside overlooking three Arab villages. None of this had bothered Avi. Shemtov was only able to prevail when his son discovered that expelling Arabs in droves by any means they could devise was the primary objective of the militant community. Avi didn't marry his wretched self-righteous monster, but he and his father didn't have much to say to each other afterward, and Berta never forgave Dan for interfering, claiming they'd have been better off with that creature for a daughter-in-law than the spoiled assimilated American who had easily persuaded Avi to try life in Los Angeles.

Berta was too preoccupied with improving their contorted family relationships to bother with Shemtov's place in history, but as he and his lifelong dream of building an ideal society withered and diminished, he yearned more intensely for the recognition of history. For an indestructible memorial he needed the perfect tools.

Benjamin Landau was his ideal instrument. Shemtov was ready to activate him. But he would have to flesh out some support at the American end if his scheme was to have any chance of success. Shemtov's old friend, Peter Bendington, once CIA deputy director for operations, had been forcibly retired several years ago in one of the agency's periodic purges, designed to appease the Congress. Since then, nothing had been the same. Shemtov and Bendington had met in the filthy waste of Europe in 1946, sharing the yield of the debris. As the years went by, they had provided each other more than a little cooperation, sifting through the interminable rubble that build the foundation for their pursuits. With Bendington gone, more or less hiding out, it was said, in his hothouse in Virginia, it was not quite as simple as it once had been to organize the necessary support. Shemtov had some ideas about an American end for his new operation. There were possible consequences he could not control. He was too experienced to try. He needed help. He had to hope that Bendington's connections were still good.

He moved to his habitual spot at the window, staring out between the leafy screen cast by the huge pine branches outside. Lights were coming on all over Jerusalem, dazzling points, each casting a small glow upon the gathering darkness. Reflecting abundant past and present life, the lights spread out farther in all directions than they used to do. He had watched them over the years as the sweeping curves of the hills became punctuated with buildings, gardens, roads. The spacious twentieth-century designs stretching out and away beyond the old walled city gave an extra concentration to the narrow cobbled alleys. Dan Shemtov, whose respect for history provided the perspective that enabled him to meet the brutal requirements of his job, thought that the lights of Jerusalem looked fragile against their desert backdrop. Losing Gershom would put out a lot of lights.

Popping a mint in his mouth, Shemtov pulled a card with two American phone numbers toward him. His first call was to New York.

"How are you, Al?" he inquired, in an English that sounded like a cultivated second language learned in any of half a dozen European capitals. "Just want to make sure my package arrived safely?"

"Sure did. According to schedule. I already acknowledged receipt."

"Well done. No difficulty taking care of it, I trust?"

"Absolutely." A brief pause. "No problem."

"Quite. One other thing. You'll be needing some facilities. There's a letter addressed to my old friend Pietro. It will arrive in the office with the other mail in the morning. It's personal. Do you remember Pietro?"

"Oh, yes, yes, of course. No problem."

"I'd appreciate it if you'd hand-deliver the letter yourself as soon as it arrives."

"Er...sure thing. But...er...is he expecting it?"

"He will be by then. Stay in touch, Al. Take care of that package. It's precious."

The second call was to Virginia.

"Mr. Bendington is in the greenhouse and can't be disturbed," he was curtly informed.

"Tell him William Butler Yeats is on the telephone and would he please be so good as to pick up the extension instrument on the potting table at his side," Shemtov said, enunciating every syllable. "At once, if you please."

He heard a gasp and then a gurgling sound and leaned back to wait. After seven or eight minutes a sibilant "yes" came over the wire.

"Things fall apart," Shemtov said, "the center cannot hold; mere anarchy is loosed upon the world. The blood-dimmed tide is loosed, and everywhere..."

As he continued, the voice in the Virginia greenhouse joined in, chanting happily, leaping along with familiar empathy.

"The ceremony of innocence is drowned; the best lack all conviction, while the worst are full of passionate intensity." Shemtov and Bendington concluded the stanza on an entirely inappropriate but mutually satisfying note of triumph.

"How are you?" Peter Bendington inquired across the ocean. "Before you respond, let me assure you that there is no reason to assume that this line is secure."

Shemtov laughed.

"It's good to hear your voice," he said. "How are the tubers?"

"Multiplying, my dear fellow. Proliferating. More rapidly now that they enjoy my relatively undivided attention."

The acid rasp of Bendington was undiminished. May his resources be equally intact, Shemtov thought.

"I'd like to see you soon, but it's impossible right now," said Shemtov. "I called to ask you to steal a few minutes from crossbreeding tomorrow when Al comes to visit. Do you remember him? Short, stocky, blond hair around a balding patch?"

"I believe I do recall. Frizzy fellow. Is he, as the cops say to the kids, carrying?"

"You might put it that way. Thank you, Peter. I'll get into contact in a short time. A very short time. Take care."

"It sounds very much as if that is advice I should be offering you."

Shemtov laughed.

"See you soon."

"Bombs away," said Bendington. Shemtov heard him chuckle before the connection was broken.

FOUR

When Benjamin Landau let himself into his Tel Aviv apartment on Jabotinsky Street, he was blinking rapidly again, stiff and aching. He was so absorbed by the audacity of Uri asking more of him, so outraged at being jerked like a Bedouin bride, that he unlocked the fifth-floor door thoughtlessly, unprepared for rooms that he hadn't seen for six months and that hadn't been lived in for weeks. It was orderly, of course. The woman who scrubbed her teacups before putting them in the dishwasher wouldn't have left it any other way. But though the furniture was in place, something was wrong. Ben took a few steps across the living room and heard his shoes on the bare floor. The oriental rug they'd bought together in Iran years before was gone.

His choking rage surged again, but he was distracted by the windows, flat and glittering as the late-afternoon sun sank over the sea. The light was strange; the room had never thrown off such garish streaks of burning light. Then he saw that the plants that had trailed a filigree of green across the windows were all gone. So were the photographs, the pictures of Roni and Ruben as babies, and the copper sculpture of a tree he'd bought for Kate years ago, in a Baghdad market, the tree whose spreading, delicate branches were to give them shade and shelter all their lives, gone to America, he supposed, with his wife and children.

He shoved his hands in his pockets and walked through to the kitchen, where everything was assembled in bleak order, cups, saucepans and empty sugar bowl, nothing at all in the refrigerator, which was shut off and emitted a stale, sour smell, no dinner in the oven, no children's cereal bowls left on the countertop, no experiments for botany class on the windowsill.

In the bedrooms, he threw open closets and found his own things, no one else's. He'd been so pleased, years ago, that he could manage a bedroom each for Roni and Ruben; he was a father who understood the need for a place to be alone. Now there wasn't a toy, a book, a battered sneaker, just routine furniture, shuttered windows, dust, desertion. He could see that she never meant to come back. It was the bathroom that made him shut his eyes for a few seconds. No toothbrushes, none at all, no cake of soap on the sink; but on a peg behind the door, Kate had forgotten a brief, bright nightgown. As he moved the door, it floated out toward him, a filmy salute.

Ben walked back to the living room. It was odd, he thought, standing in the bleak order that framed the debris of his life with Kate, that Miriam's loss still tugged more piercingly, pulled from a deep, hollow yearning. Perhaps Kate had been right all along. "You buried your feelings with Miriam," she'd said. "You just have remnants left for me; you only care down to a certain point. You must have felt more once, Ben." He had, once.

In a cabinet under a badly depleted bookshelf he found a half bottle of Scotch that Kate had not taken. An American wife and long years abroad had taught him to use it, making another difference between him and most Israelis, another difference the life of a pawn had inflicted upon him. He poured, irritable that there was no ice, sipped, waiting for the little rush of warmth. There was a tap on the door. No one knew he was there. It was a mistake. But then the bell rang. He took another sip before calling out.

"Who is it?"

"*Shalom*, Benny. I need help. It's Shimon."

Miriam's younger brother. Ben hadn't seen him for over a year. His voice sounded very quiet, tired. Ben opened the door and stiffened.

"What do you want?" he asked the trim, middle-aged man in khaki shirt and pants, his graying hair and clear gray eyes not Shimon's at all.

"I thought you might not open the door for me." Shemtov smiled. His voice wasn't tired at all now. "I believe you are very angry with Uri. Can I come in?"

Benjamin hesitated. If Shemtov hadn't used Shimon's name, he might have been able to slam the door as he wanted; but he had to be sure that Shimon wasn't in trouble. Every damned thing required a calculation these days. He stepped back and Shemtov walked in, rubber-soled shoes squeaking once on the uncarpeted floor.

They had met before, of course, Shemtov and Benjamin Landau, but only rarely and briefly. Ben knew him by sight and by the legend that surrounded him. At war again within himself, he rubbed his eyes to try to stop the blinking, shifted his shoulders and picked up his glass.

"A drink? There's no ice. The refrigerator was cut off."

"No drink, thank you. Have a mint."

Shemtov withdrew a small box from his pocket and popped a white peppermint into his mouth. It was true then. Ben had heard it often. The brilliant intelligence chief chewed mints to help him think. Ben watched him move to the long blank windows and look out upon the rush-hour traffic before settling down in an armchair.

"Is Shimon in trouble?"

"I know nothing new about Shimon." Shemtov dismissed the subject with a gesture. "Please sit down. I must talk to you."

"We have nothing to say to each other."

"You are wrong. There is a great deal you do not know."

"I don't want to know anything. I know enough. Too much. I don't want any more."

"Nevertheless, you are going to learn something new. Sit down, if you please."

Shemtov was about twenty years older and half a foot shorter than Ben and slightly built by comparison with Ben's massive shoulders and broad chest, but Ben sat down and watched him, shrugging. Twenty years of discipline denied him options in the face of that gray stare.

"I believe you refused Uri's request that you go to the United States."

"It wasn't a request. It was an order."

"I see. Would you have refused a request?"

"Yes."

"We had been certain you would wish to visit your wife and children."

"Well..." Ben hesitated. "I might want to, but no more missions. Uri wants me to combine a visit with a mission."

"It's only one brief assignment. Simple. Deliver a message. Why not?"

"I'm through with the Service. I'm not going to do any more. I've had it. I'm retiring." He heard his voice rise and stopped talking.

"Just one errand, Benjamin. You'd be in Philadelphia with your family anyway. It would pay your costs and then you could retire. We're ready to help. A new life, new work, we'll help you do what you want after this."

"No. No more." He was shouting now. He stood up, blinking, walked across the room and back again. "Can't you people understand? This Paris thing finished it all for me. Sitting in prison, knowing how you used me, watching my man die for nothing but a tricky deception—all that made something stop for me. I don't have whatever it is that was useful to you. It's gone. Can't you see that?"

Shemtov looked beyond Benjamin for a minute or two and then fixed his gray stare firmly on him again.

"Sit down, if you please. I have something to tell you."

"I don't want to know. I don't care what the reasons are, or how urgent it is, or how the life of the nation depends on me, I don't want any more of it. I have only one life and I'm not giving any more of it to your operations. I won't."

"Do you remember," Shemtov said quietly, as if Benjamin had not spoken, "the day your wife died?"

Benjamin looked at him and sat down, his shoulders and head thrown against the back of the chair, legs sprawled out in front of him.

"Three *fedayeen* came up through the trees toward the playground, didn't they, Ben? When she shouted a warning, they shot her. No one got there in time to stop them, but within seconds people had run near enough to shoot. Two of the attackers were killed, remember, Benjamin? One got away. Three of your friends gave chase, but they never found him. By the time you came up from the fruit trees, she was dead. Her mother had taken the little boy—Natan, wasn't it—from under her, and they were searching the bodies of the terrorists. It was all over, wasn't it? Except for the one who got away."

Ben rubbed his eyes with the back of his inflamed hand and then folded his arms across his body, holding himself tight. He said nothing.

"You thought that was the end of it, but it wasn't. We found the third man, Ben, just outside Metulla, late that same night. We had a number of choices, of course. We made a very careful decision. We turned him, Ben. Then we sent him back."

Still hugging himself, holding his body as if it might otherwise separate, Ben leaned forward.

"Why?" he asked hoarsely.

"We offered him his life in return for information. We've protected his family on the West Bank while we've been siphoning intelligence out of him for twenty years, Ben. Not as much as we would have liked, not always totally reliable, but good enough. More than we would have had without him."

"You let Miriam's killer go free?"

"For a time, Ben. And now his time's up. That's where you come in."

Ben shook his head, blinking.

"I don't know what you're talking about. I can't handle any more. It's impossible for me to understand how you people do things. You—"

"Ben, we don't trust him anymore. He's feeding us false stuff. We've got to get rid of him. And we've got to do it in a way that we won't be implicated. It mustn't look like an Israeli assassination. You're the man for the job, Ben. It's simple justice."

Ben shook his head again.

"We must betray him to his own people, Ben, and let them do the job for us. All you have to do is go to Philadelphia to see your family and pay one visit to tell one man what I have just told you. He'll pass it on. Miriam's murderer has outlived his usefulness. We've sentenced him. His own people will take him out. That's all we want you to do. One message. Not so terrible, is it?"

FIVE

The novelty of traveling under his own identity wore off quickly for Benjamin Landau. He enjoyed the unfamiliar sense of legitimacy only briefly before the habitual nuts and bolts of wariness shifted into place as the other passengers on the long flight began settling down for what remained of the night. Ben, too alert by then to doze, picked over the origins of all the potential watchers he might encounter during his American visit, all the legmen, stringers and ciphers who might conceivably be interested in the travels of Landau after his early release from a French prison, found guilty of espionage.

It was difficult to inspect the passengers. Most of them had turned off the overhead lights and hunched down under rumpled blankets. Ben ambled very slowly to the rear bathroom and back, trying to examine the potential for trouble in the seats off both aisles, but was forced to acknowledge that his examination would have to wait for morning. It would make no difference anyway; he hadn't yet discovered an acceptable escape from a passenger jet in flight. He would have to wait. But even in the near total dark of two A.M. he knew there were more Israeli security people than usual. He sensed their presence as sharply as if they surrounded him on a moonless midnight in the desert. He felt as if their eyes feasted upon his dry, scaly skin, and he yearned to be rid of them.

Reaching up to turn off his reading light, he felt the body of the elderly woman next to him sigh and settle and he ached to sleep also. But, along with other things most people took for granted, Benjamin had lost the habit of sleeping comfortably. Besides, his destination was Philadelphia, where he had first been twelve years ago. He was invaded by memories. Like it or not, and he did not, he was going to revisit the people and scenes of a season that had produced the framework of the life he had lived since. It was through Dr. George Zaggad, professor of Near Eastern Studies at the University of Pennsylvania, that Ben had met Kate. And it was to Zaggad that Shemtov insisted he must carry the message now.

He had first seen Zaggad staring out from posters hung all over the campus. Full lips curving quizzically under a mustache, sad dark eyes, salt-and-pepper hair perfectly groomed above a broad forehead, Zaggad was a handsome man. The posters described him as an internationally renowned expert on the history and politics of the Middle East. The posters announced a public lecture at which, ten years after Israeli occupation began in 1967, Zaggad would discuss the future of Jerusalem and the West Bank. Benjamin had never heard of the professor, but briefly free from the unadvertised program in computer sciences and sophisticated communications which his Service had sent him to study, he went along to hear the lecture.

Ben had not expected the overflowing crowd: hundreds of students jammed the huge auditorium. Older patrons were jostled and pushed as the youngsters packed themselves, shrill and partisan, into the hall. There was no seat for him, not even in an aisle. He hunched a heavy shoulder against a wall halfway down from the platform and watched as Zaggad was introduced and greeted energetically by applause just barely exceeding the boos. He leaned forward as soon as Zaggad started to speak and so did the enormous audience. Zaggad was a brilliant rhetorician. In flawless English, with just a charming trace of the familiar Arabic accent, so close to Hebrew, he delivered a history of the West Bank as though he were telling a romantic adventure story to a small circle of enraptured admirers. Then, flicking a lock of dark, silver-flecked hair back from his forehead, he launched into a postwar kaleidoscope of heroism, pain, loss and longing that poured from his lips like poetry, inflaming the minds of his listeners. Professor he might be, but Zaggad was no dried-out, fussy academic. His address ranged the sweeping canvas of centuries and came to rest on the colors and sounds and smells of today's displacement.

Benjamin, grasping for the first time that Zaggad was a Palestinian, had to admit that he was superb. He thought he had never heard so lucid and balanced a review. Even as his own commitment became clear, he dealt respectfully with his adversaries, those other Palestinians, of whom Ben was one. There was none of the fanaticism, none of the bloody vengefulness that Ben expected from the opposition and from his own side, too, for that matter. Here and there, like strands in a multicolored tapestry, Zaggad declared opinions as if they were facts, exaggerated or reduced, selected anecdotes that went, as shades of a deeper color, to the center of his thesis, which was, of course, the abuse and humiliation of his people, the Palestinians, at the hands of the Israelis. But Benjamin, admiring his skillful weaving, had to concede that he had not known there were Palestinians like this one: more than literate, highly educated, blooming with a forceful charm, a conjurer's ability to captivate. When he concluded, stepping away from the podium, an attractive man of middle height and sturdy build, the auditorium rocked with sound. Ben was a foreigner here; Zaggad was not. He was revered or detested, but he was known and accepted. He was a prominent figure on this campus, Ben could see.

Zaggad handled questions as adroitly as he had lectured. Many of the questions were confrontations, for a large number of the youngsters in the hall were passionate Zionists. There were also statements awkwardly contorted to sound like questions from within the large group of Arab students who screamed

"Free Palestine" in unison a number of times. Zaggad, his own tone evenly sympathetic, impartially cordial, turned each remark into an opportunity. The final question of the evening came from a young woman near the back of the hall. She could not make herself heard, so the professor invited her to join him on the podium. Ben watched as she walked down the long aisle, briskly composed, her neat cap of brown hair shining under the light.

"Professor Zaggad," she said in the accent Ben had learned to recognize as Philadelphia native, "East Jerusalem was declared international territory by the United Nations in the 1947 partition plan. It was invaded by Jordan and held until the 1967 war. During those twenty years, no Jews were permitted to enter the Old City. The Holy Places were neglected and abused. How does the PLO justify its 'return'? They didn't have it, sir."

Zaggad smiled and moved next to her at the podium. She did not return the smile, but looked steadily out at the ignited mob. He had to wait at least two minutes before the shouting subsided and friends pulled two angry young men apart in the left aisle. Then, turning directly to her, he answered.

"Now, Miss Abrams," he said, "we've discussed this many times before." He had to wait for the noise to subside again. "You know that Jerusalem is the heart of the Palestinian nation, its birthright, the living symbol of its legitimacy as a free independent people. I was born there, I went to school there, my father was in government there. It is my home. You know that, Miss Abrams. I want to go home, a free man."

The main event ended then, in a roar of congratulation and confrontation. But Ben watched carefully as Miss Abrams, waiting for the crowd to shift untidily away, lingered on the platform and then moved slowly down the steps to the aisle. He was waiting as she reached the bottom.

"Miss Abrams?" Ben touched her arm to get her attention. She turned and looked at him with a level brown stare.

"My name is Ben Landau. I am an Israeli, studying here. I liked your question. Can I buy you a coffee?"

Afterward he was surprised. He had sought out very few women since Miriam's murder; none had been strangers. He had not welcomed approaches made to him either. When some conjunction of circumstances had led, three or four times, to what felt like the beginning of a relationship, he'd broken it off, severed the connection. After all, he traveled so much, an entanglement wasn't practical. Besides, if you didn't have something, you couldn't lose it. But on the night he heard George Zaggad lecture, he forgot all this or at least suspended it. Afterward he thought that some quality of intensity, of involvement, or even romance, lent by Zaggad to his audience had infected him and added a special appeal to the self-assured grace of the young woman who walked with him for coffee in a student cafeteria a block away.

They found a booth and sat down, examining each other openly.

"Your English is very good," she said.

He laughed.

"I travel a lot. I pick up languages easily."

"What else can you speak?"

"Well, Hebrew, of course. Arabic. French. A little German, not much. Spanish. Some Russian."

He smiled as her brown eyes widened still further, lips pursed. She looked very smooth, all of a piece, he thought.

"And you? What do you speak?"

"Oh, I feel very inadequate after that. Spanish and just a little Hebrew."

"Hebrew? How is that?"

"I spent a year in Israel doing research for my thesis," she said.

It was his turn to be surprised.

"Tell me about it."

"Well, tell me your name again. I'm afraid I didn't hear in that confusion."

"I'm Benjamin—Ben—Landau," he held out his hand.

"I'm Kate." She shook hands.

"Kate Abrams. Good. Now, what about the thesis?"

She had studied political science in Boston and then come home to Philadelphia to teach and work on her doctorate. She'd gone to the Middle East to study the development of Palestinian insurgency, revolution, liberation, depending on one's point of view. She was working on her thesis, she told him, and now needed less than a year to complete her doctorate. Dr. Zaggad was her advisor. Ben was startled.

"Really? Isn't that awkward?"

"Why should it be?"

"Well, because... Isn't it obvious?"

"Not to me."

"He's a Palestinian nationalist and you are a Jew. You know enough to ask him that question about Jerusalem. Aren't you in conflict all the time?"

She shrugged slim, blue-sweatered shoulders and his attention wandered. Then he looked at her face again. She was smiling.

"Ben," she said, "he's an academic and so am I. It's not our business to run for election. Facts are measurable. As for opinions, no one requires us to agree with each other all the time. Zaggad is a very erudite man; he's read everything, he's been everywhere. And he's a wonderful teacher."

"I can see that."

"So he's a Palestinian. That doesn't automatically rule him out of the human race, does it? He's not a terrorist or anything like that, you know."

Ben saw a crack already opening between them and immediately moved to fill it. He was no lonelier in Philadelphia than anywhere else, he told himself, but he knew only a handful of people and those very slightly and, after five months in the city, was tired of eating alone.

"What do you do besides study?" he asked her.

"I jog. Listen to jazz. Cook complicated dishes. I make a very special bouillabaisse. What do you do?"

"None of that. Read. I don't cook, but I love to eat."

She laughed.

"I mean, what do you do for a living?"

"A living? Oh. I work for the government. Nothing exciting. I'm just here for the semester, studying computers. But I like the sound of your cooking."

He walked her home to her apartment, a few blocks west, waited while she fumbled for the assortment of keys urban Americans all seemed to carry, hoped for an invitation. It didn't come.

"I'd like to see you again," he managed, as she turned to say good-bye.

She stared at him in the half-light from the hall.

"Are you married? I'm not about to do that again."

"I was. Not anymore. What do you mean?"

"Absolutely not married, not at all?"

"Not at all," he said quietly.

"Well, call me in a few days. I'll have to see. Here's my number." She scribbled it on the back of a card and went inside, closing the door without another word.

When he phoned her two days later, she sounded delighted to hear from him. He had self-consciously forced himself to study the entertainment possibilities in the paper and found a supper club featuring a clarinetist described as cool and blue. After decoding the idiom, he guessed this would meet the need and proposed the outing. And they did have a good time, he remembered now, shifting his heavy frame awkwardly in the dark plane somewhere high over the Atlantic, on the way back to Philadelphia.

Though the years and the missions, the separate impulses of their immutably different perceptions of reality had replaced his first images of Kate, he had never forgotten her early lightheartedness, her caustic wit, the look of her, long, narrow, all of a piece, glowing with the triumphant pull of the clarinet, choosing subtly aromatic foods and a full, rich Burgundy to balance the clarinet, she said mysteriously. Afterward, they walked back through a city softened by the first light snowfall, the little flakes settling on her warm silky hair. He remembered the taste of snow upon her eyelashes, the spicy perfume on her skin, the smoothness of her sleek, lithe body; he heard the echo of her light laugh, trembled at her touch on his spine. That first night in her apartment, a slow trumpet throbbed; in the lamplight her composure taught him an ease he'd thought was gone forever. Her directness, her simple pleasure unraveled some of the old contortions of his pain, leaving him comforted, optimistic as he had not been since Miriam's death.

From that beginning, Ben set out to give Kate what he thought she needed. He gave her an evidently tough but romantic hero and an undivided companionship, unspoiled by the clamorous pain of the wife who'd come along with Kate's first Israeli lover. He was grateful to her for giving him the chance to learn that a relationship was, after all, possible again. Kate gave Ben his introduction to the soaring sounds of horns and the voluptuous pleasure of food. She also provided his introduction to Dr. George Zaggad, by taking Ben along to his seminars, inviting Zaggad to dinner, helping them to meet, allowing them to talk often without intruding her own opinions too insistently.

When Ben left Philadelphia after his semester's study, his two most important farewells were to Kate and Zaggad. With months still needed to complete her doctorate, there was never any question of Kate's returning to Israel with him, which was just as well, because Ben wasn't at all sure he wanted that. When she said she might visit him later, he understood this as a gesture to make the break easier; he had no idea that Kate was already committed. The parting with Zaggad had been simpler, of course, but not without emotion. What he had first conceived of as a potentially useful connection had become a wry friendship; he had begun by surprising himself with respect for Zaggad and ended with warm affection.

Reporting later on his contacts with Zaggad to his desk officer, Ben had emphasized the gulf between the standard Israeli view of the dispersed Palestinians and the reality of his own encounter with one of them. Zaggad was Ben's first, his most important, exposure to the notion that the other point of view might have some dignity, even some validity. When Ben called upon Zaggad at his Pine Street townhouse to say good-bye before his return to Israel, he said that he hoped they would meet again.

"In Jerusalem, perhaps?" Zaggad smiled.

"That would be nice."

"You know I cannot return there unless things change, my friend. Your people do not want me."

"George," Ben had said, standing in the doorway, looking back past Zaggad at the snow-covered strip of garden beyond the living room, "I hope they change just enough for you to come home."

"We'll see what the years bring," Zaggad had said as they shook hands.

The years had certainly brought change, Ben thought, looking around the cabin as people started to shift about in the early light. Returning to Philadelphia after a couple of wars and many missions, two children and a ruptured marriage, the betrayal of his life's work by his own people, he was on his way to see the man from whom he'd parted as a friend, a professor who had become, in the intervening years, a member of the Palestine High Command. Ben didn't want to see Zaggad anymore, but he knew this was the last stop for him, the absolute end of the journey begun after Miriam's murder. He would deliver the message. No more.

He was finished, done with the codes and secret meetings, the dynamite and rockets, the assignations in hidden corners, the ambiguity, the dual purposes, the unexplained and inexplicable. He'd done it all; they hadn't known how to value him. Using him as a decoy in Paris had ended his usefulness. He would do no more. There had to be another life for him and he would find it. He knew that he had a little way still to go.

SIX

"Ben! What are you doing here?"

Kate ran toward him the length of the deep lawn behind her parents' house, where he stood blinking in the bright autumn light. The gold leaves that had blown on her as she sat beneath a huge tree fell away as she ran. The sun shone coppery glints in her brown hair to match the burnished color crunching under her feet. Benjamin put out a hand to steady her as she drew nearer, but she was upon him, breathless, smiling, her arms flung around him, before he could stop her. He had not expected any welcome at all. Bewildered, patting her back, he looked gravely down at her to find tears in her eyes and an unfamiliar shade of uncertainty hovering about her delicate features.

"What happened? I don't understand. I thought you were in prison."

She stood on tiptoe to kiss him, then hugged him again.

"They let me out. The government gave France some terrorists in exchange. They'll try trading them for hostages in Beirut."

He'd been so angered about the publicity at his trial, so furious that photographers and newsmen had covered his return home, making his work doubly futile, that it hadn't occurred to Ben that she didn't know he'd been released.

"I'm so glad you're out. I thought it would be years and years. It's wonderful. Tell me about it, what was it like?"

Just like that. It was a long time since he'd thought he understood her, so he shouldn't have been surprised.

"Kate," he said, "why did you leave? You didn't even write. Just left. You tell me about that."

She took a step or two back and smiled up at him, grabbing his hand.

"Let's go and sit down under that tree," she said. "There's lots to talk about."

Shaking his head, blinking a little, he walked with her over the rustling ground, admiring her fluid movement, aware of his own persistent stiffness. The trees blazed above them, shot through, glittering with light against the high, clear sky. The big stone house was settled durably in its abundant setting, gracious, stable, permanent. It was a long way from Benjamin's native village, with its low-lying single-room apartments, its air-raid shelters and ammunition factory.

"What's that tree?" he asked, pointing to the shimmering thin gold leaves above.

"It's an American elm. They're dying out from some incurable disease, but this one's a survivor."

Kate released his hand as they sat down on deeply cushioned redwood chairs under the elm.

"What's the matter with your hands?" she said. "They're so rough and blotchy."

"They're much better now. You should have seen them in prison."

"Was it terrible, Ben?"

"Yes." He turned and looked at her. Beyond the sharp, sleek image, he saw her nightgown billowing out at him from behind their bathroom door. There was, he thought, nothing at all that he could depend upon.

"It would have been miserable anyway, but they made certain it was brutal. They wouldn't let a doctor near me. They threw substandard food at me. They looked away when I was beaten and abused. I gave them a wonderful opportunity to pressure our government to release terrorists with French connections." He didn't want to talk about it.

"Why did you leave, Kate?" Telling his wife threatened to whip his rage into an explosion.

"Oh, Ben," she said, looking away, "things got so bad." She reached to the ground for a handful of burnished leaves, crushing them in her fist. "You know, when you were arrested it was in all the papers, on TV. There were public debates about the trial. The children were terribly upset. Everyone we know had something to say, lots of it not very nice."

"What do you mean?"

"There were people who thought you'd been incompetent, otherwise how were you caught, stuff like that. There were people who were annoyed because you were supposed to be a trade advisor. You'd deceived them all along. You know. After you were sentenced, everyone said the French were determined to show the world they wouldn't put up with it and they'd make you serve a full sentence. Ruben was getting in fights at school all the time defending you. Roni came home crying. I got sick of it. About two weeks ago I went to see Uri."

"What happened with Uri?"

"He said they couldn't get you out. Maybe there'd be a way before the ten years were up, but he could guarantee nothing. We must learn to live without you. He said at least we knew you were alive and that we'd see you again one day."

Ben stood up and walked a few steps away, hands shoved deep into his pockets. They'd set him up and then abandoned him. Each time he was forced to recognize it was like the first time, as if the insides had been drained out of him, leaving a precarious cavity.

"I couldn't handle it," she went on. "I got so angry, I said the first thing that came into my head. I said I'd given Israel enough and I was taking the children and going home. It hadn't really occurred to me to do it, but when I got back to the apartment I discovered there'd been a bomb on the school bus that afternoon.

It hadn't exploded. They'd found it first, but it was *there*. Roni said, 'Don't worry, Mom, we were quite safe,' in that nonchalant way all you people have. Believing already, nine years old, that the army will always protect her, no harm can come to her. You know Israelis believe that. Otherwise, how could they go on?" She rubbed the palm of her hand over her eyes. "But it's demented. It's out of touch with reality. There is constant danger out there. Denying it doesn't make it go away. It may even bring it closer. Hearing her, after Uri, made me frantic. I realized that I could leave. My threat to Uri wasn't empty; I could make it true. So I did. I couldn't take it anymore, Ben."

He leaned down and touched her hair.

"You didn't write to tell me. I had no mail from you for at least two weeks before I got out of prison."

"I know," she said, tears winding down her high, arched cheekbones. "I know. I didn't want to hurt you. I didn't know what to say. The longer I put it off, the harder it got. I was so angry, Ben. With you as well as everyone else."

"With me?"

"Don't you remember how we fought before you left for France? You knew I was sick of it, sick of living without you so much, tired of the secrets and the danger, never knowing, never being able to plan, never being honest with anyone. And living in Israel had worn me down. I was fed up with it all and you, so determined to carry on."

"I never deceived you, Kate. Twelve years ago, when you followed me to Israel after you got your degree, I tried to stay away from you. When you wouldn't let go, I told you what I did. I told you what life with me would be like. I told you. I made sure you knew. I told you about Miriam. You knew I had to do what I was doing. You made the choice."

"That never included prison in France for ten years, Ben."

"No," he said slowly. "No, it didn't. Not for me either."

Handing her a handkerchief, he told her how he had been betrayed, set up as a decoy, abandoned to the French so that his Service could get the weapons intended for Iraq into Israel.

"They betrayed me, Kate. My own people." His voice cracked and strained, he told her he was leaving the Service, looking for a life where he wouldn't need to trust anyone. And where he'd have some control.

"Oh, Ben," she cried, "will you stay with me here? We'll start again and live in peace and raise the children without the terror all the time."

He couldn't answer. Blinking, he bent over and kissed her eyes; he lifted her up and put his arms around her, straining her to him. Her body curved toward him, fitting him as it always had, nudging, urging, reminding.

"Where are the children?" he murmured into her crisp, windblown hair.

"They're at school. And my parents are away. I was all alone until you came." Kate drew back a little and looked at him, all the tears gone, brown velvet eyes wide.

"Follow me," she said.

She led him under the golden elm. Behind it, a weeping cherry, its branches trailing the ground, its leaves a denser, coppery gold, made a hiding place. Parting the branches, she pulled him inside, down with her to the bronze carpet, reaching unerringly for everything that was hurt and damaged, everything that had been abused. Gently, surely, she comforted him, as she had done at the beginning. She gave him her openness, her fluid assurance. She offered him peace. Afterward, he propped himself on his elbows and picked pieces of leaves out of her hair. She knew him, he acknowledged to himself; at least Kate knew who he was. And cared. Shifting apart, they pulled their clothes into place and sat down holding hands, leaning against the tree trunk, listening to the sibilant leaves.

"Ben, let's stay here together."

"What happens when all the leaves go and it snows out there?"

"You know what I mean. Look, everyone in Israel is a casualty. In almost every family someone's been crippled or mentally shattered or blown up on a battlefield or carved up on a border. Everyone is scarred. From the last survivors of the Nazis to the

59

infants on the Golan who have to stay in underground shelters for days at a time. It's a permanent endurance test, Ben. You've done your share, more than your share. What do you think?"

"I just don't know yet."

"I know you don't entirely agree with me, but think of the occupation, Ben. It's not the country you grew up in anymore. The sleepy little Arab villages you knew then are occupied territories now, with a defiant underground resisting an enemy. You can't keep an occupation army in place for over twenty years and not be affected at all, can you? And Ben, imagine Ruben, patrolling the roads of Gaza or the alleys of Ramallah. Do you want that? That's not defending his house, Benjamin."

Everything was turned about, all the customary measurements invalidated, all his supporting structures warped and splintered. He new enough to know that he could not make decisions yet. But there would be time, and he still had a last errand to run. He turned to her.

"I have to think about it all. I'm very confused. But there's one thing I have to do here in Philadelphia. I might as well get it done and then we can go on with our lives."

"What do you have to do?"

"I have a message to deliver."

She let go of his hand.

"A message? What do you mean?"

"Just one final job. And you can help me, Kate. I have to see George Zaggad. I hope you can arrange it quickly."

He heard her sharp, indrawn breath.

"I thought you were through with it. I believed you."

"I am, Kate, I am. It's just one last little job."

"So that's why you came to Philadelphia. To see George, not me. To get me to help you see him. My God, I believed you."

"Kate, no, you're wrong. I came to see you and the children. When they knew I was coming they asked me—"

"You're using me, Ben. That's all you people know how to do." She stood up, brushing leaves off her skirt, hair tossed out around her.

"Kate, you don't understand."

"Damn right, I don't. I thought...My God, I can't believe you'd use me now."

"Listen," he said, clambering up to stand facing her, putting his hands on her shoulders. "Listen, I didn't want to do it; they forced me to. Someone's life is involved, Kate. I had no choice."

She jerked away.

"Of course you had a choice. There's always a choice. Everything we damn well do is a choice. You know that, Ben. You could have said no, you could have said, 'It's enough,' you could have said, 'Forget it, no, no, no.' "

Each scream pierced him like a shard of glass. He felt his legs weaken. He clenched his hands together. He was blinking again, his eyes watering.

"I couldn't say no. It's to do with Miriam. I had no choice." He wanted her to understand. He needed her to share it. She might be the last thing he had left.

"Miriam? Oh, come on, Ben."

He took a deep breath.

"I'm going to tell you about the job."

She stared at him.

"Sit down again with me. I'm breaking all the rules. I don't care. I want you to understand."

SEVEN

"The years have made you even more beautiful."

The resonant, familiar voice startled Kate. She'd been watching for Zaggad, staring at the wrong door; turning now, flushing at being caught planning to manipulate him more than from the compliment, she found him hardly changed. More silver, certainly, in the thick black hair, the lines across the forehead more clearly carved. But there was the same robust intelligence, the same barely restrained energy flowing warmly from him, the same promise of a huge reservoir of emotion contained beneath his vibrant surface.

"I'm so glad you could come," she murmured as he settled himself across the table from her.

It had been easy to make the arrangements; La Terrasse was three minutes' walk from his office on the campus, and it was where they had lunched on their last encounter, twelve years ago, before she left to follow Benjamin to Israel. He'd been delighted to hear from her. Of course he remembered her; he'd heard she was back in town and had seen the chairman about a position; he'd love to help; of course they must go back to their old haunt for lunch. With her rediscovered husband standing close by, it had been easy to deceive him by omission on the telephone.

Now, doubtful of her resolve, facing his perceptive gaze, she had to remind herself that her goal was nothing less than to redeem Ben's life.

"You look wonderful," he said again, staring appreciatively at her. "Let's start with a glass of wine, yes? So. Tell me all about yourself. All this time, what have you been doing?"

"Well, to start with, I got married. Do you remember Ben Landau?"

"My dear, I remember him very well. I know you married him. I heard from many mutual friends, here and there, too. But tell me, are things not well for you? I heard you came back without him. Things didn't work out?"

It was impossible. She had planned to talk about old times, common interests, old friends, and leave Ben and his needs until later. But George Zaggad had never been a person who could be controlled in conversation or anything else. He'd plunged to the center of her mission before she'd found her balance. She didn't know that she could handle him. She remembered suddenly that he was a member of the PLO High Command. He simply couldn't be the teacher she had known. A cold finger touched her spine, followed by an unwelcome rush of warmth.

"It's not quite like that," she said, making herself look at him. "I'll tell you later. Let's order some lunch. I'm starving."

He smiled slowly, shrugged and turned to the menu. She told him about her children, she told him about the teaching she had done in Tel Aviv, she talked about the book she had started about local government on the West Bank, she chatted about colleagues, changing times, diminishing grants for research, the role of the university; all the way through the salad and the omelets he smiled, asked questions, told anecdotes, the engaging, cosmopolitan raconteur, a perfect companion. When the plates were removed and the coffee poured, he waited for her to stop talking and lift her cup.

"Now, Kate," he said, "tell me all the things you have been avoiding through this delicious meal."

Her hand shook a little and she put the cup down. She glanced around; she had chosen the table carefully, in the corner near a greenhouse window, shot through with frosty sunlight, surrounded by plants, intimately tucked away. They would not be overheard.

"George," she said, "I didn't actually leave Ben. He was in prison. In France. Sentenced to ten years. Didn't you know?"

"Kate," he said, "I'm so sorry. Why did you think I would know?"

"He was charged with espionage, George."

He was silent.

"In view of your...your position in the Palestine High Command, I thought that was the sort of thing you would know."

She made herself look at him directly. His expression was patient, friendly, unchanged. He still didn't answer.

"George," she said suddenly, in a little rush of words, "I don't know who you are." She regretted it before the words were out. This time he smiled.

"Yes, you do. You know who I am."

"This has nothing to do with...Look, can I ask you, what happened? You weren't involved in politics. You used to say your role was keeping the record straight. You said you were an observer, historian...Now you're a member of the High Command. What happened?"

"You know what has happened, Kate. The October Ramadan War, the disengagement agreements, Sadat, Camp David, the West Bank, the siege of Beirut, Sabra and Shatilla, the Intifadah. A new perspective. A new view of my own contribution. Do you think the only effect of the Israeli occupation is to brutalize the occupiers?"

"I don't agree that—"

"Occupation radicalizes the victims also."

"It's wrong to—"

"We're long past right and wrong. It's like a failing marriage, stretched and jagged. It doesn't matter who is right or wrong, proving it makes no difference. Tracing the history is irrelevant.

All that matters is that it's failed. Both partners are losers. There aren't any winners. So it is with all of us who struggle over the past. It's futile. I intend to influence the future." He paused, eyebrows raised. When she didn't answer, he said, "Well, tell me about Benjamin."

"He was tried for espionage...."

"I know."

She stared at him, lower lip caught between her teeth.

"You *do* know?"

"Kate, Benjamin's arrest and trial made headlines here. He's an old acquaintance. Don't you think I read about it?"

She hated it, all of it, more than she had thought possible. Fooling herself that she could manipulate him while he toyed with her. It was like walking in the dark on rocks, not knowing when to expect a sharp edge, a slippery coat of wet algae, a loose, unstable spot where she would lose her footing. Rehearsing with Ben beforehand didn't give her any skills; she wanted to be herself, she was only comfortable speaking directly, she had no taste for deceit.

"George," she said, "there are some things you don't know from the papers."

He laughed.

"Many things, I am sure."

She was tired of it.

"Ben was set up, George. His own people betrayed him. They used him as a decoy so they could hijack weapons meant for Iraq and take them into Israel. They offered Ben to the Sûreté to throw them off the track."

She looked at him.

"That's interesting, but not very surprising." Zaggad spoke very quietly and she had to lean forward to hear him under the throb of conversation from the tables around them.

"Why isn't it surprising? I think it's amazing."

He laughed again, leaning his elbows on the table, resting his chin on clasped hands, looking steadily back at her.

"To me, my dear, it is not surprising, because I have observed the cynicism of your husband's masters so many times before. They decide they have a job to do, they do it, there is no human consideration, the result is all. It may be why they are often successful."

"Well, you may not be surprised, but Ben was shattered. He feels betrayed, totally abandoned. He says they used him and then just dropped him when it suited them."

"Hasn't he been in the business long enough to understand that?"

"He expected loyalty, George."

"It sounds as if you have talked with him, Kate. When did he arrive?"

She shook her head and bit her lip again. Throughout the conversation, Zaggad had been many paces in front of her, walking on ground so unfamiliar she could not anticipate it at all.

"Do you know that he is out?"

"Yes."

"They exchanged him for four terrorists."

"Terrorists? Those men were being held at Ramleh, pending trial. What's the difference between terrorists and revolutionary heroes anyway, Kate? I abhor violence at least as much as you do, but the situation is driving people to actions that have to be measured in revolutionary dimensions. They are driven to excess to respond to the excesses of occupation and oppression."

"I don't want to argue with you, George. I have some things to tell you."

"I see that, yes."

"Ben is very bitter. They waited for six months to get him out. He was ill in prison. He felt they should never have thrown him to the French. They should have got him out much sooner. He came back angry and resentful. He's determined to leave the Service."

"Yes."

"When he got to Israel, he discovered something by accident that made him so angry, so heartbroken actually, he decided he must do one more thing. To undo something they've done."

"And what is that?"

"He wants to see you, George. He wants to tell you what he discovered."

"Why? I should do his dirty work for him?"

"No! It's not that at all. It's something that has to do with his own life, something that happened long ago, something he has to put right before he can really leave it all behind him."

"And how do I fit into all this?"

"The information affects you, too. It affects the Palestinians. I mean to say...George, this is an occasion where your interests and Ben's happen to coincide."

"How extraordinary all this is, Kate. Tell me, why didn't Benjamin contact me himself?"

"Oh, George, he was sure you'd know he was found guilty of spying for Israel. He knows you're an important Palestinian leader. He wanted me to arrange for you to meet so that he can talk to you, so that you'll listen. How could he have come directly to you? He might have been killed."

Zaggad smiled and leaned back again, staring silently around the room. She waited. She knew she'd made a lot of mistakes, but at least she'd got the important things spoken aloud. That was something, she supposed. She shifted on her chair, feeling the aching tension behind her calves, the stickiness where her underwear clung damply to her skin.

"You'll have to tell me something more if I am to see Benjamin."

"I don't know any more."

"Then I am afraid I must refuse to hold this meeting. I see no purpose to it. I don't have any reason to think that Benjamin knows anything that would interest us."

"George. Listen to me, please. There is one other thing I can tell you."

"Yes?"

"His first wife was murdered, long ago, by three *fedayeen*. Two were killed, one escaped."

"So?"

"The one that escaped is now a member of your Invasion Committee."

"Really? How extraordinary."

"George, Ben found out about that man a few days ago, after he got back from Paris. He saw a file...well, George, that is why he must see you. That is really all I know."

Zaggad shifted sideways on his chair, turning away from her, tapping his forefinger on the table between them, eyes shifting slowly around the plants hanging from the ceiling. Then he shrugged.

"All right, Kate. I suppose I'm curious to know what he has to say. I enjoyed his company years ago. I must say I've wondered many times what he reported for the record about me."

She flushed again but didn't speak.

"Listen then. I"ll tell you where he must come if he wants to see me. I suggest tomorrow. Ten o'clock in the morning. Give him these directions very precisely. Tell him I shall be alone and I expect him to be also."

Then he gave her directions with the air of a man who had used the same rendezvous before. His tone had turned unusually cool, she noticed.

"I have to leave now, Kate. My friends are waiting for me. This has been interesting."

Watching him walk away, she saw two men who had been sitting at the table beyond them get up to leave also. By the time they reached the cashier, Zaggad was chatting with them. One of the other men paid both bills, and the three left together. She hadn't even been aware of them, but it didn't matter. She was jubilantly relieved that it was over.

EIGHT

Benjamin met his daughter outside her classroom at the end of the school day and they walked together to the big field to watch Ruben play in a soccer match. The weather had changed abruptly. Dense gray clouds hung low and a new chill disturbed the air. The carpet of leaves crunched thicker beneath their feet, but the trees, holding the last of their brilliant color, still blazed red and gold beyond the field.

Roni seemed at ease in the school Kate had found for them, a few blocks from her parents' house. Skipping along beside him, unable to hold hands because of the lesions and raw patches that still plagued him, she looked not much different from the other girls. Her English was excellent, of course. Kate had seen to that, insisting on speaking English at home since the day Ruben was born. Her compulsion had irritated him then; he had to concede its value now. And Roni's American mother had known what clothes would help her be accepted quickly in the fourth grade of the suburban school. She was properly equipped, his little princess, even down to the gaudy beaded friendship pins attached to her blue suede sneakers.

Benjamin, watching her closely, could see nothing to mark her as different, foreign or strange. Nothing that identified her as the daughter of a failed spy either, but he did look carefully at the little groups of parents settling down to cheer the boys. He watched to see if anyone recognized him. Ridiculous, of course, on an autumn sports field at a Main Line elementary school, but Benjamin had developed ingrained habits that clung as sour as the lingering odor of garlic. He wanted to be able to feel what he looked like to the other parents; he wanted to inhabit them just long enough to learn what they might discover from the way he dressed or spoke or listened to Roni's chatter.

No one there could possibly know that he was a father trying to rebuild his connections with his children after six months in prison, but this didn't stop him from checking and rechecking everyone around him just as, he supposed, he would never lose the need to turn on the radio every hour for news, keeping track of the latest bombing or the newest border infiltration. Not many fathers had been able to get to the weekday afternoon match, he noticed, and only one was unaccompanied by a wife or another child. He'd be interested to see which boy came up to him after the game.

Ruben came out onto the field with the other boys and looked around, as they all did, for parents huddled on the stands. He nodded and waved once but he did not run over for a whispered "good luck" as some of the boys did. Ben, blinking, asked Roni about her schoolwork. It was all right, she said. The work wasn't hard, but there were a lot of things different about the school. Like the computers in the big room the older kids got to use and the equipment in the gym, most of which she'd never seen before. And the bathrooms. The bathrooms were much bigger and much cleaner. And . . . there were other things. Like what? he wanted to know. Well, there was no security. You saw people walking around with big bags and packages and you knew they hadn't been checked for bombs because there was no one around who did checking. Well, of course she knew that was because there weren't bombs here in America; still, it seemed strange. And the kids . . . well, there were a lot of things they didn't know. Or understand. At first she'd tried to explain, about youth groups and training programs and the army and stuff like that, but after a while she'd decided it was better not to talk about all that. These kids were pretty dumb about things that didn't happen here, although of course they couldn't be sure they never would happen, could they, Daddy? Anyway, she guessed she liked it here. Most of the time she felt as if it wasn't the real world, but maybe something else, like a dream or a vacation.

Ben, trying not to tear at his hands, felt his eyes filling again and blinked repeatedly. He asked her to tell him the names of the boys on Ruben's soccer team, and while she did, he watched his son. Ruben was taller than the others. Broader, too, already. Bouncing the black and white ball on his dark head, running forward to take a pass, he looked older than the boys running around him, his expression alert yet guarded. He'd had to cope with a lot more than most American boys in eleven years, Ben thought, enjoying the enthusiastic cheering as Ruben scored the first goal of the game. In his son's restrained smile and conscious composure as he moved from his triumph to take his place on the field, Ben saw a filtered reflection of himself. He saw, in Ruben's nonchalant lope and steady gaze, an image of the boy he had been. But he'd been far more innocent, oddly more protected and supported than Ruben was now.

The inexorable passage of the years ached deeply inside him. He wished his son was happier. Kate might be right; he could do worse than find a way of life that would give the children the security he'd denied them this far, give them the chance to grow to their full potential, redeem their lives and let all the rest go.

Benjamin glanced around again. The solitary father, clearly having come straight from his office in his well-polished shoes and business suit, was intent upon the game. Perhaps he belonged to the visiting opposition team. None of the others seemed to know him. But then, they didn't know Ben either, although one little girl came up and whispered and giggled with Roni for a while. Roni introduced her as "Susan B. 'cause there's three Susans in my class, A, B, C, get it, Daddy?" He hugged her, but she squirmed away. She wasn't used to having Daddy around. Or was it just that she was nine? He didn't know much about it.

When he looked back at the field, Reuben was pulling a tousled boy up from the muddy ground, pushing him forward, hurtling him back into play. He didn't look toward his father at all. Benjamin, blinking, wondered if he could undo the damage he'd done to Ruben. Or perhaps it was only damage to himself? Ruben looked a lot more intact than Benjamin felt. Soon he'd have to decide how to spend the rest of his life. With surging irritation, it to occurred him that his own preferences might be a legitimate consideration. But his own preferences were currently as obscure as the sun anyway.

As the game ended, the boys ran over to the stands. Ruben, who could run the fastest, walked.

"Good game," Ben said, reaching out to touch his shoulder, intimidated by the evasion in the eyes so like his own. Watching Ruben shift his shoulder away, ruffle Roni's dark cap of hair, point out a new boy on the team, Ben forgot to watch the solitary well-dressed father and see which child he'd come to applaud. By the time he remembered, the man had left. He could see him at a distance, striding quickly between the burning trees toward a parking lot. He couldn't see a child with him.

Walking back to the house with his children, Benjamin reminded himself all the way to talk only about the game and the school and avoid the angry issues that lay behind Ruben's precarious composure. Don't spoil the day; just enjoy them, grit your teeth, they'll come around.

Kate was home when they arrived, back from her lunch with George Zaggad, jubilantly reporting the time and place she'd arranged for them to meet.

NINE

Beyond Shemtov's window, the translucent light had drained away. Without its special radiance, Jerusalem revealed more starkly the tangled web springing from her layered history. Spread out before him, searchlights played on the stone wall of the Old City, where soldiers leaned against the railing at the top of David's Tower, the glow from the great golden dome of the Al-Aksa Mosque shimmered proudly, motley crowds shuffled interminably around Jaffa Gate, traffic moved swiftly along modern city streets, the lights of the growing expanse of new roads and buildings up the hillsides stretched ever wider the illuminated arc around the city. For Shemtov, the bitter discord that surged always beneath Jerusalem's deceptively innocent surface was never more palpable than at night.

Staring beyond the window, waiting for the call that would tell him whether his operation to save Gershom was under way, he summoned the image of the boy he had recruited twenty years before. Mediterranean bronze, thick, wavy black hair, lean, hard-muscled, triangular chin and a frequent, delighted smile that even he, who cultivated a remote and self-contained mask, could not resist. The boy he had turned into Gershom had looked right for just about any assignment that Shemtov and his case officers could develop; more, he could look like any Middle Easterner. Shemtov, obsessed by an audacious program to infiltrate Israelis throughout the Arab world, could not resist that lure. He'd changed in all the years, of course, Shemtov thought, remembering the last time he'd risked meeting Gershom briefly in Rome. Still handsome, certainly, hair still full, though graying, face gaunt, with prominent cheekbones and temples, eyes hooded. He had smiled very little when they had met more than a year before, but when he did, his face was transformed back into the young man Shemtov had found and trained.

Preoccupied with shifting images of Gershom over the years, Shemtov was startled by the phone, though he'd been waiting for it. It was Tel Aviv headquarters. He clicked the switch on the underside of the phone.

"Message just came in, sir." It was the duty officer. "You wanted to know right away."

"Thank you. Go ahead, if you please."

"Job's wife has made contact, sir. Meeting set for Job for ten A.M. Eastern time tomorrow. That's five P.M. here."

"Thank you."

"Shall I forward instructions, sir?"

"No, thank you. I shall do it myself. Good night."

Shemtov, allowing himself a few seconds of satisfaction at this report, wondered if the time would ever come when he would be able to tell Benjamin that his code name had been Job for this operation. Its evocation of enduring pain suited him, of course. Perhaps, in time, Benjamin might be able to find some amusement in it. Perhaps. Shemtov dialed the second number of the orange card in front of him. Al was not in New York now. This time it was Philadelphia, Area Code 215.

"Hello, Al," he said. "How are you all? I just wanted to let you know we have definitely decided to operate tomorrow. Caesarean section, sometime before noon. It's the only way to save the infant, so we must proceed."

"Very good." The response was crisp, clear, all-American.

74

"We'll handle it. Nothing will go wrong. By the way, I took your letter personally to Pietro."

"Thank you. I assume he was able to assist?"

"Oh, yes, everything we need. Very well organized. Connections still impeccable."

Shemtov chuckled.

"I thought so. Well, I'll be seeing you soon. Good luck."

He put down the receiver without waiting for a response. Looking at his watch he calculated that it was almost six in the evening in Virginia. Peter Bendington's rare petal formations would be folding up for the night by now. Peter had been very helpful. Shemtov felt he ought to thank him immediately. No knowing when he'd need support in the States again. Pulling the phone and the orange card closer, Shemtov dialed the first number on the card, selecting his introductory remark from a reservoir of mutual interests. When Bendington's harsh whisper came onto the line, Shemtov said, "Had we but world enough and time" and laughed as Bendington completed the couplet.

TEN

Benjamin stood looking at flamboyant, spiky bromeliads and the elegant shapes of violet and coral birds of paradise. He'd seen them often enough before, of course, but that was in another world, a world where the sun blazed fire, shocking these wild colors and soaring lines into life. Here, shielded by glass from the chill wind chasing the last of the leaves under a thick gray sky, the flowers looked unlikely. He actually reached out to touch a curling edge on a strelitsia to assure himself that it wasn't plastic. They only seemed to be false.

"They grow on the hillsides at home, don't they, Benjamin?" said a resonant voice behind him.

He wasn't startled; he had been waiting for it. It had reverberated so often in his mind across the years that it remained familiar. He turned at once, smiling, holding out a big hand.

"It's good to see you, George," he said and shook hands, forgetting that contact seared his slowly healing skin. Benjamin saw immediately that the years had been kind to Zaggad, whose sturdy, muscular frame was as trim as it had been twelve years before. He looked as robust, as energetic, as exuberantly intelligent as he did when Ben first saw him. The extra threads of silvery hair and the deeper lines around his eyes did nothing but enhance his handsome intensity. Benjamin noticed all this with relief and pleasure, forgetting entirely the purpose of the meeting or the effects of years of waging secret war on opposite sides. For a minute or two the mask he had struggled to develop during the intervening years just slipped away and he looked at an old friend with simple happiness.

"It's extraordinary to see these flowers when it's so cold and dreary outside, isn't it?" said Zaggad. "Makes you wonder if they're fake. How can glass and lights produce what our sun does?"

"That's just what I was thinking," Benjamin said.

"Have you ever visited the Longwood Gardens greenhouses before?"

"No. I've never been here."

"This was a gift to the state of Delaware from the Du Ponts. American aristocracy in a way. I'm glad I've given you the opportunity to see it. Or that you have given it to me. Which is it, Benjamin?"

Benjamin had to stoop a little to meet Zaggad's eyes. He had absolutely no scruples about the message he was about to give Zaggad; it was obviously in the interests of both of them, he was betraying nothing. But some vestigial caution nudged him. After all, though George Zaggad was an old, congenial friend, he had become a member of the Palestine High Command. Benjamin had to wonder what Zaggad was thinking about him. He needed a minute to slip a mask back into place.

"George," he said. "I wanted very much to see you. You chose a good place. But it's hot, isn't it? And damp."

Zaggad shrugged. "It's a greenhouse."

Benjamin patted his upper lip and forehead with a tissue and looked around the hothouse. They were alone in the subtropical garden, though he could see people moving about through the glass sides of the adjacent unit.

"Kate tells me you know something about what's been happening to me lately?"

"Doesn't everyone? Tried and convicted of espionage for Israel, sentenced to ten years, jailed in Paris, released six months later in exchange for four so-called terrorists. A spy."

He paused and looked expectantly at Benjamin, who hunched his shoulders and shoved his hands into his pockets, but said nothing.

"I've wondered," Zaggad went on. "What did you tell your masters about me years ago? Do you know, I trusted you. I thought we were friends. I never even considered you might be spying on me. I was very naive in those days, wasn't I, Benjamin?"

"I wasn't spying on you, George."

"You're not going to tell me your career as an agent began after that, are you, Benjamin? That trial in Paris shows you have a long record. You're a senior operative. It's only twelve years since we knew each other here, after all."

"I didn't say I wasn't an operative then, George. Just that I wasn't spying on you. I wasn't. I was here for something else. I met you by accident, through Kate. We were friends. I trusted you, too."

Zaggad nodded somberly.

"Times have changed, Benjamin."

"Yes, now you're a member of the Palestine High Command. You weren't then. Or am I being naive now?"

"No, no, I was not. I believed then just what I told you, that we could work it out, your side and mine."

"And now?"

"Now?" He smiled. "Now I know we cannot. No way. Not at all."

"What made you change your mind, George?"

"What the occupation did to my people. What it did to yours. What I know of history. Sadat. Iran. Saudi Arabia. Learning to identify the scale of passion that a need for identity can build, properly used. Come, Benjamin, you aren't here for a lesson about national liberation. Incidentally, you, your people, gave us fertile soil." He laughed. "In more than one way, of course."

"I want to tell you something, George."

"I gather you do."

"No, I mean something else, before we begin."

"Well?"

"I was not here to spy on you and I did not do so. But I did report to my superiors after I returned. I told them we had misjudged the Palestinians. They are not all animals, some of them have rational aspirations, cultivated minds, great ability."

"Some of my best friends are Palestinians, right, Benjamin?" Zaggad said quietly, raising his eyebrows.

"That's not fair, George."

"I think it is. But anyway, I don't have any commitment to be fair."

"You used to have."

"Those days are over."

He walked a few steps away, toward a huge bromeliad, whose thorny spears of leaves guarded the thrusting deep pink flower bursting from its center. He looked at it, then turned back to Benjamin.

"You are not unchanged yourself, you know. We are not the men we were. Now. What is this information you are supposed to share with me?"

Benjamin, leaning against the wooden edge of the nursery table, hands deep in his pockets, stared at him.

"You don't understand," he said. "I'm not 'supposed' to do anything. I've left the Service, George."

"Oh?"

"I was betrayed by my own side. I can't go on." Looking through the glass behind Zaggad to the bleak gray scene beyond, stunned rage overtook him again. "That last mission to Paris—that was a setup. They used me as a decoy. I wasn't even told they had other agents in there. I just went on doing what they told me, a foil for the real operation. They used me to throw the French off the track; they let them arrest me. My God," he said, taking his hands out of his pockets and scratching the skin, which had begun itching again, "I had an operative who got a job in the factory so we could have access, a family man, you understand, wife and four small children, handed to the French on a carving board for dinner so the others could fly the stuff out. My man had worked for me—for them—for five years. He was shot in the head; his head was blown into pieces all over the sidewalk. Do you understand me? And I spent six months rotting in a filthy prison before they traded for me. They told Kate I was lucky to be alive, there was nothing they could do. When I got back they gloated about the successful mission; what a wonderful thing, they got the arms that were meant for Iraq, they tricked the French, aren't we all wonderful? I told them then, 'I'm finished, no more.' I told them, 'How could you do this to me, what right have you got, what do you think I am.' I told them, I said, 'I cannot understand how you could do this to me.'"

Benjamin, blinking rapidly, shoved his hands back in his pockets to prevent himself from scratching them. He shifted his stiff shoulders under his storm coat and looked about the greenhouse. His eye caught the flaring bromeliad and reminded him. He turned back to Zaggad.

"And do you know," he said more quietly, "something else happened after that. I went home, to my parents' kibbutz, in the Galil, you know? There was a young man there, a boy I helped to raise, he was like a son to me, from another time in my life. I found he had been killed, fighting hand to hand on the Golan, while I sat betrayed in a Paris prison. What for? What's it all been for? His name was Natan."

Benjamin covered his face with his hands. His tremor had returned, he was infected again by the poisonous bacteria that had attacked the wellspring of his life, he was undermined in every tissue of his system. After a minute or two he raised his head, his dark eyes misty, and looked at Zaggad. He thought he saw, mirrored extraordinarily on his face, the horror that he felt himself. Caught up now, enduring terribly again the assaults upon his being, he saw in Zaggad's alert, intense gaze the reflection of the idealism that had been his own, that and the shadows of doubt, the hazy edges of ambivalence slanting across. He thought that he and Zaggad had more in common than they'd known, they were brothers after all; and he was not sorry to have shared this moment.

Zaggad shook his head slowly.

"You've had a bad time," he said.

"There's more," said Benjamin wearily. "There's more, George. One more betrayal, the worst. Which is why I am here." He rubbed his eyes, shifted his shoulders, hunched back against the nursery table. "I can't bear knowing I have spent my life working for a cause as corrupt as the one it fights."

"Tell me, then," said Zaggad.

"Yes."

But for a minute he couldn't speak, his chest and throat and eyes filled. He rubbed his eyes again, blinking, turned and walked down the aisle and back, and cleared his throat.

"I was married before, when I was young. I don't think I ever told you that, did I? Her name was Miriam. She was murdered a long time ago, by three *fedayeen*, attacking the kibbutz. She died protecting the boy Natan I spoke about. Two of the guerrillas were killed, but one escaped. For years, nearly twenty years, I heard no more about it. Now, this last time, I learned something new."

He was not looking at Zaggad anymore. He was not looking at anything around them. Staring sightlessly ahead, he watched some image in his mind. Incredulity marked his face and voice.

"I went to tell them in Tel Aviv I was finished with the Service. There was a lot of argument, pressure, accusations, but I wouldn't listen to anything, I said I am finished. My...superior..."

"What is his name?"

"His name?"

"Yes, what is his name?"

Benjamin blinked.

"I know him as...as Uri."

"Yes. Go on."

"He said there were papers to sign, he would get them. He left me in his office. My file was on his desk. Of course I looked at it. There was a picture of me when I joined, a report on Miriam's murder, that's what made me volunteer for the Service. The whole thing in the file, just as I knew it. Except one thing. They have the name of the third man, the one I thought had got away. And there's a cross-reference for him. Do you understand? It means he has his own file. Can you imagine? His own file? It can mean only one thing. I was afraid Uri would be back at any minute, I heard footsteps in the corridor outside, there was a typewriter clacking below, I could hear water running somewhere, but I flipped through the file. Much later near the back, there was a paper numbered with the cross-reference code. It had instructions not to send me into Beirut because Kamal Hussein is now a member of the Invasion Committee of the PLO. That was dated about five years ago. That's all I had time for, but I know the name, of course. I know he's still on that committee."

"Kamal Hussein," said Zaggad.

"He killed my wife, George. He belongs to my Service, he has a file. They sent him back after Miriam was murdered. Now he's on your committee and he's reporting back to Israel. That's why I wanted to see you. Now do you understand?"

Zaggad took a step toward him.

"Some things I understand. Not everything."

Benjamin raised heavy eyebrows.

"I don't understand—" Zaggad began.

"Can't you see? You have a traitor on your hands?"

"You want to help us, Benjamin? The PLO?"

"George, that man killed my wife. I want him killed. He should have died twenty years ago."

Now Zaggad turned away, looking beyond the glass to the adjacent unit, where a school group, shepherded by two rumpled male teachers, toured the tropical plant displays. The only sound in the glass house where Benjamin and Zaggad were standing was the steady dripping of a leaking sprinkler.

"You don't mind exposing a man who gives your people information?"

Benjamin laughed.

"This man? No. I don't mind."

"It's odd," said Zaggad quietly, watching Ben. "The Invasion Committee has been investigating a leak, I happen to know."

"A leak. More like a running stream. George, they've had a killer in place for twenty years. And he's penetrated deep. You can imagine what he's delivered."

Zaggad did not shift his stare, even while he flicked hair away from his forehead, even while his highly polished shoe scraped at a patch of mud on the floor.

"Tell me, Benjamin, do you think your Uri left that file there by mistake?"

Benjamin, blinking, stepped closer.

"My God, of course it was a mistake," he shouted, loudly enough to attract a curious stare or two from the glass-walled unit next to them. He lowered his voice. "Uri went to get severance papers for me to sign, vows of silence, pending pension payment canceled. I was leaving the service. He wasn't thinking about the file. We'd quarreled, he was angry."

"Did you sign?"

"Of course. I'm through. I told you."

"You sound like a man who has something still to finish."

Benjamin took a deep breath. He was determined to close the circle that had begun for him when Miriam was murdered; he had to free himself from all this; he had to convince Zaggad.

"George, I told you. I have something to finish. Kamal Hussein, I want to finish him."

Zaggad didn't answer.

"I hope to do it this way. If not, I'll find another way."

"Well, I will think it over."

"Will you let me know?"

Zaggad laughed.

"No, really. Will you? Because otherwise I'll have to make another plan. He goes free no more, I tell you."

"Benjamin, you need a rest."

"Not yet." His voice was rough.

"I shall make an inquiry, perhaps. After a few days, you may have word from me. If you don't then it's because I have nothing to say to you."

Benjamin nodded. Zaggad raised a hand to prevent him from speaking.

"Do not communicate with me again. Don't send Kate either, it isn't safe. Anyway, I don't want to see either of you. My life is complicated enough."

"George—"

The hand came up again, a stop sign.

"No more. I'm leaving now. Please remain here for ten minutes before you leave. Good-bye."

There was no handshake. Zaggad turned and walked to the door. He stopped and looked back at Benjamin.

"Don't try to get to Beirut, Ben. Have a rest."

He was gone. Benjamin watched him walk to the next hothouse and go in. Ten minutes later, when he left, he saw through the glass that Zaggad was still talking to one of the teachers, leaning over the proteas and waving his hands about, while the other teacher talked to the schoolboys in the corner opposite.

The parking lot was gray and cold. Benjamin strode across it toward Kate's mother's white Oldsmobile, raising the collar of his parka against the chill. A noisy family group walked by, little children tugging at their grandparents, while their parents hurried ahead. The children were trying to make the old folks swing them along; their shrill, insistent voices and clattering footsteps irritated Benjamin, distracting him from his effort to reconstruct the encounter he'd just had with Zaggad. He wasn't sure whether he had convinced him to act against Kamal Hussein. He couldn't interpret Zaggard's reactions. Walking into the cold beyond the greenhouse, it occurred to him that he would have no way of being certain that Miriam's killer had been caught. Whose word could he trust, after all? Regrettably, not

Zaggad's, even if he was ever to hear from him again, which seemed unlikely. As for Shemtov, Benjamin knew perfectly well what his word was worth. Watching the children force their grandparents into their pace, toying with the notion of going to Beirut himself to hunt Kamal Hussein, Ben arrived at the car, unlocked the door and slid in, pushing his collar down, switching on the engine to start the heater.

"Just sit quite still for a moment," said a voice behind him. A cold circle of metal touched the back of his neck.

Staring ahead, he watched three men approach, appearing from behind the school bus that must have conveyed the boys in the greenhouse next door and perhaps the teacher with whom Zaggad had been so intently engaged. One of the men walked a step or two ahead of the others, bouncing on the soles of his feet, as if his movements had been learned to compensate for his shortness and chunky frame. He looked very serious, Ben saw, square jaw in a salmon pink face, pale eyes steady under frizzy yellow hair. The other two men were both taller, darker, narrower. One had a badly pockmarked face; the other looked younger, relaxed, almost jaunty, hands in the pockets of tight blue jeans.

It was this one who opened the door next to Benjamin and gestured for him to get out. Perhaps they wanted Kate's car, Ben thought. As he slid out of the seat, the other two men walked over to the passenger side of the car. The man with the gun climbed out onto the pavement next to Benjamin, hands in his raincoat pockets. Ben, turning to get his first look at him, told himself there was no way he could handle four men, at least one armed, no sense—

"Mr. Landau," said the man with the gun. Benjamin stiffened. It wasn't the car after all. The man's accent and appearance were American. A lot of well-groomed brown hair, good teeth in a pleasant smile, a direct stare from untroubled blue eyes, an assured stance, aided no doubt by the bulge in the raincoat pocket, in which a hand held the gun pointing at Benjamin.

"It's very cold out here," he said. "So get back on board. Back seat, please. In the middle."

"What's going on? Who are you?"

The gun poked through the pocket and jabbed his stomach.

"Just get in," its owner advised.

Benjamin climbed back into the car and was immediately flanked by the gunman and the man with the pink face and frizzy fair hair. The other two got into the front. The car started moving immediately, out of the parking lot, onto the highway.

"I'm entitled to know what's going on," said Benjamin.

"No," said Frizzy. "You're entitled to nothing."

He sounded very hostile and he glanced at Benjamin with contempt, lips pursed together. Unmistakably American also, plaid shirt pulled taut over a beer belly, jeans, boots, windbreaker, salmon complexion, balding in a small saucer among the frizzy hair. Benjamin couldn't see the faces of the men in front. They could have been from anywhere. Neither had spoken a word or offered any other means of identification. The man with the American accent and the gun in his raincoat pocket gazed serenely ahead. Frizzy's contemptuous stare returned repeatedly to Benjamin.

"Where are we going?"

"You'll find out."

Ben jerked both elbows out and shifted forward. The gun was pressed into his side immediately and the stocky man with the pink face locked his hands in a painful grip. Seven inches shorter than Benjamin and without his large frame and huge shoulders, he was surprisingly powerful. Benjamin kicked out impotently at his legs.

"Now listen," the gunman rasped, barely moving his lips, disgust rising from him, "I don't want to sit next to you, believe me. I sure don't care to talk to you."

"What are you talking about?" Ben shouted.

"You have to come with us. We have a long drive. Nobody's enjoying it. If you keep talking I'm going to hurt you right away. So shut up. Okay?"

The man on his left sniffed loudly in agreement.

Benjamin sat still then, trying to work out who they were and what they wanted. It stretched credulity too much to doubt that they were connected with his meeting with Zaggad, but these men on either side of him were not Arabs, he was sure of that. Besides, if for some inexplicable reason Zaggad wanted to kidnap him, he wouldn't have waited until he was getting into the car, surely. Why would Zaggad want him anyway? Benjamin leaned forward, trying for a good look at the men in front, some way to identify them, but his guards pulled him back roughly and the stocky man banged his knee with a clenched fist in a way that made him realize he could get badly hurt.

Benjamin's rage, lodged like an extra organ within him for twenty years, hugely enlarged by his months in prison and by multiple betrayals, gathered with an intensity that demanded expulsion. He marshaled his depleted reserves to force himself to be silent. He was aware that his exhausted system could not withstand the physical abuse that the man on his right seemed eager to deliver. It was too much, he thought bitterly. It never stopped, there was never an end. This meeting with Zaggad was to have been his last gesture, but here he was again, captured, manipulated, impotent. And he didn't even know who wanted him or for what. He swung for many miles between an absorbed concentration on controlling his rage and an effort to calculate which enemy these men represented. It made no sense, he thought again and again, between blasts of fury that overtook him like a high wind on a mountaintop. He was certain only that these were not Palestinians; not their emissaries either. He could think of no one who might need to kidnap him.

They were speeding toward New York, Benjamin noted, watching the road signs, looking ahead to the smog, urban disorder strewn out beyond. After a while, he thought that they were making for Kennedy Airport, a notion that produced clenching new rage.

After well over two hours of silence, Frizzy reached into his pocket and pulled out a small book which he threw onto Benjamin's lap.

"My passport?" Benjamin jerked upright, incredulous. "Where did you get it?"

Frizzy stared stonily ahead.

"Where did you get my passport, godammit?" Benjamin shouted, clutching the stocky man's arm. His hand was immediately gripped by the other, crushed painfully. His knuckles cracked with a brittle sound and he grunted.

"Don't you talk to me like that," Frizzy said, and dropped Benjamin's mangled hand.

"Might as well tell him, Al," murmured the man with the gun. "We'll be there pretty soon now." His expression altered. Benjamin thought he was restraining a smile.

"Okay." The man called Al leaned forward now so that he could stare directly at Benjamin. "We got your passport from Kate, of course. Where else?"

Benjamin opened his mouth, but he couldn't speak. Blinking rapidly, he tried to concentrate.

"How...how?" he managed after a moment.

"Oh, we had no problem getting it," the other murmured quietly.

"But wh-where..."

"You're going home, Landau," said the driver, in the Hebrew of an Israeli. "You're under arrest."

"Under arrest?" Ben repeated slowly. "Under arrest for what? What are you talking about?"

"Treason," spat Frizzy, whom they called Al.

"You're crazy," Ben retorted, voice and reason returning in the face of this outrageous nonsense.

"Passing information to the enemy," said Al, with a twist of his small mouth. "Giving Zaggad the goods. That's treason, you filthy, rotten scum."

Benjamin leaped at him, his huge hands grabbed the frizzy head on both sides. He pushed it back against the seat, but in the instant the gun was pressed into his side, the other man had an arm around his own neck. All three froze in that tableau. The car moved steadily forward. Then Benjamin's hands loosened reluctantly. They all settled back, helpless to alter the course they'd begun when they climbed into the car.

There was a long silence. Then Benjamin said quietly. "Surely you know I'm on a mission?"

The only reply was a mocking chuckle from his left.

"I'm under orders, man," Benjamin said, his voice rising. "I can prove it.

"You'll have your chance in court," said the driver.

"What authority do you people have?" Benjamin asked, hurtling into the new reality.

The man on his right leaned forward and took a folded card from the driver. Holding it carefully in front of Benjamin, he showed him. Benjamin, blinking, banged his fist on his knee. They had authority. No doubt of it.

"But Sh...my chief, surely your people have checked with him? I'm acting on instructions."

"You'll be able to try that after we get you locked up" came crisply from the front.

"Well, let me tell you, I'm not going with you. I'm not getting on a plane. I'm not leaving the United States. I'm married to a U.S. citizen. My children are here. I'm not going back to Israel now."

"Landau," said Al, his voice resonant with satisfaction, "you are going to get on that plane, using your own passport and be escorted back to stand trial for treason."

"I am not."

"Oh, but you are. You have no choice. We are holding Kate, Roni and Ruben hostage for you. They will be released when we have you in the air. Not before. We don't want any scenes at Kennedy, Landau. You're going and you're going quietly. That's why we're holding them. To make sure. Get it?"

He smiled broadly for the first time, his skin reddening, as Benjamin sagged beside him.

ELEVEN

No one expected Shemtov to be there, but they showed no surprise when he walked into the narrow basement room of the old Arab house. The hidden guards outside must have been startled also; their chief wasn't in the habit of strolling into the communications room at all hours, let alone after midnight. The only one who didn't remain impassive was Shai, the boy hunched on a stool in front of the big machine, and that was because he didn't know enough. He'd heard of the legendary Shemtov, of course, but had never seen him. He would have expected him to be bigger, somehow, more imposing. When the compact stranger in unmarked fatigues came in, Shai swung around on his stool, his bushy black eyebrows raised high, a mocking grin curving below his high sallow cheekbones.

"What the—?" But he was quick on the uptake; he saw the others nod respectfully, murmur politely. He turned back abruptly to monitor the blank screen, a flush staining his face like streaks of crayon. After a minute or two, the gray-haired man sat down on a chair against the wall, leafing through the papers Gabbi, the commanding officer, had handed him. The night's yield, so far. Nothing much. Then Gabbi came over to Shai, bending low to whisper into his ear, "This is the chief. Just do your job quietly." So he knew, and had to struggle not to turn around and stare.

Shemtov's composure fitted him like his own skin. The urgency of his anxiety bubbled from somewhere deep inside him, beyond muscle and bone, in the tissues where the ugly choices were made. By now they might have decoded the letter for which Gershom's messenger had been hung. If they had, they might have found out there was a leak directly from the Committee. How fast could they trace it to Gershom? What was he doing to protect himself? There'd been no word, of course. Nothing, since the shrill alert of the hanging near Sidon.

The machine shuddered and the light clatter began, like delicate high heels on a marble floor. Gabbi moved to stand behind Shai. The boy touched a key, a light blinked and the decoding began.

"It's New York, Dan," Gabbi said quietly. Shemtov was across the room in a second, bending over Shai's shoulder to read the words as they came through.

"Job securely aloft" were the first words.

Gabbi nodded. Shemtov made no effort to suppress a slight sigh of welcome for the next phase of his operation to save Gershom. The machine tapped on.

"Retinue released. We're in place. Orders?"

"Put it on hold," Gabbi told Shai. He handed pencil and paper to Shemtov, who scribbled off a response and gave it at once to Shai to transmit.

"Well done. Maintain full surveillance both subjects. Report urgent all activity."

Shai pecked it out on the keyboard, pressed the encoder, watched the lights until the tapping began again. When the screen darkened, Shemtov turned to Gabbi and inclined his head toward the door. They went up to the hall on street level and into a room fitted out as an austere office toward the back of the high-ceilinged stone house.

"Congratulations, Dan," Gabbi said in a level tone, without a smile.

"Too early for that yet, Gabbi. There are things to do right now, if you please."

Gabbi pulled a notepad out of his pocket.

"Get a couple of your young men onto the phones, Gabbi. Let's see, Amnon at *Ma'ariv*. Gluck at the *Post*. I suppose Ben Dror or someone like that at *Ha'aretz*. Anyone else you can dredge up. TV, of course. Tell them Benjamin Landau is being brought back under arrest from the United States on charges of treason. No details available. Give them time of arrival at Ben Gurion Airport. Absolutely no attribution. If they don't like it, they needn't bother to go out there, they can be pipped to the post by the others, that's their problem."

"Okay," said Gabbi, taking a step toward the door.

"No, wait. There's more. You get Uri in from Tel Aviv. He should be at the airport. He can represent us."

"You mean you're not going?"

"Oh, absolutely. I'm not going. Nor are you. That could be very dangerous. Benjamin mustn't see me now. No. I shall come into it later. Quite a bit later. Send Uri. Then phone the P.M.'s office and tell them we've got him. They can notify the cabinet. This will be the biggest security case in Israel's history, Gabbi."

Gabbi bit his lower lip.

"We don't have many traitors, Dan." He didn't trouble to disguise the irony.

"Don't be bitter, Gabbi. We have no choice."

Shemtov stared at him, but Gabbi was glancing down at his notes.

"Any other calls?"

"I must call Aron Levy myself." A shadow of distaste disturbed his expression just briefly. "There will be more news from America soon. I shall have to get Levy over with."

"I'll leave you here with the phone, then." Gabbi avoided meeting Shemtov's gray stare.

"If you please."

Shemtov glanced at his watch. Almost two in the morning.

Smiling slightly, he dialed Levy. He had to be courteous, he supposed, but at least he could wreck the night's sleep for Levy.

"Good morning. So sorry to disturb you," he said as soon as he heard Levy's voice. The voice of a policeman, he thought disdainfully, knowing and hating the fact that Levy thought of him as a rival. The audacity! "I wanted to inform you. Have you heard the news?"

"Not yet, Dan. I was asleep" came the fuzzy response.

"Well, our man is en route. We've had excellent support from the American end. I assume you're ready with a full contingent for his arrival?"

"Oh, yes, of course." The policeman's voice was getting stronger every minute. "My boys in the arresting and escort party are all furious with your man, naturally. They despise a traitor. I've already issued very stern warnings about maltreatment. Fair trial and all that. Some of the boys would like to take the flesh off him as soon as he lands."

"Quite so," Shemtov murmured. "Er...have you informed the press?"

"Well, I didn't think we'd want that. No exactly something to be proud of. I assume the P.M. will want it hushed up, at least until the damage is contained. I took it for granted..." He ran on like a fountain.

"Quite so. Well, then. I just wanted to alert you that the arrest has been made and it's over to you for a while. Thank you."

"As to legal counsel—"

"As we discussed, let's have a hold on everything. Everything. For the first few hours. But if he mentions any names, legal counsel or anyone else, I want to know, right away. If you please."

He was smiling again as he replaced the receiver and hurried back down to the basement. Gabbi and two of his men were elsewhere, making sure that Benjamin Landau's arrest for treason would get sensational coverage. Shemtov toyed again with alerting some of the foreign correspondents, and again rejected the idea. It was an unnecessary risk. They were certain to pick up the news through the usual interlocking connections. He could see, he could taste the headlines in the United States, Damascus, Cairo, Amman—and in Beirut, where they would count the most.

Shemtov walked over to Shai, picking up the tearsheets stacked on the table next to him. Messages had been clattering in while he'd been making sure that the world and Aron Levy knew how damaging Benjamin Landau had been to Israel's security.

"Job's wife telephoned vacationing parents. Very distraught. Parents returning immediately. Urged her to do nothing. Violent reaction, refusal, broke connection. She immediately called our consulate, placed urgent message on tape for return call for reasons of quote utmost security unquote. Then attempted to contact Andrew Payne, known to be family attorney. Payne unavailable. Message left with answering service."

Shemtov flipped the sheet over, read the next one.

"Sisera driving alone on highway to New York."

The ridges on Shemtov's forehead deepened. He looked at the next one.

"Job's wife called Harry Monk, pediatrician, requested special favor, house call, children hysterical, refused to explain further on phone."

Shemtov shook his head, reread it, picked up the next one.

"Sisera pulled over to roadside, made two calls, unidentifiable, from phone booth, drove off in direction of Manhattan."

Zaggad's trip to New York must be connected with his meeting with Landau. It must, Shemtov thought, warmth rippling through his veins like a shot of brandy. It might be working, the operation might really save Gershom. The machine clattered and he turned to read over Shai's shoulder again.

"Sisera parked car in large lot off Lexington, walked to East 65th Street, was admitted to opposition mission before ringing bell. Is carrying overnight bag."

The room was silent then, Shemtov gazing at some invisible

configuration in space, Shai watching while pretending not to. Gabbi came in just as the ticking of the printer began again.

"Pediatrician visited retinue for half an hour. Job's wife, holding revolver, saw him out, locked up, many lights switched off. Then telephoned FBI to announce her husband had been kidnapped, demand immediate assistance. FBI assured her message will be transmitted to appropriate authority and advised her to call local police. She broke connection abruptly. Called Sisera's house, no reply."

The clattering stopped, but the machine gurgled loudly and began almost immediately.

"Attorney Payne returned call. Refused to go to house, too late. Changed his mind when she told him Job and passport have been kidnapped, she and children held for several hours. He promised to visit immediately."

Shemtov sighed, looked at Gabbi, shrugged.

"Just as you said, Dan," Gabbi nodded. "Everything right on schedule."

Shemtov pulled a little box of white mints out of his breast pocket and offered it to Gabbi and to Shai, popping one in his mouth without a word.

"Job must have been very effective with Sisera," Gabbi said abruptly.

Shemtov closed his eyes for an instant.

"He's a highly skilled operative. Brilliant, really. And this time, he's got a powerful personal goal."

Gabbi's eyes widened suddenly. He knew nothing of this. But he didn't ask. Shai, however, had none of the inhibitions of long experience or moral ambivalence. He swiveled around on his stool, looking openly at last at the steady, tanned face, the gray stare, the composure of the legendary Shemtov.

"May I ask a question, sir?" he said, disregarding Gabbi's frown and the slight smile at the corner of Shemtov's mouth.

"You can ask," Shemtov said.

"Wasn't Sisera a Canaanite general, sir?"

Shemtov was smiling fully now, a rare, sunny burst of approval.

"Yes, indeed. A very brave and courageous one. He was also, I should point out, an intellectual, a man of sensitivity, the most trusted aide and advisor of King Yavin."

They all turned back to watch as the clattering started up.

TWELVE

When the plane lurched, losing height, Benjamin pressed his body hard against the back of the seat. He didn't want to look down. He didn't know why, but he resisted the land stretched out below; he didn't want to see it until he had to. Battered, bludgeoned, nearly numb, he had endured the long wait at Kennedy Airport and the twelve-hour flight in virtual silence. Feeble efforts to get information out of his guards, haltingly, apprehensive undertaken, had been fruitless. Between them, he'd subsided into a dazed, sullen quiet, dozing, waking cloaked in drifts of patchy fog, utterly unable to sort it all out. Waiting within a cage of numbness for the anticipated confrontation with Shemtov, he wanted to alert his senses as the plane descended. He wanted to make himself ready.

He had not been permitted to shave. Apart from splashing his stubbly face with tepid water in the bathroom, the door held open by a guard, he had not washed since leaving Kate's parents' house about twenty hours and several lifetimes ago. His clothes were rumpled and grubby. There was no cheer as the plane touched land, no excited burst of song that invariably accompanied an Israeli plane landing on the soil of the redeemed homeland. The crew on this special government flight and the guards accompanying Benjamin didn't feel like celebrating.

He walked to the exit door behind one, ahead of the other. Now he felt an urgency to descend. He expected Shemtov. It had not occurred to him to expect anything else, so he was totally unprepared for the gathering on the tarmac. Standing bewildered for a moment at the top of the steps, he was the single target of photographers' flashes. His large frame silhouetted against the young clear light of dawn yielded images for the world to inspect: images of a big man, battered, alone, staring ahead with a look of confused horror so intimate it was an obscenity to record.

He saw, at first, only the television cameras, the notebooks, the mob on the usually empty tarmac. He was nudged from behind. He started to go down; his eyes, blinking rapidly, searched for Shemtov below. He could not find him, could not identify a single face. No Shemtov. Gabbi, then, representing him. Lifting his head high to peer over toward the back of the crowd, he bit his lip. No Gabbi. He heard nothing. He thought there was no sound at all, from any of them, until he reached land, when he was grabbed on each side by armed police. There were a lot of them, but only two were needed to separate him from everyone else. They started to lead him forward, toward a convoy of cars parked on the tarmac, when he heard the shouted questions.

"What did you get from it? What was it worth?"

"Where's your *khaffieh*, traitor?"

"How much, Landau? How much?"

He jerked at the guards. He tried to turn and identify the bodies attached to the voices, but there were too many.

"Any comments, Ben?" That was an American accent.

"How will you plead?" That was from somewhere in the Middle East.

He could tell that many of them were silent, doing their jobs, making judgments, not making judgments. What did he care? It was all some dreadful foulup. He had to see Shemtov. Then, nearing the cars, moved inexorably forward by the police, he saw, standing to one side, a face he knew. Uri, it was Uri, his case officer, the man who'd run him in Paris, set him up for the Sûreté, brought him home when it suited him, set him up for George Zaggad in Philadelphia, Uri watching him expressionlessly as he wrenched free from his jailers' grip and swung around toward him, skin flushed, blazing with fury. Their hands were firmly on him before he stopped in front of Uri, looking down at him, struggling for words.

"What have you done to me?" Benjamin was hoarse.

Uri's eyes flickered, his shoulders lifted in a tiny shrug.

"Where's Shemtov, goddammit? I demand to see him." Benjamin lunged toward Uri, but the police restrained him easily.

Uri was motionless, impassive.

"Why?" Benjamin roared suddenly. Behind him cameras clicked, flashes cut arcs of hard light.

"I'm sorry, Ben," Uri said quietly, turning and walking toward the terminal, not looking back, not once, as Benjamin was pushed into a car between two policemen and driven off in a convoy whose sirens shrieked for most of the twenty-minute drive to the prison at Ramleh.

THIRTEEN

The raucous wail of a bugle blown by a shallow-chested novice woke Shemtov at three in the morning. Surfacing anxiously, he snapped upright on the awareness that only two people in the world could make his gray telephone ring; and one of them was his Prime Minister, whom he had left dithering, preparing for sleep three hours before. Very convenient that Berta remained in Bat Yam with the children as she preferred.

Shemtov swung his legs over the side of the bed, turned on the lamp and kicked the scrambler switch on the wall before pressing the phone to his ear.

"Yes?"

"I am Gershom."

"Ah." The deep sigh was fear as much as relief. "Where are you?"

"In a phone booth on the Piazza Navona."

"You're in Rome? Are you all right?"

A quick, indrawn breath, like the eerie rustle of a pine when a bird shifts invisibly in its darkest recess.

"At present, yes."

There was a little silence as each waited for the other to speak. They were unaccustomed to communicating by telephone.

Routine methods allowed time for reflection between responses; or occasionally, reassuringly, the other man's expression and gestures could be searched for amplification. They both began talking at once, were silent again. Then Gershom asked, "Did you hear about the hanging north of Sidon?"

"Yes. But I haven't received your message."

"The message," said the distant, melancholy voice, "is being decoded on Hamra Street. Akman took care of the messenger."

Shemtov sighed.

"I was afraid of this. Is that why you're in Rome? Do they know where—"

"Listen," said Gershom in his straightforward way, "you have to take me out. They'll know who I am in a matter of days. What I am, I mean to say. They may know already. I can't go back."

This was the only time he'd ever asked. Never before, in twenty years. Like a patient informed that his brain scan has identified a dreaded disease, Shemtov absorbed the confirmation of his gravest foreboding. Gershom had not suggested leaving Beirut during the Yom Kippur War in '73 when his Palestinian comrades, like him construction workers for the Maronite warlords, had abandoned their ladders and cement to rush south, brandishing stolen rifles and braggadocio, preparing to invade Gershom's homeland. He hadn't suggested it, ever, in all the years, not even during the interminable hot summer of the siege of Beirut in '82, when he'd clung stalwartly to his Bourg al-Barajneh sidewalk café, which was well known by then as a gathering place for troublemakers, Palestinian intellectuals and spies from five continents and five hundred factions. Steadfast, constant like the Mediterranean tides, Gershom had stayed, pouring thick Turkish coffee sweetened to dense syrup into tiny cups, serving his customers, drawing them into the network he nurtured with the same exquisite care his first love gave to a bunch of infants in the underground shelter of a besieged northern kibbutz.

Gershom listened—he had elevated listening to pure art—but he also talked. By then Tewfik Mahmoud was a member of the elite five-man Invasion Committee, making the plans that he filtered back to Shemtov, clear as water purged and purified in the Dead Sea project. He hadn't hinted at evacuation even after the Sabra and Shatilla massacres, when several of his oldest friends and their wives and children were slaughtered exuberantly by Gemayel's militia while Israel blinked spastically, turning the powerful binoculars of her army units toward the heavenly firepower of that autumn, rather than the explosions in the festering camps. Gershom had never before so much as murmured that he'd had enough. The end of his mission had never been discussed.

"It's over," he said now, as Shemtov dug inside himself to search out the priorities. "Where can I go?"

"Steady now," said Shemtov firmly. "Tell me what's going on, will you? Why are you in Rome?"

"We were coming before all this. It's nothing to do with it, just lucky that it gives me a chance to talk to you. Otherwise—"

"What are you doing in Rome, Gershom?" Shemtov cut in.

"I'm here with Walid. It was planned before, when we heard from the American. It's nothing to do with Hanouri's chauffeur."

"What American?" asked Shemtov sharply. Gershom talked to many people, but never to Americans that he could remember.

"He is called Rich."

"CIA?"

"Who knows? That's what we're supposed to believe, but I doubt it."

"What do you think he is?"

"A merchant, I think. He's offering us some new kind of weapons, everything dirt cheap."

"Is he indeed? Gershom, what does—"

"When I see you, I'm going to tell you all about it," Gershom interrupted mournfully. "It's very interesting. But now, tell me the way to get out. I must leave it all behind now. There's no time."

Shemtov was becoming alarmed about using the phone for so long. His line was absolutely secure, of course, but the phone in the booth in Rome could be picked up if it occurred to someone to try. It wasn't a risk he should go on taking. He needed Gershom's information about the American. Urgently And Gershom had to be informed about Shemtov's diversion, the name-dropping by the embittered Landau to Zaggad in Philadelphia that made it safe for Gershom to return to Beirut.

"I'm coming to Rome in the morning," he said.

"No, no. Don't come near me. My danger is enough. You mustn't come."

"Gershom, we can't stay on the phone. There's a lot we must—"

"No, out of the question. I can't risk it, don't come near. You owe me that, at least. You know you do."

It wasn't only the thin connection distorting Gershom's voice. Shemtov heard a high desperate chord of terror, as if Ghershom hung scarred and bleeding from a tree, legs writhing, twisting up to avoid flames leaping beneath. Sweat bubbled at his own hairline, beaded his upper lip, dampened his armpits and his crotch.

"What was in the message you sent, Gershom?" He needed time to plan.

"I was telling you about coming to Rome with Walid. I was hoping you'd meet me here. I haven't seen you for more than twelve months already. But not now, not now, you mustn't come anywhere near me now."

A sudden switch from Hebrew to Arabic. Unprecedented. High-pitched, as near to babbling as Shemtov had ever heard him.

"I won't come if you don't want me to, don't worry. Don't worry about it," he said soothingly, sorting through fragments for a makeshift operation.

"You must take me out. Don't you see I can't return there?" Gernshom, who never raised his voice, was strident. "Do you know what they're going to do to me? Think of it. Think how they'll—"

"I have," Shemtov announced calmly, "a plan. I've been

preparing it since I heard about the murder. I have a way to protect you. You'll hear from me within twenty-four hours."

"Don't send any one of your people." Gershom's voice was thicker now, almost muffled. He had returned to Hebrew, though.

"Trust me. It's foolproof, you'll see. When have I ever steered you wrong? Stay in place. I'll clear this all up in a few hours."

"Please."

"Eliahu," said Shemtov commandingly, using his name for the first time in over twenty years, "Eliahu Golan, this is an order." Then, with implacable authority, he said, "Trust me," and broke the connection, rubbing the moist phone on the sheet to dry it before getting up to splash cold water on his face and neck, dress, and drive to Tel Aviv.

FOURTEEN

They handled Benjamin Landau strictly according to regulations. They did not abuse him physically. They did not malign him. They put him through routine procedures in their laconic style, but with careful attention to detail. They did not interrogate him. They did him no harm, unless it could be said that handling him like a contaminant, avoiding all but essential conversation and ignoring his questions and pleas for Shemtov was harmful. They took their time removing, labeling and locking away his leather belt, shoelaces, keys and wallet and the small recorder that looked like a flashlight and was even more unreliable.

It was hours before he was alone, in a small cell with a barred window, from which he could see brush and high cement walls and hills, pink and hazy beyond. He had no idea what would happen next. He ached. Every muscle, every bone, every tissue, it seemed, had been violated; every movement hurt. He sat down slowly on the edge of the iron bed, wincing, eased cautiously down on the gray blanket to find a place for his sore body. The rash was back on his hands and arms, but he was too exhausted to lift one hand to scratch the other. Repeated blinking had left his eyes burning dry, but for the trickle of moisture at their corners. It was all another terrible mistake, he thought, drifting into a shocked sleep.

He woke when a man sitting on a small chair next to his bed cleared his throat. Thinking at first that it must be Shemtov, peering through the dying light at the gray figure, Benjamin struggled to sit up, blinking out of his daze. It was not Shemtov. This man was taller, his nose jutted from his face like a rocky outcrop, what remained of his hair, curling in ringlets above a prominent forehead, was very dark, and there were purple plums for eyes, fleshy lips. Not Shemtov at all. Benjamin rested his back against the gray wall behind him. He knew the face. He'd seen his picture. He waited.

"Benjamin, I'm Aron Levy, Internal Security."

He leaned back, licking his lips. When Benjamin remained silent, he sighed deeply, lifted thin eyebrows above the plummy eyes and drummed his fingers upon his knee.

"It is necessary for us to talk," he said.

"I wish to see Shemtov," Benjamin responded.

"Ah, yes. I know. I hear that is what you have been saying. You will, I suppose, in the course of events. For the present, you will have to make do with me."

Benjamin was bewildered. Shemtov had sent him on the mission, his final one. He needed Shemtov to extricate him from this misunderstanding. He was not free to explain to this man. He was not permitted to expose the mission.

"So, tell me, why did you do it?" Levy gave a little upward jerk of his chin as if to say, "Come on, you can tell me, it's quite simple."

Benjamin stared at him, trying to concentrate. An inexplicable series of mistakes had obviously been made; he must resist his exhaustion, his confusion, his pain, and put things right. The situation was not irretrievable. He swung his legs over the edge of the bed and sat forward, leaning his big frame toward the security chief, hunting for the right words.

"Look, I intend no disrespect, sir. I am not free to discuss the

106

mission with you. I was under orders from my chief. I have to
see him to get this cleared up."

Levy's expression altered. He appeared to be smiling, since
prominent teeth were now briefly visible.

"Landau," he said impatiently, "did you or did you not meet
George Zaggad in a greenhouse in Philadelphia yesterday
morning?"

Ben shrugged. He didn't know what he should say.

"Will you answer me?"

"Am I being charged with something?"

The teeth again. The light was fading rapidly from the cell;
long gray shadows stalked the land outside. Benjamin could not
find the edges of Levy's head.

"Yes, Landau, you are being charged with treason."

He licked his lips and, as he did so, the electricity came on. A
recessed, screened-off bulb yielded pale light.

"Don't I have to be charged in court?"

Levy clicked his tongue against his upper palate loudly. He
stood up, took a step away, which brought him almost to the
door, then turned back.

"Yes. Eventually. You will be charged in court."

"Then I demand a lawyer."

It was a smile. There was no mistaking it: the lips drew back
across wet teeth, lines shifted around bulging eyes. It was a
smile, not a grimace, almost certainly. Tall, paunchy and
powerful, Levy erased it as quickly as he had before.

"So. A little reality set in, eh? You will have a lawyer. In due
time. Anyone in particular?"

Ben said the first name that came to mind.

"Isaac Harari."

"Mm." Levy bent his head, studying the stone floor, revealing
a fleshy second chin beneath the hard-edged one thrusting
aggressively forward.

Harari's name occurred to Benjamin as the only important
lawyer with whom he was even slightly acquainted, having met

him two or three times with Kate's father. Monty Abrams and Isaac Harari were high school and college buddies. Harari's decision to emigrate to Israel after World War II did nothing to damage the old close ties; Kate's parents' loyal Zionism took them often to Israel, and Harari's political and diplomatic skills were even more frequently put to use in the United States.

Harari's name seemed to sting Levy into confused silence. Isaac Harari was, after all, a member of the Knesset and of its State Security Committee. But who could be more appropriate as Ben's advocate than a man whose connections with his Service were unassailable? Ben was quite satisfied with his impulsive choice. It was the logical one, though Levy appeared nonplussed. Raising his head, he glanced at Ben.

"I'll look into it," he said slowly.

He moved to the door, his hand on the knob. Then, like a rash bursting up to the skin, malicious curiosity rippled over his face and he turned back to Benjamin, his forehead gleaming.

"You know what they're saying out there, Landau? Do you?"

Benjamin shook his head.

"I hear you betrayed an agent. An Israeli spy. An agent working for us inside a top committee of the PLO. He gave us the best intelligence we've ever had. And you betrayed him to George Zaggad in a greenhouse in Philadelphia."

Benjamin shook his head wearily.

"Because you were bitter about a few months in a French prison, Landau? That's all it took to sell us down the Nile? Or is the rest true, too?"

"The rest?" Ben whispered hoarsely.

"That you had some personal motive. Revenge. Some incident from your youth. The rumors are blowing like the *khamsin* over the desert." He was almost spitting.

Ben hurled his body off the cot, fists clenched, blinking. Levy opened the door, revealing two armed guards.

"I'll look into your request for a lawyer, Landau," Levy said curtly, before the door banged behind him.

Caged, Ben took two steps and slumped against the wall. Three huge spotlights glared from the high towers near the wall outside, blasting through the darkness beyond his barred window. He heard footsteps, then silence. Assaulted by rage, he slammed his large palm against the door. His stomach lurched convulsively. He kicked out against the unyielding iron cot. Then, limply tired again, he sank down on it, tears suddenly erupting to wash the dryness from his burning eyes.

Where had it all gone wrong? What had he done to bring himself into this intractable cage? He blamed himself, he was sure that he had made some unforgivable mistake, he must be responsible for his solitary agony, but he didn't know how. If only he could identify the cause of his distress, if he could somehow pinpoint the action or the words or the thought that had made all this happen to him, he might be able to come to terms with it. In a rising wave of revulsion against himself, he lay facedown, weeping silently.

He heard the door open and a little metallic clang as the plate with his evening meal was placed on the floor beside it. He didn't raise his head until he heard the door close. He clambered slowly off the cot, shifting his shoulders up and down, shaking first one foot, then the other, trying to put himself back together. He ate slowly, taking gulps of the sweet, weak coffee, careful to chew every bite, trying to avoid the cramping spasms he'd suffered in Paris.

Unsought, sporadic flashes of memory jumped at him. The contemptuous sneer of the American, Al, in the car on the way to the airport in New York; the flaring strelitsia curved behind Zaggad in the greenhouse; Kate's neat brown head shimmering in a veil of spun-gold leaves; all the security on his flight to New York; Shemtov chewing mints in the apartment on Jabotinsky Street. What was it Shemtov had said, exactly? Why was it so important to get the name of the Palestinian to Zaggad? There had been a reason why Ben could not resign just then, he was the only man who could do the job. His final job.

He would have to go back to the beginning, go over it all, seek out every nuance, every subtlety, find the explanation, for there had to be one, somewhere. But when was the beginning? He couldn't be sure if it was Uri, bringing him in from the kibbutz to try and get another mission out of him, or Shemtov, finding the only way he could to force Ben to go to Zaggad. Or was it before, when they sprang him out of the French prison? Or when they allowed him to be captured? Jolted by a vision of Miriam so powerful that it opened raw the painful buried wounds of his loss, he forced himself to contemplate going back, all the way, to her death, which had evidently set in motion not only his own clandestine career, but that of another, more deeply concealed source of intelligence.

Benjamin reflected that Levy's accusation that he had betrayed Israel's best agent hardly squared with Shemtov's original, declared intention of exposing a turned Palestinian, who happened also to have been Miriam's murderer.

There was a great deal to think about before he encountered Isaac Harari, which he assuredly would. Despite the events of the previous twenty-four hours, this was still Israel, after all, the bastion of democracy and idealism he had served so long. Sometimes wires became crossed or objectives distorted in the daily struggle for survival, but the nation was built firmly upon principles of justice, fairness, civil liberty, redemption. Benjamin brought all the instruments of his covert life to a fresh analysis of the events that had delivered him home to charges of treason. He wanted to be ready for Harari.

FIFTEEN

Gershom sat in a rented Fiat braced for death. He needed to plan his escape before his double life destroyed him; instead, he was driving up and down the Roman Hills, listening to the final proposals of Rich, the chattering American with apparently unlimited resources.

Gershom was invaded by fear. Images of destruction behind his eyes dwarfed the grand, sweeping hills; the serene golden light was an illusion barely masking the gashed flesh and clotting burgundy blood which stained his vision. A dozen times or more Gershom had closed his eyes and clenched his hands together in the face of an oncoming car, heard a shrieking collision, a shattering windshield, high cries of pain. He'd looked out and down to the brooding valley and felt the rush of air as the car hurled off to the side, turning in the air, crashing, crumbling into flames. He'd twisted around to search behind, watching for assassins following, hugging the same interminable curves, disguised assassins who might be anyone, serve any master, commit any savagery. He waited for the grenade hurled at the Fiat's roof, the machine gun poking black from the window of a passing truck, a crash from behind, in front, above. Through it all, the American talked.

"I'm telling you, we can deliver the stuff. You guys are overdue for some help, we know that. This'll do it for you, you'll find that out. It can be done. You can take the West Bank, let me tell you."

He gesticulated as he talked, sweeping his hand expansively about the steering wheel as if he were waving commandos into place in Ramallah, in Hebron, in Jericho. In Jerusalem. All the time, though, Gershom endured his private consciousness, the car lurching out of control, exploding from a hidden bomb, smashing into a rocky outcrop ahead.

"Three weeks from now, you could be ready to go. No reason to delay. The money's no problem. I know you guys have some princes in your pocket. Those cats don't like the Shiites any more than you do, not one bit. Anyway, you can have the stuff on account, pay later. My people know you're good for it. No reason to delay, let me tell you."

Rich swiveled his damp, glistening head all the way around to smile at Walid, jammed uncomfortably into the back seat. Gershom concentrated on concealing his fear.

"Why you're offering us?" asked Walid, snapping the tab on a beer can, a small explosion that Gershom had to identify before he could lean back and feign nonchalance.

"Because the time is right, man. The West Bank's ripe, there's turmoil over there. Now's the time to chase the Jews out of there, take it back. Give me a beer, will you?"

Both hands lifted from the wheel to snap the can open. The glossy head, with its thin strings of black hair lacquered in place, leaned back to take the first long swig. Gershom restrained himself from grabbing the wheel.

"Quite frankly, it would take the heat off us in the Gulf. Shift attention a little bit, you know what I'm saying? But that's by the way, a little bonus, kickback, call it whatever the hell you like. Thing is, they're ready for you over there on the other side of the river. They're sick and tired of the occupation. See, the youngsters have never known it any other way, its been that way since they were born. You know they've grown up angry. And disappointed in their parents, let me tell you. They're ready to join you, throw the foreigners off their land. That's how they see it, you know that. You can go home and take it back. I'm telling you right now, it's yours for the taking. Go home."

Go home. The words whispered mysteriously through Gershom's memories, tantalized his senses, intriguing enough to overtake his terror. Go home. Home. Where was that? It certainly wasn't the West Bank, which hadn't even been part of Israel during Gershom's life there. The West Bank towns had been conquered only a few months before Gershom had left for Beirut via Cairo, where he had established his stolen identity. The West Bank wasn't even a part of his Israel.

So where was Gershom's home? It wouldn't be Kafr Kassem, the little village near the pre-'67 Jordanian border, though for twenty years Gershom had schooled himself, his Tewfik Mahmoud self, to believe in it as the home he'd fled with his bitterly bereaved mother in October 1956, after his father and brothers were massacred by the Israeli Border Patrol.

Gershom had gone to look around Kafr Kassem during his early training, long ago, trying, because Shemtov demanded it, to imagine what his life would have been like if he had grown up there, but all he saw was a docile, cozy village, built into the sunlit hillside, doors painted bright pink and blue to ward off evil, dark-eyed children squatting placidly on corners. He couldn't see the village serenity evaporate in the sudden ratcheting of machine-gun fire, the bicycle wheels tumbling on the reddish dirt, the bodies collapsed in dusty light, fast, crumpled, finished. Gershom had read everything that Shemtov provided, though there wasn't much about Kafr Kassem. The Israeli authorities didn't exactly expunge it from the historical record; unlike their adversaries, they were defiantly, proudly, not in the business of rewriting history. But they tiptoed softly around it, if they approached it at all, which they didn't if they could avoid it. Trying to incorporate Shemtov's cover story within himself, Gershom learned that the massacre at Kafr Kassem had erupted on the eve of the Suez War.

When Egypt's charismatic Nasser nationalized the Suez Canal, blockaded the Strait of Tiran and the port of Eilat and raised the pitch of the routine cries for *jihad*, for holy war, to shrieks, Israel, France and Britain planned a joint operation against Egypt. Poised to invade the Sinai desert, nervous of disruption because of frequent terrorist infiltrations, the Israeli army ordered a wartime curfew on the jittery Jordan border, from five in the afternoon until six the following morning.

In the area around Kafr Kassem, where two thousand Arabs lived in generally acknowledged cooperation with the Israelis, the border police received the curfew order at three-thirty in the afternoon. The mukhtar was advised some time after four. The orders required the police to shoot any Arab on the streets after curfew. No arrests were to be made. It was impossible to inform everyone from the village who worked in nearby towns or in the fields. Asked by subordinates what to do about Arabs returning from work unaware of the curfew, Colonel Shadmi said there must be no softheartedness. "May Allah have mercy on their souls, *Allah yarchanu*," he said.

In seven villages, subordinates softened the orders, delaying the curfew, escorting workers home, forbidding firepower. But at Kafr Kassem, when fifteen villagers rode their bicycles toward home at five-twenty, they were instructed to dismount. Alarmed, they tried to flee. They were shot and killed. Villagers returning from work in the backs of trucks and wagons were shot on sight. By the time the army became aware of the massacre and halted it, forty-seven Israeli Arabs had been killed, including a number of women and children.

Although the tragedy was covered up by censorship at first, eleven officers were eventually tried and received sentences of up to seventeen years, though no one served more than three and a half. Generals Dayan and Tsur of the general staff were not even questioned. Colonel Shadmi was fined one piastre. "You'll still find Palestinians griping about 'Shadmi's piastre,'" Shemtov told Gershom; over the years, Gershom confirmed this time and again. Kafr Kassem was a code for betrayal, for vicious, frivolous carelessness with Arab life, for murder with impunity. For state-sponsored terror. The name reverberated with the same grief and shame and humiliation for the Palestinians as Deir Yassin and Quibya.

Gershom thought Kafr Kassem belonged on the Palestinian Roll Call of Infamy; it was their Maalot, their Munich, their Mahane Yeduda market, their Lod, Metulla, Mishmar Haemek, their Etzion Bloc. But Gershom was extremely uncomfortable with the comparison, because he knew that Kafr Kassem was a rare perverse exception, whereas the number of Jews killed at the merciless hands of Arab terrorists was huge. But measuring suffering, loss and inhumanity by body count made Gershom feel deeply ashamed. In fact, it made him feel wicked. He would have liked to have talked this over with someone who was qualified to measure ethical conflicts, but he didn't know anyone like that. Certainly, there was no use discussing this with Shemtov. Although he would certainly grasp the issues that troubled Gershom, he'd say exactly what suited his operational needs, nothing more, nothing less.

However important Kafr Kassem had become to Gershom, it certainly wasn't home. Shemtov had chosen it as the cover story for Gershom's early years because it would instantly identify him as a brutally aggrieved Palestinian, and because, in the aftermath of the 1967 Six-Day War, the body of the boy who had been named Tewfik Mahmoud at birth in Kafr Kassem had been found along with the bodies of several Egyptian soldiers who had been killed defending Ismailia. Tewfik Mahmoud's papers and his life story were available for Shemtov to graft onto Eliahu Golan. It was an especially convenient cover because his mother, Amira, had died at her brother's home in a village near Ismailia the previous year.

Kafr Kassem wasn't really home and Ismailia, which Gershom had visited only briefly to learn enough to sustain his new identity, certainly wasn't. Nor was Baghdad in Iraq, where he had really been born, third son to a prosperous Jewish merchant, who lost everything in the pogroms of the early fifties and fled destitute, part of Operation Ezra, to Israel, his obedient wife and five children accompanying him to the indignity of a tent in a dusty, confusing absorption camp.

Baghdad wasn't home and the transit camp certainly wasn't and Gershom didn't feel that his home was in Holon where his father eventually settled down, in a small square stone house with two rooms and three citrus trees, a guard dog and five chickens and from which his mother, no longer obedient, had shortly fled. Of her own volition, Gershom reminded himself, as he always did, repeating the words like a prayer, a talisman of reassurance. Of her own volition, reappearing at odd intervals once a year or so, unhinged and demanding.

Gershom supposed that his home might be Dafna, the settlement near the Lebanese border where his father had sent him to grow up to be a man. The old man had dispersed the children about the country as if scattering his seed to explore and compare the nourishment of different regions, different ways of life. As a result, Gershom and the others had each grown up alone, virtual strangers to one another, the idea of family just that, an idea, nothing more. He supposed going home might mean Dafna, with its brisk air drenched through by the warm tart breath of oranges, the ground thick underfoot with crunchy pine needles, the settlers always intent upon any shiver of movement on the heights above, the children huddled into shelters where infant cries punctuated the shelling and the smoke didn't usually penetrate.

Gershom wondered if home hadn't actually become his little cafe in Bourg al-Barajneh, or the apartment near the Roache where the sun sliced between the slats of the blinds and painted stripes upon the face of Razan as she lay there, even now, waiting for him.

"For us, it's very strange to operate with the United States," Walid was saying, crumpling his beer can with a loud enough crackle to return Gershom to the moment in the Fiat with the American, Rich.

"Look, man, our interests coincide. You can see that."

Gershom glanced at the American. His jovial expression was

glued in place like his hair. He licked his lips and held forth again. The man talked a lot.

"Walid, come on. My government wants a peaceful solution. Same as you. The road to peace is the end of Israeli occupation. You have to show strength, I kid you not."

He slapped the steering wheel a couple of times for emphasis. Gershom watched the road curve away.

"Let me tell you," Rich continued relentlessly, "the Jews are so busy fighting each other they don't know what's going on. They've got their own little war going on now with the religious. They're fighting each other in the streets. I've seen it. With my own eyes. My own eyes, let me tell you. Those creeps come out with their pasty skin and thick black clothes and that hair hanging down the sides of their faces and throw stones at the folks going to the movies. The army is busy with them these days."

They were winding downhill by then, the translucent light sheering away into a pastel haze, the hills darkening behind, the curves hiding the approach of cars from above or below. Gershom knew that his fear of collision or assassination were simple disguises for his terror of discovery. That was no fantasy, it was likely and imminent. But naming the cause of his fear did nothing to lessen it. For miles around the hills he sat absorbed in the ruminative anticipation of one disaster or another, hearing the conversation between Rich and Walid only when he could loosen for a few seconds the menace that hovered, like the closing light, about him.

"The time might be good for us," he heard Walid acknowledge.

"Yeah, your people are fed up, kids getting killed in demonstrations regularly, more land stolen from the old farms, they're digging up the olive trees to pour cement for army barracks. No way to live, Jewish settlements all around, can't go anywhere, blue tags on the cars, get stopped and searched all the time. All the time. They're ready. The youngsters have been raised for revolution. You know that. It's time."

A car was approaching, a large silver Mercedes climbing the

narrow path up the slope toward them. Its surface shone in the gathering dusk, its square body filled the road. Gershom clasped his hands together, and shifted lower in his seat, braced for the impact. Even Rich stopped ranting and leaned forward over the wheel. When the car passed without squeezing them off the road, Gershom rubbed the back of his neck and turned to look at Walid, who sat unconcerned.

"I can't see how we are going to throw out the Israeli army. They have the power."

Rich smiled, his sallow, fleshy face puffing out with satisfaction.

"You'll have the power. The gas will do the job. No way they can handle it. They're not prepared. They'll have no choice. They'll have to retreat."

"Gas?" said Gershom.

"Not too much. A couple of drops at crucial spots. Your West Bank can be wrapped up quicker than a camel bends for a prince."

"I didn't know about gas," said Gershom.

"Of course you know. I was just telling you. It's a toxin, man. That's what it's all about in these little wars. Nothing to worry, I'm supplying masks for your boys, of course."

There was a little silence. Walid cleared his throat rather loudly.

"Remember, Tewfik? Gas at the bases, he was saying?"

"Oh, yes, sure," Gershom agreed. "Is it the same stuff the Russians used in Afghanistan?"

Rich peered intently at the road, tapping the steering wheel several times with his right index finger. Gershom felt Walid nudge him just below his shoulder and knew he shouldn't have asked.

"Now you guys know it's not Russian stuff, don'tcha?" Rich chided. "Where'm I gonna lay hands on that shit? But the same net effect, I promise you, the same results or I'm Mohammed. Squash any resistance from the heroes of the IDF."

Gershom didn't care what the Americans helped the Palestinians do on the West Bank. It no longer mattered to him. He only cared about staying alive. He was reduced to that. Nothing more. He had to start by getting out of the car. They had already passed the outskirts of Rome, meeting streams of single-minded Roman drivers darting wildly in and out of traffic lanes, grabbing every vacant inch on the road, honking on pointless principle. He'd heard Tel Aviv had become just the same. In a few more minutes he would be free at least of the clammy, talkative American. He had to get away. Shemtov wasn't going to get anyone to him, that was obvious. He had to take care of himself. He had to get away, hide, think. As the little Fiat approached the bottom of the Spanish Steps, the American delivered his final barrage.

"Let me know what your people decide as soon as you've consulted. You know how to reach me. We can be ready to go in hours, remember that."

He stopped the car abruptly and shook hands with Gershom and Walid.

"See you soon," he said, smiling, gleaming moistly. "En route to Jerusalem."

Out of the car at last, moving up the steps, they blended into the disorderly assemblage that gathered there every evening, shoppers, tourists, businessmen, students taking the last light. Gershom's legs and shoulders ached, he stopped to rub a calf twisted by a cramp, he looked about. Walid urged him upward.

"Come on, I'm sick of folding myself up in that little car. We must have a party. Some fun. We've earned it, after listening to that American big-mouth for hours. I'm thinking we should find us some girls to play with later."

Energy exploded from Walid's sturdy thick-chested frame, his large head, topped with its wiry bush, his darkly darting eyes and sensuous mouth. His shoulders looked as if they would burst from his denim shirt, his body thrust against his jeans, his stride quickened. He'd worked; now he wanted to play. Gershom felt steadier as they climbed, some of the strain draining away, the tightness receding from his chest.

"Why where you asking about the toxin? He's never telling us where he gets it."

Walid was looking at him oddly, catching his elbow and halting their progress on the steps. A warning alarm trilled in Gershom's distracted mind. He shrugged.

"Something funny about it," he said.

"Yah, he didn't want to talk. Like he hijacked it from the other side."

What other side? Gershom wondered. He wasn't sure who Rich's masters were. He didn't want to think about it; anyway, he had more important things on his mind. Like staying alive.

They moved on again and the moment was over. But there would be others, more difficult ones, more, more, until the last, Gershom knew that. Some slip, some small error, some barely perceptible loss of control and then he would be exposed, finally open to their judgment. They climbed all one hundred and thirty-seven shallow steps, past the postcard stands and the tinsel souvenirs, the displays of religious ornaments and the shiny reproductions of Roman glory, picking a path through the swarming crowd. The jeans and T-shirts looked less out of place here than in St. Peter's Square or near the massive pillars of the Coliseum. Rome had more than one face. Like he did, Gershom thought.

They stood at the top of the steps, their backs to the French Church of Trinità dei Monti, looking down at the densely packed mob lounging on the steps. It was less crowded at the top. In the center of the piazza below, three weary tourists soaked their feet in the Barcaccia Fountain. Gershom wanted only to be alone, to plan his escape from Walid, from the Palestinians, from all of it. Walid wanted girls.

There were lots of girls on the steps to interest Walid, many looking about with the air of sniffing the wind that Walid now assumed. A woman with a screaming baby strapped to her back jumped up and down to quiet it. A group of tourists peered into one another's shopping bags, squealing approval. Five or six swarthy men argued loudly and obscenely about the postal and railroad strikes, while three nuns looked on severely. On the pavement below the steps near the fountain some teenagers passed a reefer around, lolling against a stand from which greasy concoctions were sold on paper sheets during the day. The sounds of squealing tires, shrieking brakes and car horns throbbed continuously behind the shouted conversations on the steps and street. Gershom, toying with ways to separate himself from Walid, leave Rome, get away, tried to think of an accessible temporary hiding place.

He stood high enough to avoid the odor of fumes from the Roman exhausts, but he could see them billowing upon the air above the litter of cartons, papers, cigarette stubs, wrappers. Across the piazza on the Via Condotti, lights pricking on in the stores revealed the evening shoppers, the women with their hats, their stylish clothes, high boots, gleaming jewels. In and out of Bulgari, Gucci, a stop for a drink at a round marble table at the Antico Cafe Greco and then on to Ferragamo and Valentino, the rituals of generations of fashionable travelers, as far removed from Gershom as his own early impulses were now.

Threading his way among them, a man pushed himself along in a wheelchair, carrying a bulky package on his blanket-covered lap, shifting forward to steer his chair. Gershom watched him idly; he and his wheelchair were discordant on that sleek, high-stepping pavement, glossy couples arm in arm, women polished to a bright sheen, the wheelchair clumsy, bulky, its driver hunched forward, dark hair resting on his shoulders, something oddly coordinated as he seemed, from Gershom's high perspective, to thrust a hand beneath the blanket, pushing it aside with the other. Staring now, Gershom saw him plant both feet firmly on the sidewalk below the chair. He stood, lifted high the square package that had rested on the blanket on his lap. He wasn't a cripple after all, Gershom observed and then making the quick, jolting connection, he shouted.

"Down," he screamed, tugging at Walid's shirt and pulling him down, both of them flat on the second step just in time, just as the bomb in the bulky package ripped through the crowd, as the screams and thuds began, bits of flesh scattering, sighs and smoke shuddering through the piazza and up the steps.

"Was that for us? What do you think?" Walid wondered aloud.

"Maybe. Who knows? Let's get out of here. It's like Beirut."

They clambered upright. They found their way back down the steps as fast as they could cut a pathway between frightened, broken bodies. The empty wheelchair had turned on its side on the pavement, its occupant long gone. Sirens shrieked the approach of police and fire engines. A few people ran out from side streets to help the wounded, but Gershom and Walid strode away rapidly toward their hotel, two long city blocks beyond, ignoring the shrill, curious crowds.

"Who was it?"

Gershom shrugged.

"It may not be anything to do with us. After all, this is Rome. It happens all the time these days. Someone out to get someone, make trouble, draw attention, let's keep moving."

"Yes, but—"

"Let's just get back to the hotel in case there's anyone hanging about who's sorry we didn't get hit, like all those people back there."

Gershom had time to realize that he had saved Walid's life. The irony was that when his treachery was revealed, when his message was decoded, Walid would scream for his blood at least as shrilly as the others. It was no use, he could not go on, the divisions had become too blurred, the reward trivial against the costs of endurance.

They slowed their pace as they walked into the hotel lobby, sauntering in and looking about as if they had just come from a leisurely day inspecting sculptures and fountains. As they crossed the foyer towards the elevator, a tall blond woman with a bright smile and a very short red leather skirt walked up to Walid and touched his arm.

"Hullo, I think you need some company tonight," she said, in a husky, Italian-accented English. "Some dinner, some drinks, some other things we could enjoy, yes?"

She swayed, smiling. Walid put his arm round her immediately and looked at Gershom.

"Well," he said, "my friend..."

"I have a friend also. A friend for your friend," she said, with a throaty chuckle.

"I don't think—" Gershom started.

"Ah, come on," said Walid. "It's been a long day, hasn't it?"

"Yes, I think I'll just—"

"Look," the blond interrupted, "there's my friend, isn't she lovely? She knows how to help a man relax. Just right for you, I think."

Gershom looked across the foyer to the girl she indicated, a girl with a small, dark head of closely cut curls, a cool stare and a package of mints in her hand. He swallowed hard.

"Okay," he said then. "Okay. Call her over."

SIXTEEN

They both stared at him as he hesitated in the doorway. Benjamin had not expected his parents. When the guards led him from his cell down a long empty gray corridor, he expected to find Isaac Harari, for whom he had prepared a complex series of interlocking hypotheses about his arrest for espionage, including the theory that he was a pawn in a duplicitous bureaucratic battle in which the legendary Shemtov must finally have been bested, perhaps by Levy, chief at the rival service. But it was not Harari who waited in the whitewashed room, from the walls of which glaring light shed by the square window bounced onto the eyes. It was his mother and father who waited, his mother ramrod stiff in a straight chair at the metal table, his father slumped heavily against the wall at the window, so that looking at him involved looking also into the eye of the burning sun.

The guards nudged Benjamin and he stumbled slightly, moving into the room. The door banged shut behind him.

"Benny, what happened?" his mother asked. "You can tell us," she urged immediately.

He looked at her. Her iron hair stood spikily around her head like a fence, guarding the creases in her chamois skin; her dark eyes were dull, the pouches beneath weighted them down, her hands twisted upon her lap.

"What have you done?" Lazar demanded. "How could you do this?"

His voice was gritty, he cleared his throat raspingly, the heavy folds of his neck wobbled and shook. He heaved his bulk away from the wall and walked over to the table. He banged his fist upon the gray metal.

"What have you done, Benjamin?"

Ben closed his eyes and took a deep breath. He shoved his hands into his pockets and sat down apposite his mother.

"Look," he said quietly, "it's all a mistake."

"I told you," his mother said at once to Lazar and tears spilled from her swollen eyes.

"What kind of mistake? We don't make mistakes. Arrested for treason? A mistake? Sitting in Ramleh waiting to be tried for betraying your country? A mistake? What did you do, Benjamin? What did you do? I demand to know."

"Lazar," his mother whispered.

"Quiet," he roared. "I must know."

"Mother," said Ben.

"No, answer me, Benjamin. What have you done? What is this traitor? How did this happen? My boy, my only child, accused of betraying his country? My country, you understand. I helped to build it. With my own hands. Your mother's hands. The ministry knows what it's doing. This is Israel, don't forget. What have you done?"

Benjamin stood up, his massive shoulders looming over them. He kicked the metal chair and it fell in a clatter to the floor. He kicked it again and drove it clanging into a wall.

"If you want me to answer, you will have to keep quiet," he said evenly, blinking rapidly.

Lazar grunted. He sat down heavily on the remaining chair, spilling over its edges, his fleshy features shifting, shame, rage and terror at war in his eyes.

"I have not betrayed my country," Benjamin said sharply. "I have served it loyally. You know that. How can you doubt it?"

"Benny." His mother was sobbing now. "You don't know what they're saying, the papers, the radio, everyone." She put her hands to her chest, palms flat, as if holding her heart in place.

"What are they saying?"

"You were angry because they didn't get you out of prison in Paris quickly enough for you," his father said contemptuously. "We know that is true. You should never have been caught. Why weren't you careful?"

"What are they saying?" Benjamin shouted.

"You went to America. That's true, too. You met a high-up Palestinian swine there in secret. Is that true, Benjamin?"

"I was on a mission," Benjamin said sharply.

"A mission! What mission? A mission to give the name of a man who spies for Israel? For years we have a man inside, who tells us what they are doing, so we can be ready when they come to kill us with their rockets and their grenades and their Russian bombs and you give them his name? That's a mission?"

His voice had soared to a shriek. He bent over, coughing, his throat rasping, panting.

"I was instructed to do it," Ben shouted. "Can't you understand that?"

"Then, Benny," said his mother, her body trembling, "why did they arrest you and bring you back to prison?"

Lazar snorted, blew his nose loudly, folded his arms awkwardly across billowing flesh and nodded slowly.

"Well, why?" he prodded, a prosecutor haranguing a jury. "Could it have been that you were also acting out of revenge, maybe? You had some crazy idea we betrayed you to the French? We don't betray our own, you know that. You should know that, mister. How many times have we traded dozens, hundreds of Arab terrorists for one of our own? You lost your mind, maybe? You spend a few months in jail and pin it on a man who risks his neck every day for us all?"

The floor beneath Ben was shifting, the objects in the room moved of their own volition, the sun altered course, zigzagged blindingly. He tried to speak, but could make no sound.

"Ben," his mother said, "they're saying on the radio this goes back into your past. Maybe an old grudge, something to do with the animals who killed Mariam. They say they're tracking it down—"

Benjamin screamed. He saw her shining black hair matted with congealing blood, her long legs splayed out awkwardly on the sandy playground, scraped by grit, her shoulders hunched up to protect her neck, the body of little Natan breathing beneath her shelter. Natan, dead now too. He screamed again and rushed to the door and banged upon it. As the guards led him away, he thought that only Shemtov could have made this information public, and he screamed silently inside himself, again and again, as he flung himself down upon his cot.

SEVENTEEN

As soon as the El Al plane lifted off the runway at Kennedy Airport, Kate Landau started worrying whether she was making a mistake. She didn't know whether her marriage had a future or not; she certainly couldn't resolve that while Benjamin awaited trial for treason. But flying to Israel to try to clear him of the absurd charge of treason might not be helpful. It might even, in one of those unexpected contortions that so often marked his Service's most ambitious schemes, actually turn out to be harmful.

The trouble was, there weren't any rules for the wives of spies. At least none Kate had ever heard about. For years she had to make them up as she went along. Now, as the plane lurched upward, she was gripped by panic that she had refused to give in to her parents' objections. But Kate was absolutely certain that Benjamin was innocent, certain as she had not been, could not be, when he was arrested in Paris. Although her fierce resolution to leave Israel rather than raise her children as human buffers was unaltered, she did feel bound to go and organize support for Benjamin now.

Benjamin's trial for espionage in Paris had unveiled the truth about him to Kate's parents for the first time. Until then they had believed, along with everyone else, that Benjamin was a purchasing agent for the Israeli government, a commercial occupation requiring a great deal of tedious travel. Privately suspecting that their son-in-law was procuring arms, Kate's parents had repressed their resentment at his frequent absences and at the marriage that took Kate so far away from them.

The unvarnished—and unspoken—truth was that it would have been extremely awkward for a lifelong supporter of Israel, a president as a matter of fact, of a major American Jewish organization, to object because his daughter wanted to marry an Israeli. Particularly when the Israeli was not black, not orthodox, not gentile, not married, not descended from those orientals who were visibly different from Jews of the western variety like Monty Abrams and his family. Benjamin could not be disqualified on any of these grounds. On the contrary, he was more than presentable, frankly he was even desirable as far as skin, features and physique were concerned; and he was the son of *chalutzim*, of those pioneers of eastern European stock who had been the acknowledged aristocracy of Israel from the instant of its U.N.-anointed birth, when Kate was only a few weeks old. Almost immediately Monty had left Iris to cope alone with Kate and had gone to Israel to volunteer his surgical skills.

Five Arab countries, with armies outnumbering the Haganah by thirty to one, were invading all the long borders of the precarious new country. The Jewish people, so nearly obliterated a few years before, was again threatened with extinction.

Monty had valuable war experience. After completing his surgical residency he had been attached to the U.S. force that liberated Dachau. Stationed later in the U.S. zone in Berlin, his experiences powerfully reinforced the convictions handed on to him by his immigrant parents, that a Jewish national home was the only chance for survival, let alone dignity.

When Kate was old enough to understand, he had explained why he had gone to repair the wounded at Tel Hashomer Hospital in Haifa in 1948. "You and Israel are the same age," he reminded her. "I couldn't stay safe over here while they were fighting to keep that precious infant alive. Israel is my front line too. I learned that in Europe before you were born. And it's your front line. Without it, we're all finished."

Monty still kept in touch with some of the concentration camp survivors whose wounds he'd patched in a makeshift hospital tent thrown up in the stinking air near the gates of Dachau. Every time Monty and Iris visited Israel, at least once each year, Monty was reunited with Avner, who had clawed his way from Dachau through the displaced persons' camps of Europe and Cyprus to join a new settlement near the Gaza Strip. Named Yad Mordechai for Mordechai Anilewitz, the fallen leader of the Warsaw ghetto revolt, it was one of the first villages attacked by Egyptian forces at the beginning of the war of liberation in 1948. Avner had helped defend it with the same survivor's ferocity that brought him back, after it fell, to rebuild it. He lived there still, patriarch of a sprawling family. His story held a place of honor in Kate's family history, repeated and celebrated until it assumed the force of legend.

After Benjamin's kidnapping near Philadelphia it had not been necessary for Monty to instruct her to go straight to Avner. Kate would have gone to Yad Mordechai even if Monty hadn't pointed out, several times, that Avner had the right connections. *Protectsia*, frowned upon by Monty as the moral equivalent of insider trading when employed by unsuitable people, became a desirable asset in the person of Avner. Avner, Monty announced firmly, had *protectsia*, influence in the right places. If Kate insisted on going to help, she might as well do it right.

Monty urged Kate to go to Avner for help even though he and Iris had abandoned their self-imposed restraint. As soon as Benjamin had been arrested in Paris, they had launched a persistent campaign to get Kate and the children back to Philadelphia. Patriotism notwithstanding, an Israeli son-in-law in prison in Paris was not Monty's first, second or even fiftieth choice. In the privacy of their bedroom, he and Iris speculated about Benjamin's competence. Monty shared with Iris his intention to encourage a divorce once he had his daughter back in the States.

There hadn't been time for that. Kate had been home for less than a month when Benjamin was released, bitter and disillusioned, plunging almost immediately into even more disgraceful and humiliating antics, choosing Philadelphia of all places to betray his country to an Arab swine. A terrorist. And now here was Kate, insisting on turning right around and running back again. That was how Monty, and therefore Iris, saw the matter.

Their rage at Kate's defiance did not prevent them from taking care of Ruben and Roni during her absence. After all, Kate had become something of an Israeli herself by now; she didn't leave them with a lot of choice, did she? Monty's fury didn't interfere with his insistence that Kate must contact Avner the instant she set foot on Israeli soil. And no power on earth could have prevented him from flinging into the air the name of Isaac Harari, hurling it out in front of him with an expression of righteous satisfaction, not unlike that on the faces of Palestinian adolescents as they hurled jagged rocks at Israeli adolescents. Isaac Harari was Monty's oldest friend as well as a member of the powerful Knesset Committee on State Security.

Isaac Harari was a shrewd, experienced attorney who'd held just about every post in government worth having in the glory days when his party had run everything. He had returned to the country of his birth as representative to the United Nations and later as Israel's ambassador. For forty years or more, when Isaac came back to his hometown on private visits or for fund-raising appearances, he stayed at the home of his boyhood friend, Monty Abrams. After all, hadn't they gone to school together, hadn't they actually walked the streets of Wynnefield together, concentrating, at different times, upon the frightful news billowing across the ocean from Europe, the professional options available to them after graduation, or the relative merits of the boobs of Susan Miller and Janey Fried?

When Monty went to med school, Isaac combined law with

Middle Eastern studies. When Monty went to the front in Germany, Isaac went, for reasons never made entirely clear but not difficult to guess, to Egypt. And when the United Nations drew a line dividing the ancient land of Palestine, the first spokesman for the new state of Israel was Isaac Harari. Why wouldn't Monty Abrams throw that name at his daughter with all the satisfaction, all the righteous complacency he could summon? His oldest friend was in a position to find out what kind of case could be made against Benjamin. There it was, pure and simple. *Protectsia*. Influence. Power. Monty could command it. He was proud of it.

In fact, Monty had no doubt that his son-in-law was guilty of treason as described in front-page stories in Philadelphia, New York and Washington, as well as Jerusalem, Beirut and everywhere else. It stood to reason, didn't it, that if the Israeli authorities said so it must be so? Why would they arrest him and announce that he would be charged with treason unless they had irrefutable evidence? Somehow the word had leaked that Benjamin told secrets to an Arab, a high-up in the so-called Palestine National Council, a terrorist. In Philadelphia, nothing less. Where would the *Inquirer* get that story if it wasn't true?

But Isaac Harari was a leader of the Knesset, a mastermind of behind-the-scenes intrigue. He'd do what he could for Kate, no doubt about that, though he wouldn't compromise Israel's security. Kate should remember that and be humble—for God's sake try to be polite for once, have respect—when she called upon Harari.

Kate didn't feel polite, hunched against the window to get as far away as possible from the seat next to her, occupied by a stale-smelling, black-suited, hairy fanatic, whose chanting devotion evidently imposed no restriction upon his moist, salacious inspection of her. Kate didn't feel polite and she didn't feel respectful. Contemplating her arrival at Ben Gurion Airport, she did feel humble; she had no idea how to behave. She didn't know what was expected of her, by Benjamin, their friends or the authorities. Who knew? Nobody, certainly not Benjamin, had ever told her the rules of behavior for the wife of a spy accused of treason.

Kate wondered whether they'd ever told the rules to Nadia Cohen. How was Nadia supposed to behave when the Syrians took her husband Eli from El-Maza prison to Damascus's El Marga Square, the Square of Martyrs, and hanged him? Were there any guidelines for Nadia when she watched on television as the hangman placed the noose around her husband's neck? When did they allow her to know that Eli had been Israel's master spy, the most valuable, most famous in her history, masquerading for years as Kamil Amin Taabes in Damascus, intimate of President Al-Hafez, whom he had befriended while he established his cover in Buenos Aires?

When he came home to Nadia to visit once a year, did they tell her the etiquette for occasional sex with the man who'd provided the Israel Defense Forces with the exact emplacements of Syrian firepower in bunkers on the Golan Heights before the Six-Day War? Did anyone ever tell her the rules for raising three children alone while Eli dined at the Mohajerine Palace, rode horseback on the Golan Heights with Lieutenant Maazi, or tapped out his messages in his Damascene stone house, his aerials ticking explosively? Those aerials had ultimately betrayed him, but they didn't use those methods to transmit information any more, Benjamin had assured Kate, when, trying to measure the degree of his own danger, she inquired about Eli Cohen, going to his hero's death believing himself abandoned, "Hatikvah" upon his lips, while his wife heaved herself at the television screen in their apartment, littered with a debris of toys, sweaters and schoolbooks.

Eli Cohen's daring accomplishments had thrilled and inspired Israelis for more than twenty years but didn't elevate the temperature of Kate's ambivalent patriotism. His story had filled her with horror, dread and sadness since she had first heard it and it did so now, more than ever. For wasn't Eli Cohen, the ultimate hero, the very symbol of the price that had to be paid for nationhood? Who was Eli, but the most brilliant, the most provocative of Israel's fallen, martyred in defense of glorious ideals that had bent or withered in the pursuit?

Kate had not earned her doctorate in Middle Eastern history at the University of Pennsylvania for nothing: she knew perfectly well that Israel's successful strike against the Syrians in 1967 had been the result of Eli Cohen's intelligence; without it, the northern settlements on the slopes below, including the one where Benjamin had grown up and where his parents still farmed, would have been naked, spread wide open for a merciless Syrian storm. Eli Cohen had prevented that. But the Six-Day War had other consequences. No one had foreseen it, no one had planned it that way, but the occupation of the West Bank and Gaza had followed as surely as the swift victory.

Did that mean that one should never undertake anything because one could not predict all its consequences? Kate heard the question as clearly as if Benjamin were leaning urgently toward her across the dark cabin while the other passengers slept around them. "The state doesn't have the duty to protect itself? Hmm?" She heard his wry voice, saw his big shoulders hunch toward her, dark eyes widen mockingly, his broad, strong hand stretched out to her; she saw it all as clearly as if he sat there with her. Just for an instant. Then he was gone again, locked up some place out of reach; and it occurred to Kate that for once Benjamin, having so rapidly exchanged a French prison for an Israeli one, might not insist that his government's judgment was perfect. His superiors, Kate reflected, might have at last accomplished what she herself had never been able to: convince Benjamin that they were fallible, often inconsistent, sometimes self-destructive. Benjamin might be willing at last to question his knee-jerk acceptance of whatever patriotic line was billowing, like the hot dry wind, the *khamsin*, across the land.

Not that Benjamin's automatic submission to official propaganda was unique or even unusual. It was a nearly universal condition in Israel, as institutionalized, as ubiquitous as cucumbers and olives and bursting juicy Jaffa oranges. The absolute obligation of every citizen to endorse unequivocally the actions

134

of the state's military and security apparatus was still barely less entrenched that it had been when Kate, doing the research for her doctoral thesis on the growth of Palestinian insurgency, had lived in Israel for a year around the time of the Yom Kippur War, before she ever set eyes on Benjamin. That was when she first encountered that built-in compliance, so surprising in a nation of individualists and eccentrics, so powerfully woven into the national character and its legends of survival.

Kate had taken some fruit to her friend Shula and her four children on the third evening of that war and so been caught in their apartment when Ezra came home from the southern front. Anxious to leave Shula and Ezra in privacy, alarmingly aware that it must be a very tiny country indeed if its tank drivers could come home from the border for a night's sleep, Kate stayed long enough to hear Ezra jubilantly describe the destruction of the *aravim*, who were, he triumphantly reported, throwing off their sandals and running back across the desert sand toward Africa the way they'd come. Within days it was painfully clear that this was simply not true; a few weeks later the desperate condition of the reduced Israeli force trying to hold the crumbling Bar-Lev line in the face of the overpowering Egyptian onslaught was acknowledged by Israeli leaders, as were the terrible shortages of food, medical supplies and even arms, until Kissinger released supplies, while Nixon cowered in the White House, crippled by Watergate.

But Ezra had believed everything he told them that night, no doubt about it. A lifetime of conditioning blinded him to the men burned alive in tanks in the Sinai, the savage losses at the passes, the terror in the inadequate bunkers. It simply did not occur to him that the army had been unprepared for the Egyptian and Syrian invasion until the finger-pointing re-criminations of government and army leaders made headlines and opened the door to national debate.

Kate had tried to discuss all this when she first knew Benjamin in Philadelphia, but Benjamin was enraged that Kate considered it an irony that a nation of volatile individuals should automatically accept self-serving government pronouncements. The idea that methods of ensuring national security were debatable was not open to discussion, even between them.

A lot had changed since then, of course, in their own lives and in the life of Israel. The disastrous incursion into Lebanon, officially defined as the removal of terrorists to forty kilometers beyond the border, had enlarged into the protracted summer siege of Beirut. This had ultimately shifted the average Israeli perception of official statements. Even so, Benjamin would not have been so shocked that he'd been set up as a diversion during his mission in Paris if he'd learned anything much about questioning authority. Did he still believe his superiors? Did he still believe in their impeccable judgment, even now, when he had been kidnapped and jailed, accused of treason by his own officers? Surely even Benjamin would have some questions by now?

Kate was certain she'd figured out some answers. Benjamin had obviously been framed, either to protect a senior officer or as a useful counter in some intricate power struggle. Nothing so surprising in that, it was quite consistent with what Kate knew of the service which, in spite of its illustrious record, had been obliged to conceal some dismal and far-reaching disasters as well as damaging personality clashes.

She had known for some time, quite independently of Benjamin, who had refused to speculate about it, that his chief, Dan Shemtov, was engaged in a virulent rivalry with Aron Levy, head of Internal Security, for ultimate control of the combined intelligence services. It seemed to Kate quite likely that Levy, knowing that Benjamin Landau was a valuable asset of Shemtov's, had arrested him in the course of an operation to humiliate and embarrass Shemtov.

When Kate first thought of this, she wondered why Shemtov would have permitted such a valuable operative to be incarcerated in prison in Paris, but then she realized that it must have been Shemtov who had arranged for him to be traded and freed. This confirmed her theory of Benjamin's special value to Shemtov and consequent usefulness to the spiteful Levy. She did not, of course, expect to be able to convince Benjamin that this was what had happened to him. But she did intend to propose her theory to Isaac Harari, in whose sophistication she had much greater confidence.

Stiff and chilly, Kate stretched her legs out against the seat in front of her, made aware, by the movement all around her and the light beyond the window, that she had spent the whole long night, nearly the entire flight, absorbed in the ironic naiveté of her husband and the rehearsal of her representations to Isaac Harari. She needed to freshen up before landing. Preparing to leave her seat, she found the moist mahogany eyes of the pilgrim next to her shifting like puddles over her face and figure.

"I know who you are," he whispered suddenly, fingering the prayer shawl which lay about his neck and shoulders. "Did you help him?" he hissed, a little ball of spittle held out toward her on the end of his bright red tongue. "Aren't you ashamed? You've been with a pig who talks to Arabs." Blisters of saliva burst between damp red lips.

It hadn't occurred to Kate that she'd be recognized; she hadn't thought about the way people might judge her. She stood up and pushed past her neighbor, feeling grubby when her legs brushed against his. As she walked down the long unsteady aisle to join the line at the bathroom door, the eyes of other passengers stuck like burrs upon her skin. Kate understood that she would not be anonymous anymore, never private in Israel, where, in spite of deep divisions on the burning issues of the occupation and of religion, there would be absolute unanimity on the subject of Benjamin Landau.

EIGHTEEN

Shemtov detested the cats parading about the Hebrew University campus as if they'd inherited Mount Scopus. He had no idea where they came from or what attracted them to the high, bright peak, with its commanding view of the great domes, gleaming gold among the stone walls and towers and minarets of Jerusalem, the sunlit trees and rooftops studding the saffron slopes down toward the Garden of Gethsemane. Below the wide spaces and brilliant light, the shimmering reflections of infinite memory, beneath the false lull upon dazzled air, the cats were always there, slinking about on their own vicious business, hissing and arching spongy flesh until the outlines of their vertebrae rose hideously.

From his boys in Beirut Shemtov had often heard that cats stalked the streets off the Rue Hamra also, at home in the rubble of war-scarred decay. Here, they preened in a bracing breeze that swept clean over the stone symmetry on the mountaintop. Shemtov despised them; but he wanted to walk about up there and would not be intimidated by a bunch of cats or anything else, not even the disturbances erupting daily now on the road behind the campus and on the slopes between the splendid old stone houses, owned for generations by Arab families and permanent abrasive reminders to acquisitive Jews that Arabs still held the finest real estate in Jerusalem and kept their sheep on it.

Smoke hung streaky between the university and Hadassah Hospital, from the fire the *shabab*, the Arab boys, had set that morning, three old tires smoldering to barricade the road above the Arab village of Silwan and concentrate, immobilized, fresh targets for the rocks they'd carved from the hillside. The army had come and gone, the boys had fled, the wounded had been carried into the hospital, the relatives herded shrieking and wailing into a basement waiting room, but the smoke still lingered. It was not sufficient to prevent Shemtov from taking his afternoon walk. He wouldn't like to disappoint a friend who might expect to find him there.

Shemtov wandered for a while between the grassy squares behind the dormitories, where students lay about, pretending to study, flirting lazily, drowsily wrapped in the open-ended time-to-burn illusion of the early autumn semester. They barely glanced at him as he moved among them. Past the courtyards, he came upon a massive level terrace. Huge blocks of light and dark stone patterned its floor, the tall windows of the administration building provided the back wall, and the front lay open to the golden city on the hillsides, the mosaic of its rose gold stone gorgeously crowned by the stately Dome of the Rock and of Al-Aksa Mosque. Shemtov leaned out over the wall at the perimeter, tracking one or two streamers of smoke that signaled disturbances in the distance.

Students and an occasional teacher walked across the terrace, but paid no attention to the trim figure in khaki leaning on the low wall on fists bunched so tight that, if anyone had looked, he would have seen the sinews in his arms raised like knotty mauve cords. Shemtov didn't look around, not even when he heard footsteps coming closer. He pressed his fingertips a trifle harder into fisted palms and waited to discover if he'd guessed correctly.

"It seemed that out of battle I escaped. Down some...dull tunnel..." The odd murmur came haltingly from a slight figure whose narrow fingers rested briefly on the top of the wall next to Shemtov's knuckles and then disappeared into the pockets of well-tailored olive slacks.

" 'Some profound dull tunnel,'" said Shemtov.

"Excuse me?"

"You left out a word, it's 'some profound dull tunnel.'"

"Er...I'm sorry. You were expecting me, perhaps?"

"Well, I was expecting someone. It might just as well be you. How's Bendington?"

"Could you...er...I'm sorry, but..."

" 'Let us sleep now,'" said Shemtov briskly, waiting for recognition to smooth the high creamy mocha forehead of Peter Bendington's messenger. " 'Strange Meeting.' Wilfred Owen."

"Thank you, sir. I am honored." Simmering dark chocolate eyes glowed against flawless smoky skin. "I bring greetings from your friend."

"Did he tell you who I am?" Shemtov's identity as chief of his Service was supposed to be a secret, even in Israel. He was never photographed, never referred to by name in the media. He never gave interviews, never made public appearances, never traveled openly.

"No, no, certainly, he would never do that. But I am guessing for myself. I have been, as they say in America, I have been around."

Shemtov began to identify the crinkles in his lilting accent. Some years in the States lay like powdery dust upon the Arabic and French that inhabited his cells.

"Who are you?"

"Raymond Mansour. The Datepalm." Self-congratulation rose from his skin like steam off rose petals. "My restaurant, sir. In Georgetown."

"And before that, Paris for a time, perhaps? And originally, Lebanon, I think."

Mansour nodded, enchanted by Shemtov's discernment.

"Where in Lebanon?"

"My village is north of Junieh. My ancestors have been there for hundreds of years."

"How long have you been away?"

"Not long, not long at all. At least once each year I return. Sometimes more. But for nearly twenty years I didn't live at home anymore. I left after the little king chased the *fellahin* from Jordan to trash my country." His voice dropped, his eyes moistened, his lips trembled as the Palestinians invaded his thoughts.

Shemtov nodded.

"What have you come to tell me?"

Raymond Mansour looked out toward the middle distance where multilayered houses hugged the hillsides, splashed by deep fuchsia and copper bushes sprawled sedately, as though they had always been there.

"That's all new, isn't it?" He fluttered his narrow fingers at the development to introduce himself. "Every few months, something new, isn't it?" he cleared his throat and smiled brightly at Shemtov. "I have come, really, to ask you more than to tell you."

"Well?"

"What is George Zaggad doing in Beirut?"

"I thought he'd retired."

"No, no, he's very busy. He's a member of the High Command."

"I don't mean Zaggad. I'm talking about Bendington; he's retired, hasn't he?"

Wide, ingenuous eyes gazed warmly at Shemtov.

"He has friends. Enemies. He owes a little here, trades something a little there." Taupe fingers fluttered, bent, spread, sliced the air.

"Mm. Tell me, by the way, are you returning immediately to the States?"

"Oh, no, sir. Not at all. I go from here to Cyprus. Then home.

Home to Lebanon. It's not safe to fly into Beirut now, of course. So I go by sea. A cruise to Junieh."

"What will you be doing in Lebanon?"

"I'm visiting my family, naturally. As usual. And then, one or two errands. My masters are curious about recent movements."

Shemtov looked steadily at him until he shrugged and murmured, "I mean Zaggad, Tewfik Mahmoud, Khalidi, Kamal Hussein—they're interested in them."

"Your masters? Bendington? The Company? Who?"

"Both, sir, they're all interested. But your friend has sufficient information to be able to define his questions more precisely than my immediate superiors, sir."

"I see." Now it was Shemtov's turn to gaze out across the hills, where the sky looked as if the color had been hurriedly hosed out of it and clouds formed a pair of pyramids that thickened while he watched.

"They're all interested in Zaggad?"

"The news from here about Landau's arrest excited everyone, naturally. By the way, sir, your friend wanted me to tell you he is pleased he was able to help with capturing Landau."

Shemtov, fishing in his breast pocket for his little package of mints, waited, but Raymond did not find it necessary to spell out Peter Bendington's trading posture.

"Have a mint," urged Shemtov, shaking one from the box into the palm of Raymond Mansour's hand. Deftly, he shifted Gershom from the front-row seat in his mind, moved him out of sight. "Zaggad is in Beirut to look into rumors that there's an Israeli spy in the Invasion Committee. They've had a leak for some time. Now, he's been advised there's an operative reporting to us."

Raymond drew a deep breath and let it out slowly, dramatically, climaxing with a long, piercing whistle as his lips pursed.

"Someone's been doubled? You've been crossed up? Or Landau went solo? A rogue? Will you tell me that? One of the five on the Invasion Committee? My God, if it's true, it's a sensational scandal. Is it true?"

Shemtov popped another mint in his mouth, took Raymond by the elbow and moved him along the perimeter wall.

"Let's walk while we talk," he suggested. "It's getting chilly." He pointed at the crusty cloud banks churning above their heads. They walked in silence for several minutes. Shemtov was distracted by speculations about the risk that Gershom's fear would draw attention to him.

"Well," said Mansour, "tell me this, then. Will you charge Benjamin Landau? Will you bring him to trial?"

"Certainly," said Shemtov. "We must. Of course we must."

"With what, may I ask?"

"Oh, you may ask. Treason. Have a mint."

He shook out a couple of mints and walked on.

"Are there any messages I can take from you to Beirut, sir? Your friend authorized me to offer. Anything I can do?" Mansour said courteously.

Shemtov shook his head. He'd already given Mansour his message and could only hope he'd deliver it to Zaggad.

"Thank you, there's nothing at this time. But perhaps... How long before you return to the States? Perhaps you could share your findings with me first?"

"I'll be only about a week, ten days. Just time to see some friends, pass on some requests, convey some news. And that reminds me—"

"Yes?" Shemtov leaned slightly forward into the breeze. He didn't want to miss a word now.

"I do have an item for you. There is no one answering your description of Rich working for the Company at this time. But there was. Less than two years ago, Richard Dorman took early retirement at the suggestion of the new director, sir."

"Tell me," Shemtov said as softly as if he were crooning a lullaby, "tell me how my retired friend can possibly know that."

"Through myself, sir, my services. I can know that. I have access."

"Thank you." Shemtov could now place Raymond Mansour in his level of CIA seniority. "Anything more?"

"Yes. Richard Dorman was never a Middle East player, sir. His territory was Central America. He was stationed there or at the desk for many years, Miami and San Salvador, sometimes Mexico City. Not Beirut or Jerusalem, not at all."

"Thank you very much, Raymond."

"May I know, sir, is this matter connected at all with the business of Landau, Zaggad, all these matters?"

"It could be. We have to find that out. You might bear it in mind."

Shemtov hesitated and then decided that if Peter Bendington hadn't told Raymond that Rich had been offering toxic chemicals to the Palestinians when he met them in Rome, then he wouldn't either.

"What's this Rich been doing since he retired?"

"Exactly what he was doing before," Mansour smiled appreciatively. "He buys and sells. Only now he takes the profit, instead of the Company."

"What...er...merchandise?"

"Whatever he can get, whatever's in demand, you know sir, whatever the market will sustain." He touched his fingers to his mouth as if to prevent a full-bodied laugh from escaping. "The Company always has stuff to dump. How much can they store?"

"Well, thank you. Come and see me on your way back if you can."

"I'll be happy to. I hope to be seeing Zaggad, find out if he's discovered the leak."

Shemtov heartily approved of Raymond meeting Zaggad. Raymond would almost certainly tell him that Shemtov had charged Benjamin Landau with treason. If Zaggad still had any doubts about Benjamin's denunciation of Kamal Hussein this should settle them. And it should send the heartening message to Gershom, back in Beirut from Rome by now, that Shemtov's operation to save him was proceeding smoothly according to plan.

"I wish you luck. I don't know that you'll be able to see him."

"Oh, I think I will. I know him well. We're old friends." He allowed himself to laugh at last as he turned and walked around the building, waving gracefully to Shemtov just before he disappeared from sight.

NINETEEN

Two taciturn guards came to take Benjamin from his cell. They didn't tell him the name of his visitor and he didn't ask. He didn't want to give them the satisfaction of ignoring him.

By his fifth day of solitary confinement his only conversation, apart from his miserably disconnected one with his parents, had been with interrogating officers from Levy's staff, who clearly had not been taken into Shemtov's confidence and so were unaware of Benjamin's mission. When they alternately blustered and pecked away about why he'd met Zaggad and what he'd told him, Benjamin demanded the lawyer Isaac Harari, immediate release or, at a minimum, removal from solitary.

They were keeping him isolated, they assured him bluntly, for his own safety. Their chief wanted a defendant who was still breathing when his case was tried. Didn't Benjamin realize that he'd be killed or at least permanently crippled if ordinary prisoners got their hands on him? A traitor was despised as much, maybe more, in Ramleh prison as on Ussiskin Street or in the market in Beersheba or the citrus groves of Moshav Avichail. In this threatened little nation, where survival was a daily challenge and everyone knew almost everyone or at least everyone's cousin up and down the narrow sliver of land they called a country, people took treason seriously. Betraying the state meant betraying each and every one of the crooks and swindlers, the *archi parchi* and rabble, in Ramleh. Did Benjamin think they were waiting to welcome him into a prison soccer team, squabbling already over who would get his height and bulk? Forget that. He'd be banging his head against something a lot harder than a ball if they let him out. Concrete, for example. He wasn't even allowed to eat in the hall with the others.

The guards didn't speak to him; they sniggered and gurgled revoltingly if he asked them anything. So why would he ask for the name of his visitor? He hoped it would be Harari at last. He had asked for him every day since his first request to Aron Levy. He didn't believe even now that they would withhold legal help forever, but he was becoming alarmed by his own impotence: they could make him wait until his mind warped and broke. He'd already given up expecting Dan Shemtov; he recognized that he was powerless to affect the agenda, but welcomed, as a measurable sign of sanity, his anxious craving to know who was setting it.

As the guards nudged him down the long, deserted corridor, he concentrated on the priorities he'd painstakingly pieced out in the first day or two of his confinement, before the ruminative muddle overtook his mind like rampant morning glory, taking hold and spreading, strangling the roots of every other plant around. Reveal nothing. Ask for Harari. Don't give them anything, anything at all; they twist anything you say, make it mean something different, use it against you. No one believes you, he reminded himself again and again. No one believes you.

Benjamin was so undermined after five days in solitary that he had to concentrate to follow the rules he'd made. When the door swung open into the sizzling whitewashed room, he was so locked into his need for Harari that he didn't even notice Kate until she stood right in front of him, trying to put her arms around him. No simple matter if he didn't cooperate, considering he was seven inches taller and at least sixty pounds heavier, in spite of the weight he'd dropped while making a comparative study of the world's prisons.

His arms hung limp at his sides and he looked over her head at the square barred window, through which the sun glared unforgivingly.

"Ben, Benny," Kate whispered. Her fingers were dry and warm on his cheeks. She raised herself on tiptoe, but he turned his head away sharply before she could kiss his mouth. Her lips just grazed his jaw.

"I must see Harari," Benjamin said slowly, obedient to the inner legislator that possessed the only voice on earth that he could trust. "Harari and Dan Shemtov. I have nothing else to say."

"Ben, it's me. You can talk to me!" He did realize that she sounded appalled, shrill and bewildered. "I came all the way from Philadelphia to help you. You can talk to me, Ben. Look at me."

He looked at her.

He hadn't forgotten, in spite of the tormenting tricks his memory had played since he'd begun trying to reconstruct his life, that Kate had left Tel Aviv and gone back to Philadelphia when he was in jail in Paris. If she hadn't abandoned their home when he was incarcerated, she wouldn't have had to make the long journey to see him now. Or maybe if she hadn't gone to Philadelphia Shemtov would not have sent him there with the message for George Zaggad. To a meeting she had arranged. He hadn't forgotten that. Benjamin allowed himself a brief congratulatory silent salute. He was not, evidently, so damaged by solitary that he couldn't recognize an enemy trap as apparent as a rock on a desert hill partly covered by straggling gray stalks of weeds, through which bits of copper wire and metal glinted in midday sunlight. He could recognize a mine in pitiful disguise. He wasn't that far gone.

"Why did you come?" he inquired, in a voice near enough to normal that it would have fooled most people.

"To help, of course," said Kate sturdily, but the thin pale skin around her eyes creased and her lips trembled because she wasn't fooled, she knew he didn't trust her. Well, he couldn't help that, could he?

"Listen," Benjamin said, lowering himself stiffly onto one of the small, straight chairs next to the metal table. "I must see Isaac Harari, that's all. You remember him?"

"Of course. I've already arranged to see him. Later today, actually. Also Avner. And my father says—"

"Avner?" The table clanged and shook as his hands slammed down on it. "You're out of your mind. What do you know? What can Avner think? They don't even let me go in the exercise yard with ordinary prisoners because they might—"

He stopped abruptly, not at all to protect Kate from the knowledge that there were people who might kill him, but because he suddenly remembered his decision to give away nothing, talk of nothing but Harari. Here he was, providing them with new material.

"They might what, darling?" She came up behind him; he felt her fingers gently stroke his hair.

"Nothing. Never mind."

"Anyone who knows you knows you're not a traitor, Ben. Soon everyone will know it. Avner won't believe it for an instant."

Why had they sent her? Benjamin ignored his wife's words, tuned them out like a commercial on Jordanian TV, and devoted himself to fathoming their motives. Perhaps she was supposed to make him do something? Something that would put him in prison in New York, perhaps. Or Madrid? Budapest, maybe?

He shook his head a little, trying to shift his thoughts out of the densely matted morning glory into open space. A small self-mocking smile raised one corner of his mouth briefly. As soon as Kate noticed, she put her hand over one of his, still lying on the table. He flicked it off like a mosquito. Maybe they'd sent her because they expected him to talk to her so she could tell them what he said. But of course they wouldn't need her to tell him, they had every electronic device everyone else did, and a few extra, too. The steaming little matchbox of a room was bugged, they could hear everything, they were listening right then. So he growled, "Get Harari. That's the only thing to do," so that they would know that nothing would distract him, he would reveal nothing, he would not give them even an inch of string to reel him in with, he would keep them wondering.

"I've got an appointment to see him this evening," said Kate. "Ben, I think I know what this is all about. I think it's part of a struggle between Shemtov and—"

"Quiet," he roared, so loudly that tears filmed her eyes and rolled down her cheeks before the vibrations in the room subsided. She pressed her palms to her face. Benjamin waved his index fingers around in front of his ears in explanation, but Kate closed her eyes against this fresh evidence that he was deranged.

"Kate," he whispered then. "Do you have pencil and paper?"

She fumbled in her bag and produced a checkbook register and an eyebrow pencil.

"Bugged," he wrote. He then tore the scrap of paper into tiny pieces and swallowed them.

Kate nodded gravely. Benjamin wasn't the only one who needed Harari. She didn't know how to handle her husband and wasn't doing him any good as far as she could tell.

"Is there anything you need next time I come?"

"Harari," he said loudly.

"I don't know when they'll let me come again."

Benjamin shrugged, then said "Harari" again, in case she hadn't understood.

"Ben," Kate said suddenly, "remember under the elm tree—"

"Quiet," he roared, terrified that she would repeat what he had told her there.

He said "Harari" once more, as Kate touched her lips to the top of his head. When she went across and banged on the door for the guards to let her out, he felt sweeping relief that now he could relax. He wouldn't have to be quite so disciplined, quite so guarded. All he had to do was wait for Harari.

And while he waited he would try to reconstruct what Shemtov had done to him.

TWENTY

Benjamin's innocence sounded less convincing to Kate when she heard herself defending it to Isaac Harari. It also seemed, somehow, less relevant. It was absurd, but Kate felt as if she was missing the point although, while she reviewed Benjamin's reverses since his arrest in Paris, the great man nodded and, from time to time, beamed silent signals of his grasp of all the implications by piercing the distance between them with his ice-blue eyes. They were the identical color of the sheer surface of the slice of ice upon which huge prawns rested pinkly in the restaurant on the cliff above Caesarea. They were astonishingly clear against the stained, muddy skin around them, weary testimony that Isaac had seen it all before. And didn't much care for any of it.

Kate didn't hesitate to discuss Benjamin's mission with Harari. The attorney was a former chairman of the Knesset Committee on State Security and currently its most senior member; he knew a great deal more than she did about the contorted workings of Benjamin's Service. She did feel awkward about how much Ben had allowed her to know, but when she had walked into the sloping garden surrounding the apartments, the fruity tartness of laden trees, the searing reds and oranges of hibiscus and oleander had emitted an authority, a certainty, that reminded Kate that Benjamin's freedom was the purpose of her visit. This was no social obligation requiring the pretense of ignorance. Kate had been married to Ben for twelve years. She was a Ph.D., a professor, a mother. She knew what her husband did for a living.

Climbing the two curving flights of stone steps to the Harari apartment, the vibrant flowering gardens of Beth Hakerem shielded Kate in an illusion of control, quickly jarred when Ellie opened the front door. Kate had been so preoccupied with preparing what to say to Isaac Herari that she'd forgotten all about Ellie.

Ellie, whose relation to Kate all her life had been as close as any devoted aunt, administered a rapid but skillful cross-examination about the health and well-being of all Kate's family before she stepped far enough back inside to permit Kate to enter. Then, bustling about as if this were nothing but an ordinary visit for afternoon tea, she nudged Kate into the cluttered kitchen where she began the preparations for the adopted ritual, scattering sugar about as she poured it into a flowery bowl, dropping crumbs when she set out cookies on a dented tray, fidgeting and jiggling everything she touched as usual. Ellie had always reminded Kate of a squirrel, with her bright eyes, cheeky, quizzical little face, industry and cheer, a friendly squirrel but, nevertheless, a rodent, devious, with a seam of malice.

Kate resented that Ellie didn't mention Benjamin. The papers were too full of his flamboyant capture for her to be unaware, but Ellie had harbored reservations about him from the first time Kate had introduced them. Since they were inevitably the traditional reservations of an affluent suburban American matron, and therefore impermissible for a nonmaterialistic Israeli, Ellie had only muttered briefly that the gap between Benjamin's background and Kate's own was broader than the Jordan River and had then refused to be drawn into discussion, but Kate remembered the slight whenever she saw her. It occurred to her that Ellie might have chosen not to mention Benjamin's current predicament to spare her pain, but she dismissed this impatiently; she was thoroughly sick of conscientiously seeing both sides of every question.

When the tea was steeping, Ellie left it and Kate in the living room and vanished into the secluded privacy of the large apartment. She returned shortly, ushering in the great man with a flourish that synchronized with the brass-band fanfare that had heralded his arrival exclusively for her through the fifty years of their union.

"My dear, how nice to see you," said distinguished uncle to favored niece. "I've just been glancing over a rather challenging brief," he added with a small self-deprecating chuckle.

His inquiries about the family were less stringently all-encompassing than Ellie's. But Isaac managed to make it perfectly clear that they would not discuss Benjamin until after their tea. His digestion, however, was unimpaired by the smoke just over the next hill, hanging thickly beyond the right side of the square window; he speculated whether it was caused by burning tire barricades or burning rubble after a house in an Arab village was leveled. Munching cookies, which he first dipped carefully into his tea, Isaac tried out a few observations about the inflammatory coverage in the American media of exaggerated tensions within Israel between Jews and Arabs; the real tensions, he assured Kate, were between the crazy religious fundamentalists and normal people. This had long been a favored theme; Isaac enjoyed his blistering verbal assaults upon the believers who denounced the state as premature in the absence of the Messiah and zestfully beat Saturday moviegoers.

At last Ellie removed the tea tray, announced her intention of taking a little stroll to visit some neighbors, rattled the doorknob and crisply closed the outer door of the apartment behind her. Isaac gravely invited Kate to tell him how he could help her. She should begin, he instructed, by telling him all about it. Assume he knew nothing. Suspending for the time being her concern about what he did know, Kate obeyed.

Feeling constrained by some unspoken order not to waste time, she reached into her bag of academic skills and selected only what she thought important, subduing her own judgments and speculations as far as she was able. The great man did not interrupt her. He listened very attentively.

While addressing his concentrated dignity, Kate had to fight the distractions of his appearance. He was wearing creased khaki shorts, much laundered, which ended just above his bony knees. He was sitting in an armchair across from her, his bare seventy-year-old legs, pallid and remarkably insubstantial, sticking out at odd angles. By contrast with his smooth, almost bald rounded head, his chest, revealed in the deep open V of his khaki safari jacket, was dotted with silky wisps of fine, snowy hair. Kate struggled against awe and intimidation by this man she'd known all her life, her father's closest friend, a former foreign minister, ambassador, and, it was rumored, intelligence chief. She presented him with the facts as concisely as she could, ending with a painful description of Benjamin's behavior during her visit with him in Ramleh that morning.

"Before I left Philadelphia I planned to come and ask you for advice. And then, when I arrived, I discovered that Ben has been asking for you since they kidnapped him." She stared at Harari, but he didn't answer at once, so she added, "Will you take him on, Isaac? He—we—need you very badly. This is a horrible mess."

Isaac tapped a nearly transparent forefinger against the faint mauve line that straggled down from temple to wispy yellow eyebrow.

"Benjamin asked the police for me? Asked Levy personally? By my name? You're sure?"

"Oh, yes," Kate nodded. "Absolutely."

"You must be very sure, Katie, absolutely certain. He asked for me by name?"

"I'm certain." She was adamant.

"But, Katie, how can you be certain? Forgive me, you have only his word. You say yourself he's a little bit nuts. Maybe he never mentioned me until he saw you?"

"Isaac, I know Benjamin. He's not that crazy. He asked for you as soon as he saw Levy. He's been asking ever since. Five days now. That's all he wanted to say to me, 'Get Harari, get Harari.' I'm positive."

The finger lightly tapped the length of the delicate vein.

"I believe you. I know nothing of this, you understand? It's news to me. I know about Paris, as it happens. All about it. But I didn't know he'd asked for me now from Ramleh. So."

Harari looked used-up, muted, worn and sparse, but he bristled with vehement energy when he leaned forward with his elbows on his knees and fixed the cool shining blue ice of his gaze upon Kate.

"I know some things. Some things I don't know but I can guess. Some things I don't know, I can't guess. So that's how it goes. Answer me some questions, Katie."

He sounded as robust as she could have wished. Kate smiled, a little tremulously, for the first time since she'd seen Benjamin.

"Has Benjamin seen Dan Shemtov?"

"No."

"Tell me again how Shemtov persuaded him to see George Zaggad in Philadelphia?"

"Shemtov told Benjamin that one of the *fellahin* who murdered his first wife, Miriam, had been turned and sent back to spy. Shemtov said he couldn't trust him any longer; the best way to get rid of him was to betray him to the Palestinians. Ben knew Zaggad, he was the ideal officer to go and give Zaggad the name."

"The name?" The forefinger curled in a beckoning gesture.

Kate swallowed.

"Katie. The name."

"Kamal Hussein."

A long silence. Harari's only movement was one light stroke of the pastel vein.

"And this is exactly what he told Zaggad?"

"I think...I think he told George Zaggad he saw a file he wasn't supposed to see. When he went to sign retirement papers, he saw the file, pieced the information together and realized that Kamal Hussein was one of the terrorists who killed Miriam?"

"And which version is the truth, Katie?"

She stared at him, an unwelcome warmth seeping under her neck and cheeks. She hated and despised the convolutions, the blind alleys, tricks and manipulations of Benjamin's work. She'd always hated it, but hadn't learned to admit it for a long time. You never knew where you were with these people, you couldn't count on anything they said, you couldn't depend on them to stay the same. They were unreliable. The same old story. The deception became a total way of life. It wasn't only Ben's work she despised. It was his life; face it, she hated the life. In the part of her mind that she was expert at suppressing, this had been a factor in her return to Philadelphia when he was in prison in Paris. She couldn't stand his life anymore. Now, here she was, deep in it again, sucked into it as if her feet were sinking into the thick mud on the shore of the Dead Sea.

"Did he see his own file, Kate? Did he?"

She looked at the rose and purple Persian rug at her feet. An intricate, wavy black line twisted through the shapes of flowers, turning them back upon themselves.

"Was Kamal Hussein Miriam's murderer?"

Her shoulders shifted in the slightest shrug. She did not raise her eyes.

"Did Benjamin know Shemtov's real purpose? Did he believe him? Did you?"

Kate's neat dark head snapped up. She met the glassy blue stare full on, she straightened her back.

"I guarantee that Benjamin believed Shemtov. I never even thought of all these questions you're asking, but I'm sure of that. I told you, Ben was furious. He'd been betrayed over and over. First he was sacrificed in Paris. He was determined to resign from the Service. Then he learned they'd spared his wife's murderer. Imagine his rage, try and imagine it. The only reason Shemtov could make him do one more mission was because it was to trap a terrorist who killed Miriam. Nothing else would have persuaded him."

Harari nodded gently.

"I see," he said, finger tapping the exact spot where the vein faded into the pale luminous skin around it. "I see. And you, Kate? Did you believe it?"

"Of course. Ben believed it. I believed it. He said it was his last mission before leaving the Service forever." She caught her breath. "Are you saying it isn't true? Isn't it true, Isaac?"

"That's one of the things I'll have to look into, isn't it, Katie?"

"Then you will take Benjamin's case?"

"Oh, yes." There was no hint of a smile, no softening around the eyes. "I'm curious about many things you've been telling me. Also I'm very disturbed—very disturbed—no one has been in touch with me. No one tells me Benjamin is asking for me for five days already. No one." He wagged his finger at some invisible adversary behind Kate's head. "We have laws. Never forget we have the rule of law. The rule of law. Even alleged traitors are entitled to legal protection."

"I'm glad to hear it. You'd never think so, the way they're treating him, would you?"

"Katie, this is Israel. What's the matter with you? We're not sitting in some rich Arab kingdom with sheiks and camels, where they chop off the hands for adultery. Unless it's a prince, of course. Oh, not at all. Here in Israel we have to produce our prisoners, charge them in a court of law. There is evidence, lawyers, so on and so forth."

"Not always, Isaac." Kate felt awkward arguing with the great man, but she couldn't just let it go. "That's not true for Palestinians held in administrative detention for up to six months without trial."

Kate had to say it, but Isaac Harari didn't have to respond. He answered what he wanted to answer, nothing more, nothing less.

"Yes, here we indict suspects. Even alleged traitors. They must be represented by counsel in Israel."

"Isaac, you don't believe Benjamin is a traitor, do you?" The effort to keep her voice low made it tremble. She cleared her throat.

"I've seen no evidence of it. I'm going to do my best for you,

Katie. And for him as well. I've admired his work for a long time, remember. I've been watching him even longer than you've known him."

This remark laid a hush upon the air so embracing, so conclusive, that Kate, astonished by its implications, understood that she was supposed to accept it without questions. It was not in her to do so.

"Isaac, did you know Benjamin when he was recruited? When he joined the Service after Miriam was murdered?"

There was no indication that the great man had heard the question.

"Did you? Because..."

Harari rose, spindly legs far more fluid than they appeared, and stretched out a firm hand to help Kate up. He ushered her toward the door, murmuring avuncular appreciation of her visit, apologizing that he was too busy to offer her dinner, sending good wishes to the family, especially his dear friend Monty. Only after he had the door open and Kate squarely in the hall beyond did he invite her to telephone the following evening. He would inquire. He would look into it. He would telephone Ramleh to arrange an interview with Benjamin. Meantime, Katie should get some rest. Things were out of her hands; she did realize that, didn't she? The situation was out of her control, taking on a new momentum; there were mirrors, screens, veils to be penetrated; Katie should leave it to him, keep away from Ramleh, Shemtov, old connections. Rest. Rest. And be in touch with him the following evening. Rest, he said again, waving her away down the stairs, away and out among the flaming shrubbery, dazzled with light as the sun gathered intensity before its plunge down to the horizon beyond the golden hills.

TWENTY-ONE

As if trapped in a cable car swaying up the sheer side of a mountain in darkness and high wind, unable to remember the purpose of his journey or what waited for him at its end, Gershom slowly lurched terrified from sleep. Eliahu Golan or Tewfik Mahmoud? Gershom wasn't sure. It was becoming increasingly difficult to know.

He kept his eyes closed against sleep's ghastly parade of scattered limbs and squashed heads, crusted unevenly by foul green salt and strewn about among jagged rocks and orderly heaps of sorted effects. There was a pile of gold teeth, another of leather goods and several large mounds of weapons, including the very latest technological advances. For example, there were at least a dozen objects that looked like bright silver Frisbees, but were in fact state-of-the-art cluster bombs which, even when hurled by hand, fragmented so furiously that just one was sufficient to kill or maim more than a thousand people.

Which mountain? Gershom hovered between a memory of a childhood cable-car ride up Masada, his father stretching thin, corded arms up toward the peak, shrieking high above the wind to celebrate the defiant martyrdom of Jews who chose suicide rather than surrender to the Romans and a more recent memory of a risky, adult climb up Mount Hermon, slithering on its icy slopes between his two selves. Eli or Tewfik? Gershom rose to consciousness grappling between unwelcome memory and present fear to identify the place he inhabited now.

He knew he wasn't in Bourg al-Barajneh. He lay in a place too quiet, too protected, its air too fresh for the crawling, pocked and rutted camp south of Beirut, though he was irritated by a nagging awareness that he should go there to open his café, which was probably still standing. At least he hoped it was. Its front wall had only just been replastered, the holes in the roof boarded over after another explosive street battle had torn bits of it away. No, he wasn't lying in the congested camp, where cats prowled the alleys, hissing, and little boys, who'd learned from infancy how to bypass the U.N. schools, strutted about, waiting impatiently to become fighting men as soon as they were nine years old. Unless they were extra tall.

Eyelids still glued tight together, Gershom touched his stomach, slid his hand lower toward his groin, springing with wiry pubic hair, much darker, much coarser than the thick smooth salt and pepper on his head. He certainly wasn't covered by the army issue blue cotton pajamas he'd had to wear at Ansar, the prison camp near Nabatea in South Lebanon where the Israelis had held him for a few bitter weeks during the siege of Beirut in '82. He'd clung, ironically, to his Tewfik Mahmoud identity, keeping it somehow, painfully, intact while sleeping in a tent with twenty-four other Arab prisoners or lining up at night on dry, dusty brush, waiting for the ritual search and harangue. The Jews never spotted Tewfik, but Gershom's tolerant humor had been at its lowest, its meanest ebb in Ansar. He wasn't there now. His ebbing terror held a different, singular threat.

And he wasn't in Rome, whose great stone spaces, broad arches, golden light, bombs and babbling American he'd left with trepidation three days before, persuaded by Shemtov's convincing little ambassador that he should return with Walid Toucan to Beirut as if nothing had happened, as if his anonymous messenger, a family man working for money to buy food and medicine, had not been hung from a tree near Sidon by Akman, efficiently using the occasion to stage a seminar for the next generation of fighters.

Gershom must return, Shemtov's ambassador had urged. It was safe for him to return. Safe and essential. The pinnacle, the mountaintop of his life's work was in his sight at last, she assured him; this was the time when he could make the kind of difference he'd always wanted. Save the next generation from war. She returned to him the phrase he'd given Shemtov during training twenty years before, when he was searching for a way to describe his ultimate goal. He hadn't succeeded for the generation that came after him, he knew that, though he knew he'd made a difference to their ability to win; now, maybe, he could spare their sons.

As if that were enough of an anodyne for the terror that ripped his sleep and had to be stroked to quiescence whenever he awoke, Gershom obeyed Dan Shemtov. He was, after all, a man long accustomed to following instructions. He'd often made independent contributions but always within the boundaries defined by Shemtov. Gershom's imagination flared most creatively when confined by distinct and limited options. If there'd been any occasion in the past twenty years when he'd wanted to defy Shemtov, it had been in Rome, after Akman murdered his messenger and turned his message over for decoding. But Shemtov, who'd been sculpting Gershom's thoughts for almost half his life, knew how to summon his obedience. To return Gershom to Beirut, Shemtov had sent a girl to tell him about Benjamin Landau.

She told Gershom that her name was Maxine. She spoke Hebrew in a South African accent so pronounced that Gershom identified it easily, in spite of the interference of water gushing from every faucet in the bathroom of his suite, just in case he'd missed a bug when he conducted his systematic search before permitting her to speak. Gershom received the news that their chief was running an operation to divert suspicion and ensure his safety in Beirut with the skepticism he'd developed for survival.

Maxine responded with an account of the travels and troubles of Benjamin Landau, including his delivery to George Zaggad in America of the name of a colleague of Gershom's as the traitor leaking Palestinian plans to Israel.

"Zaggad is no imbecile," Gershom whispered harshly into Maxine's right ear. "Why would he believe Landau?"

"Because Landau is in solitary confinement in Ramleh awaiting trial for treason," Maxine said softly, eyes flashing, head forward, all urgency. She slid off the edge of the tub, hiked her shiny purple skirt higher up her thighs and stuck her hand under it. While Gershom stared amazed, she tugged from transparent skimpy panties a copy of the government's charges against Landau. Although the print was smudged from lying in close proximity to Maxine's overheated skin, it was clear to Gershom that Landau was to be charged with betraying an Israeli spy on the Invasion Committee.

Gershom was astonished. As a matter of fact, he was moved and inspired to discover what Landau was suffering on his behalf. He understood that it was a measure of his own value that Dan Shemtov would put into play, endanger and humiliate Benjamin Landau to save him from a traitor's slow death at the hands of the Palestinians. Landau had sought out the prestigious George Zaggad and then allowed himself to be "caught," "kidnapped" and held in solitary confinement, so that Gershom could return to Beirut. All this, so that Tewfik could learn everything about the ambitious plan to take over the West Bank with the aid of Rich, the babbling American. And keep information flowing to Dan Shemtov.

He understood that he must return. Such drastic steps for his protection would never have been taken unless his presence in Beirut was crucial. Not to return would be a betrayal of Benjamin Landau. Shemtov had expected Gershom to come to this conclusion. Gershom knew that, of course, but it didn't alter what he thought. Why should it? Shemtov was right, nothing new in that.

"Whose name did Landau give Zaggad?" he asked Maxine.

But she couldn't tell him. She only knew it was one of the other four on the Invasion Committee. She didn't know who it was or of course she would tell him. No, it was no use pressing her; the chief hadn't told her. She had no need to know and neither did he. Gershom didn't like that, but he wasn't in a position to do anything about it. Given Benjamin Landau's generous heroism, he had no choice. He had left Rome with Walid Toucan as planned.

So he was in the apartment then. Razan Hussein's apartment, which he'd been sharing with her for more than two years already, the most settled time with any woman in all the years since... since he became Tewfik Mahmoud. He was in bed, not with Maxine, who'd comforted him playfully in Rome. Just to prevent Walid from becoming suspicious, they'd assured each other. Now he was in bed with Razan, whose crisp, ferny smell he inhaled on a deep sigh. Gershom's exploring toes touched the firm flesh of Razan's twenty-four-year-old calf and his cheek pressed gratefully against clean, fitted, pastel yellow sheets, bought halfway round the world in Detroit, Michigan, by Razan. She went back to the States every six months to visit her mother. She'd returned less than two weeks before Gershom left for Rome.

Terror receding, gradually giving way to his customary guarded calm, Gershom opened his eyes to Razan's honey-colored skin, an extra golden glow on its satin expanse bestowed by the American substitute for linen. Razan's back was decorated with neat stripes of pale amber, drawn by early light glancing between half-open window shutters. Razan refused to close them tightly, although the apartment was in the front of the pink stucco building, only one floor up from the side street off the battered, bustling Rue Mazra. But security wasn't everything; life was too short to wake in darkness, Razan declared.

She constantly reiterated her newly acquired slogan, having exuberantly carried it back from the States along with the lemon-colored sheets, her vastly increased assurance and her renewed American passport, which enabled her to visit Jerusalem and

Jaffa to deliver important messages personally. Gershom didn't know what they were. Afterward, she had crossed the bridge into Jordan and flown from Amman to Damascus, where Tewfik had driven to meet her, luxuriating in the return to his bed of this lovely, assertive girl, just the age his daughter might have been if his life's circumstances had ever permitted him to father one. If the matter were ever discussed between them, which Tewfik Mahmoud certainly would not permit, Razan would insist that life was too short to worry about that. Any of that.

She was certain that life was too short to stay away if one had business in the southern suburbs, even when rival Shiite factions were shelling each other and recklessly exploding homemade mines in alleys and on rooftops among tattered laundry hanging limp in the damp, turgid air; life was too short for respectful silence in the presence of revered leaders like Ahmed Khalidi, her father or Tewfik himself. Razan preferred not to waste her time, but to speak her mind openly. She was no traditional, retiring, obedient young girl; she was an energetic woman who had grown up in America and gave no man automatic reverence, not even Tewfik. Especially not Tewfik. Life was too short for secretive glances from behind the veil, too short for the chauvinism of most Arab men, too short for the everyday conventions that were still the standard for demure Palestinian women.

Razan was a freedom fighter herself, a poet of the liberation. She was not, of course, a member of the Invasion Committee, though with father and lover filling two of its five positions she considered that she did have some influence. In her own right she was a leader of the Struggle to Return. Her inspired slogans and directives had shifted thousands of women out of long skirts into blue jeans, lifted veils as well as chins and knees and injected the rage needed to keep smashing paving stones into sharp-edged rocks for their little sons to hurl at Israeli soldiers, settlers and hikers.

Life was too short for passive acceptance, Razan exhorted the young women and girls who flocked to her consciousness-raising classes in Uzai and Ramlet al Baiga on the Mediterranean shore. She'd led classes in Jaffa and in Jerusalem, too, not far from Al-Aksa, in a slanting old house behind a jewelry store filled with the blue and green stones of Eilat and the new copper, thin and bright, from Timna. The Jews who owned that store thought the house belonged to Christians. But it wasn't Jews who sold the jewelry and it wasn't Christians who owned the house. Who knew who anyone was, especially in Jerusalem? Some people, not most of course, but some people could be whoever they wanted to be. When Razan explained that to him, Gershom smiled and tucked it into the recess of his mind where he kept ironies. Eliahu or Tewfik, who ever knew?

Did she think that life was too short to explain to him how her father was able to provide so liberally for her? Or did she really not know, as she claimed? Where did Kamal Hussein get the funds to keep his daughter in her own apartment, while he lived a few blocks away in a larger, even more comfortable one with whatever woman he took home with him? There was ample room for his privacy and for Razan's. With his long index finger, Gershom lightly traced the line that separated Razan's high round buttocks. He felt her shiver.

Razan's parents had lived apart nearly all her life, but when she arrived in Beirut filled with nationalistic fervor from Detroit, where her grandparents and mother had resettled, Kamal had welcomed his stunning daughter, the ardent revolutionary, with proud excitement. And unlimited support. As if he'd inherited a fortune. He'd obviously come by resources he'd never had in the twelve or fourteen years he and Gershom had worked together. He couldn't have had vast sums of money—dollars, no less—without Gershom knowing. They were good friends, even living together for a time during their years as construction workers before Gershom opened his cafe in Bourg al-Barajneh.

Of course, Kamal Hussein had made good money from his import business. The perfume, silks, and leather goods from

Paris had found a voracious market, in the fashionable stores of the big hotels along the Corniche and the glamorous boutiques on Rue Hamra in the days of Beirut's elegance.

But Kamal had taken a beating like everyone else when the persistent, intractable civil wars drove the tourists away, impoverished the Lebanese, and scared off even the big bankers and traders. They sent their women to Paris and London almost all the time after war became constant; they picked up their trinkets easily enough in Europe, where they could shop without risking a sudden spray of shells, a sniper on a crumbling rooftop, an explosion from an innocent-looking Mercedes, or a narrow heel caught in a gash on the pavement or in a torn segment of floppy flesh. They'd come to take it all for granted, of course, but not to the point where the heels of their Italian leather shoes sank into a stomach or mud-slick intestines. Kamal had certainly complained incessantly about how badly his business was hurt by the ceaseless battles, where it barely made a difference which adversaries were fighting. Or who was on whose team that day. Or who lived or died.

So it was strange that during the last three years Kamal Hussein seemed to have more to spend, more to enjoy, more to give away, especially to Razan. She traveled to the United States twice a year, lived comfortably in her western-style apartment, drove her sporty red Merc convertible up and down the country, treated her classes to fruit or baklava, sometimes even wine. Gershom had known her almost as long as she'd been in Beirut. During those thirty months she had not earned a cent, though of course Razan had worked intensely hard for the Struggle to Return, on her poetry, which was published in several countries already, and even fund-raising in America among the staunch Arab communities, for support for the exiled Palestinians.

Razan stirred, then settled a little closer to Gershom, close enough that the sleek skin of her back grazed his chest with each breath. A long strand of glossy black hair teased his shoulder. The heel of her foot brushed his ankle. He curved his body to the outline of hers and edged closer. He had not told Shemtov about Razan. He was supposed to keep Shemtov informed of any personal relationships or connections he made and he had always done so. He'd had no difficulty with that, none at all. And there'd be no difficulty now, of course, except that the circumstances had not been propitious for him to explain Razan to his chief. There had not been a suitable opportunity.

At the beginning of his life as Tewfik, Shemtov had discussed the problem of women very openly with Gershom. Too openly, really. The chief had been quite outspoken and had embarrassed the principled, lonely and inhibited young man. Eliahu's experience had been limited to some fumbling experimentation with a girl he'd grown up with on the kibbutz where his father sent him as a child, and several thrilling encounters with a superior officer in the army who had directed his efforts on border patrol in the Sinai desert and also in a sleeping bag. On a chilly night, after a shooting chase across the border, a bad scare from snipers in a cave beyond the Arab village and the capture of four terrorists, under a sky darting with silvery shivers, Eliahu discovered that with a woman there were many different things that could be done and more than one way to do them. Above all there was the delicious pleasure of doing nothing. His commanding officer took care of everything. Eliahu's compliance was perfect reciprocation, arousing them both to a lavish sensuality that only Razan, in all the years between, had ever superseded. And so it was only Razan who beguiled him into a continuing relationship, the only woman he'd ever lived with.

Long ago, Shemtov had explained that he would need women. He shouldn't be ashamed or afraid to take Arab women; it would help his cover while providing the release every normal man needs. He would be away a long time—neither of them had any idea how long in those early days—and he must not increase his isolation by avoiding women. The thing to resist was getting emotionally involved. That would be very dangerous. The more intimate and intense the involvement, the greater the risk of exposure. The role of choice for Tewfik was the eternal Don Juan, the elusive philanderer, the charming womanizer.

Chuckling, Shemtov pointed out that he was giving Gershom a license that all men ardently desired, a license to enjoy variety, permission to escape the domestic trap. Relationships with women, like friendships with men, must only go down to a certain controlled point. Beyond that, they were dangerously invasive. For almost twenty years, Gershom had complied. It had not been difficult. He was a man accustomed to discipline, a man whose work was fruitful and whose life was intact because he obeyed the rules. Besides, the role of seducer, gallant adventurer, came to suit him. Shemtov's prediction proved accurate. Gershom enjoyed variety, found pleasure in pursuit, calculated the conclusion of his romances with satisfying precision, becoming more and more adept at painless separations. He tried to make them painless for his women, too, and often succeeded.

If anything, evading deep emotional ties to his friends was harder to accomplish. While there was nothing sexual in those friendships, there was a quality of close camaraderie which threatened Gershom's ultimate privacy. He was always aware that his intimate friendship with his four comrades on the Invasion Committee caused him great vulnerability, the largest threat to the secret of his divided self. He and Shemtov talked about this whenever they met, Shemtov always striving to remind Gershom of the danger, helping him to sustain the invisible fortress that he'd erected to protect his true identity.

Gershom had never intended to become deeply involved with a woman; he didn't realize it was happening to him until Razan suggested he move into her new apartment. It wasn't the first time a woman had invited him to live with her, but it was the first time warmth spread all through him, leaping up into his face to make his eyes fill and his lips tremble, actually tremble with yearning. He'd still been far too disciplined to submit immediately. He'd think about it, he told her, shuddering as her tongue traced his inner leg from ankle to crotch while he lay stretched out on his back, limbs flung wide, on her wide, white bed. It took a month to convince himself that his twenty years of experience made the risk negligible. While he worked the same harsh territory for all the time it takes from birth to high school graduation, he'd learned enough to handle it, to stay intact even while permitting her intimacy. He was entitled to some comfort after his long, lonely alienation from everyone and everything that belonged to his real life. This was his only chance of life on this earth; it wasn't a rehearsal. With a trembling smile he recognized that the truth was that he couldn't resist Razan Hussein.

But there'd been no opportunity to tell Shemtov about her. He'd been worrying about it for some time, especially since the idea of having a child started to haunt him. When he sent the message about going to Rome, he'd thought Shemtov would meet him there, as he'd done often before. Then he'd be able to explain about Razan. But Walid's ambush of his messenger put a stop to that plan. Then, calling Shemtov in terror from Rome, asking to be taken out, Gershom had wanted to ask for Razan to be brought to him, until he remembered that when Razan discovered who—what—he was, she would come near him only to destroy him. When Maxine told him what Benjamin Landau was enduring to save him, Gershom was warmly aware that not betraying him and the Service would also return him to Razan. He had not so far forgotten his priorities that Razan alone could make him return, but she was an enormous inducement.

His fingers, trailing up and down over the firm curve of buttock sloping down toward her center, detected a quick tightening, a slight internal jerk, a poised tension. Razan pressed against his hardness, upper body flung forward away from him, to gain an angle from which she could grind against him. He wanted to slide inside her from behind, but before he could shift away enough to do so, she flung herself around and over him, forcefully kneeing his hip until he lay flat beneath her, open to her, waiting for her to receive him. She straddled his narrow hips, knees pressed down on either side. She leaned forward to bite his lower lip, hair fanning out about his head, tantalizing his shoulders and chest until, too aroused to tease him any longer, she raised herself up and sat firmly on him, tilting backward, bouncing sweat-shiny breasts taut and high with nipples staring at him like a second devouring pair of eyes. He lifted his head to lick them but she pushed him down, and leaned further back, smiling her private pleasure.

The phone rang. Intent upon their heated ride, they ignored it. It stopped seconds before Razan, with a high cry, felt his pulsing spurts inside her and flung herself down on top of him. The tears that so often followed her release seeped down his neck to his collarbone as the phone rang again. After eight long peals Razan climbed off him and crossed to the bathroom. Gershom reached for the phone.

The conversation didn't last long. It didn't take much time at all to remind Gershom who he was and how close to exposure as a traitor. An Israeli spy, moving freely among them, trusted even in their secret, hidden center. He tried to tighten Tewfik's skin around Eli's Jewish bones, he masked Eli's inquisitive eyes with Tewfik's somber determination, he savagely rehearsed the names and places of his Palestinian history. But Gershom knew that whatever Shemtov's manipulations accomplished, he was as precariously exposed as if he stood alone, balancing in high wind and darkness in the center of a cable car without sides, shuddering up the sheer side of a mountain.

When Razan returned from the bathroom, Gershom lay with his hands clasped behind his head, staring up at the ceiling as if he were searching there for stars.

"Where's your father?" He didn't care how abrupt he sounded. Or how preoccupied.

"In bed, I suppose. It's not even seven yet." She shrugged. "Who was phoning so early?"

She sat on the side of the bed and rumpled his thick wavy hair. He jerked his head, only slightly and only once, but Razan drew back immediately.

"That was Akman. Looking for your father. Among other things."

"What are you talking about?"

There was no reason not to tell her.

"Akman says George Zaggad will arrive later today. He's driving from Damascus."

"You knew he was coming. He often comes."

"He told Akman he wants to meet with us, our committee."

"Why? What for?"

"Who knows?" said Gershom and remembered to add. "You know I can't talk about the committee."

She sighed and tossed her hair, folding her arms under her breasts. But he didn't wait for her standard speech about her access to the deepest secrets of the struggle.

"Thing is, Akman tried to reach Kamal to make arrangements about the meeting with Zaggad, but there's no answer to the phone. Where could he be at this hour, Razan?"

"Ah, Tewfik, you didn't answer the phone the first time it rang either. Come on. Maybe he's making some lady happy, too busy to answer."

Gershom managed a smile, but while he showered and dressed he worried about the meeting with Zaggad, whose brilliance he respected. Everyone in every faction respected Zaggad. That's why he was on the High Command. And that, no doubt, was why he'd arrived to explore Landau's information. Gershom wished that Shemtov had told him whose name had been given to Zaggad.

It was difficult to detach himself enough to play the game, but he tried to figure out who Shemtov would choose to sacrifice. Not Walid, surely, who loved life so infectiously, who threw himself so wholeheartedly, so courageously into everything he did? Ahmed Khalidi, maybe? But he was the oldest of them and had suffered much greater deprivation for much longer. Perhaps he deserved to be spared. Certainly it couldn't be Kamal Hussein. Shemtov would surely think of Razan and...but Gershom remembered that Shemtov didn't know about Razan and would have no reason anyway to spare her. Shemtov surely couldn't have chosen Akman. There would never be a way to pin the leaked information on him. He was too upright, too loyal; there were no chinks in Akman's armor.

Trembling suddenly, Gershom grasped that only the death of one of these dear friends would save his own life. Looking for reasons to save them was suicidal. He would, he thought sadly, be so much better able to deal with Zaggad and with his brothers in the struggle if he knew the name Landau had offered, the man Shemtov hoped to sacrifice.

He was eating the fruit and yoghurt Razan had set out when the phone rang again. She ran though to the bedroom to answer it. Gershom followed her immediately and heard her say yes several times, each time more faintly. That was all she said. When she hung up, she covered her face with her hands, bending her head until her glossy hair fell forward like a screen.

"What is it? Razan?"

She dropped her hands. Deep frown grooves sliced between thick eyebrows. Her eyes were narrow crescents.

"Tell me," Gershom insisted uneasily.

"It was Akman." Razan rubbed the palms of her hands jerkily over her hip bones. He'd never seen her do that before. "Akman went around to Papa's apartment to tell him about the meeting with Zaggad, but he isn't there. The door was wide open. Most of his things are gone. A lot of clothes. Even that nude statue he bought in Athens, the one he likes so much. It's not there. I can't understand it." Her hands pressed hard against her hips, up and down. "Akman says it looks as if he's... gone."

"Impossible," Gershom said. "I was with him last night, remember. He'd have said something."

She caught her lower lip between her teeth. Her hands were still for an instant, fingers splayed wide.

"He was fine last night," Gershom said quickly. "He was fine. He can't be gone."

"Well." Razan turned away sharply, went to the kitchen and lifted bunches of grapes from the colander where they'd been rinsing. "Akman says there's an envelope addressed to me. He's bringing it over here right now. We'll soon know."

Waiting for Akman, Gershom, who felt that the meeting with Zaggad about the leaks was worrying enough, tried not to be alarmed by the glittery flush on Razan's high-cheeked face or by the constant rubbing of her palms against her hips, so fiercely that she seemed to be trying to eliminate them.

TWENTY-TWO

Shemtov did not expect to see Isaac Harari until much later in the day, but when he looked up from the swaying coffin, he caught the pale, frigid stare of the American. Harari would always be an American to Dan Shemtov, though the older man had lived in Israel more than forty years and spent them in public service. Harari's gaze was fixed, not on Shemtov, but on the pallbearers, straining under their burden, augmented in the last minute or two by the extra weight of the pregnant wife of their murdered comrade. When Tami hurled her upper body across the top of the light pine box, the legs of Yaron's youngest brother buckled. He straightened and jerked forward along with the others, toward the fresh wound on the slope ahead that had been prepared to receive Yaron's mutilated body.

At the instant he sensed Harari's marble stare, Shemtov realized that he should have anticipated that Harari would be at the funeral; he would have done so if he were not distracted and preoccupied with Gershom's safety. He and Harari were both at the funeral on the West Bank for the same reason. This new victim of the latest version of Arab terror was the son-in-law of an old, mutual political friend. Seven months ago, Shemtov and

Harari had both attended the wedding ceremony of Tami and Yaron on the lawn between the settlement recreation center and the field where they trudged now in the dry dusty air. The field was ringed by armed settlers. Their vigilance, their bitter rage, had not kept Yaron alive; they were damned if they'd allow anything, anyone at all, to disrupt his funeral.

Shemtov and Harari were not the only outsiders at the funeral.

The entire settlement community had turned out, of course. There were several hundred of them now, amazing if you looked back to the early eighties when ground was first cleared by nine or ten families looking for the quick commute to Jerusalem and subsidized building costs. In defiance of the Camp David accord, or at the very least in defiance of its spirit, this was one of many new villages offering the convenience of suburban Jerusalem. It wasn't a political statement from religious fanatics, fundamentalists claiming their biblical heritage, like the settlement farther south into which Shemtov's son had almost married. This one was mainly for professionals and business people who worked in Jerusalem and enjoyed the comforts of suburban living. As well as being, of course, part of the facts on the ground, the human factor with which Israel was occupying the West Bank. The distinction between zealots and yuppies, however, wasn't a significant one for Palestinian villagers nearby.

Shemtov, moving among the crowd toward the new grave, as usual looked detached, as if he were alone, as if he had nimbly elevated himself several feet above the mourners. Glancing about, he thought that there might be more than five hundred settlers if you counted the children who trotted solemnly beside their parents, absorbing, like so many sponges, the fury, the fear, the utter hatred that spun poisonously in the air around them. But there were also scores of outsiders, members of neighboring settlements, city folk, relatives from all over the country, army friends of the young couple, their parents' friends and old political and military allies, come to mourn and also to replenish their individual pain, refueling the beakers of their souls with suffering so that it would never get used up, as the level of oil in the lanterns of the Maccabees had never dropped below a certain point. They accumulated suffering for their survival.

Shemtov was not anonymous at the graveside, not by any means, though he would have preferred it if he had been. But he knew almost half the people there; and two thirds at least knew him. And pointed out the legendary chief to anyone who didn't. That's Israel. Everyone knows everyone, more or less, in certain circles. Some would say, certain privileged circles. The army, government, defense, intelligence, that nearly incestuous, intertwined circle of those who make the decisions, those who really run things. They were all connected in some way, related to each other's former wives, sleeping with someone's lawyer, descended from a common well-meaning but incompetent ancestor who had lived, four or five generations previously, on a wintry border between nations of bitter enemies. It didn't really have much to do with party political allegiance, in spite of the divisive animosities. No matter how you voted, if you were part of the central elite, you didn't avoid its celebrations. Or its funerals.

The notion of an Israeli aristocracy would have been anathema to its idealistic founders, but it was an indisputable fact of life, confirmed by the testimony of everyone it excluded, not least the striving, embittered "orientals," darker, less literate, less modern. (There were those who went to great lengths to avoid saying "less civilized" and those who didn't bother.) Sometimes scratching, frequently banging raucously upon the walls of intellect, dignity and privilege they were determined to scale, these descendants of immigrants from Arab and African countries knew all about the aristocracy in the Promised Land. As did Dan Shemtov, who was a part of it. Otherwise he would not have been at Yaron's funeral. He had neither time nor taste for the event.

Though he followed the procession and heard Tami's searing cries, though he watched his old political ally, Tami's father, grimly support his wife with an arm around her shoulders for what must have been the first time in fifteen years, even as his insides lurched when he was briefly unable to block from his mind the hideous images of the way Yaron's life had seeped away, even brushing aside guiltily the sudden, hot rush of relief that it was not his own son, ripped up as if his flesh were nothing but potato peelings, dead in that box up ahead of him, even then, in his core, Shemtov willed himself to a pink stucco building with wrought iron trim off the Rue Mazra in West Beirut.

He wanted to be there, invisible, as he watched over Tewfik Mahmoud and Razan, daughter of Kamal Hussein, whose passionate connection had been mentioned to him in passing by one of his boys nearly two years before. Tewfik, dedicated strategist of the Invasion Committee, proprietor of the Kassem Café in Bourg al-Barajneh, was far too well known for his liaison with the daughter of Kamal Hussein to go unnoticed. Razan herself was too fiery, too assertive, too politically radical, in spite of her flaming sexual appeal, to be ignored by the assorted purveyors of information who drifted in and out of Beirut. The gossip that filtered back to Shemtov about Tewfik and Razan was sporadic and thin, but certainly more substantial than anything Gershom had provided him on this subject. The Rue Mazra was where Shemtov's anxiety led him. He needed to know if Gershom was there. He needed the phones, computers, technicians who might have news of Gershom for him. He didn't want to be on the West Bank at all. Ever, actually, though even the thought was heresy.

But of course he was there, and so was Harari, watching their old *chaver*'s widowed daughter, hair sweatily plastered across her face, sprawled clumsy across the coffin, banging her fists upon the light, smooth pine, screaming, "We'll get them, we'll get them all," until the young people began to chant with her, as passionately as if they swayed deep in the burning heat of a rock concert, utterly oblivious to everything but the harsh joy of submerging their selves in the communal will.

Yaron, a social worker attached to the mayor's task force for rehabilitation of crippled veterans, had been in Talpiot, counseling a twenty-year-old double amputee, recently returned from military hospital to his parents' apartment. The ugly yellow brick building squatted within inches of that ring of land the Palestinians called occupied and certain Israelis called liberated. Yaron walked sadly out to his green Volkswagen, burdened by his inability to comfort the boy who'd lost both legs on patrol in the security zone north of the border, in southern Lebanon. When Yaron opened his car door, he was jumped by two young men, waving narrow-bladed knives at his eyes and neck. One blade bit the skin beneath his chin, leaving a thin line of blood down his neck from jaw to collarbone. They accused him of trespassing.

"This is Palestine," they jeered. "You're a foreigner here. Why do you put your feet down on our soil?"

They pushed Yaron onto the back of an open truck, among the cucumbers and tomatoes that had not sold that day in the Mahane Yehuda market. They tied his wrists together with hairy yellow twine. They tied his ankles with it as well, so tight that his feet turned purple and numb very quickly. A third man drove the truck toward a network of small villages near Hebron.

Forty minutes later, at the outskirts of Dehaishe, the truck halted on a dusty shoulder, quickly attracting a crowd of small boys who had been practicing throwing rocks in a stand of pine trees nearby. They laughed and cheered as Yaron was pulled from the truck and hurled out onto the ground. Their enthusiasm must have encouraged Yaron's captors, who jumped around him, shouting and snapping the twine in the air above his head. His captors turned him facedown on the gritty sand, while the driver joined his knotted ankles to the back bumper of the truck. Yaron lifted his head up off the ground as the truck's engine rumbled and throbbed, but when it moved forward, jerking him along, his face scraped the gravel again, scraps of skin and pellets of blood staining the earth as the truck gathered speed, though it never exceeded fifteen miles an hour.

The little boys raced alongside, shouting approval and urging speed, watching everything closely enough that several of them were later able to provide details to the community and to the police. The truck made its way along the main roads of three adjacent villages; by the time it reached the second one, brush word-of-mouth brought old men out of their roadside stores and women and children from the stone houses behind, to line the street. Some folded their arms and stared; one or two started forward, as if to intervene, but were pulled back by cooler judgment, their own or a neighbor's; and others applauded as Yaron's flesh was slowly soiled, ripped and destroyed, his head flopping in the dirt and his chest, from which the last fragments of shirt, hair and skin fell entirely away, scraped to bleeding pulp on the punctured, potholed macadam.

In spite of the rather vivid reporting of a couple of little boys, from whom they were able to extract the names of at least two of the three murderers, and whose thrilled approval had given way to guilty, sickened horror, the Shin Beth had not yet caught the scum, who were variously reported to be in hiding in the Old City, across the border in Jordan, or heading north for Lebanon, sheltered by a network of PLO guerrillas installed in safe houses along the coast.

It was the not the first time this grotesque new form of terror had been practiced by West Bank adolescents. Shemtov knew it wouldn't be the last. Pelting rocks, hurling grenades, burning tires for barricades, the knife in the back in the crowded market, homemade explosives in grocery bags and under seats in school buses, burning matches tossed down in precious forests, nails with cut-off heads hammered into tarmac to trap army vehicles, rusted screws twisted into oranges. And now the public humbling and shredding of innocent captives. The battle was joined every day, new fronts opening like infinite Japanese folding papers. Survival demanded scrupulous vigilance. Avenging Yaron's awful death wasn't Shemtov's responsibility, for which he was truly grateful; but it was a jolting reminder, not that he needed it, heaven forbid, that Gershom's life must be saved. Which was why, after all, he had agreed to meet Isaac Harari later that day.

Of course he didn't want to. He seemed to spend more of his

time than ever doing things he didn't want to. He would have preferred to stall Benjamin Landau's nominated defender until Gershom was secure, but Isaac Harari was too formidable to be evaded any longer. He'd certainly stirred things up the previous evening when, after an apparently emotional meeting with Landau's American wife, he'd driven his shabby maroon Audi over from Beth Hakerem to Rehavia without so much as a warning phone call. There he found Aron Levy sprawled in a reclining canvas chair while his wife and daughters leaped about, conscientiously weeding around tomato plants and date bushes between running inside to bring him newspapers, cold drinks, bowls of nuts and bunches of grapes.

Later, Levy stridently informed Shemtov that as soon as he saw Harari, standing grandly at his iron gate as if it were a canal he intended to blockade, his stomach growled and heaved, heralding a spastic dyspepsia that lingered for hours, that might, as a matter of fact, be permanent. Levy's stomach had known instantly that Harari's visit was not social, not friendly and not good.

Aron Levy had not enjoyed referring Harari and his grievances to Dan Shemtov. He had not cared at all for Harari's derisive wisecracks about strings, puppets and magicians. The old man had even mentioned Svengali in connection with the ubiquitous Shemtov. What a nerve he had. Levy had not relished, far from it, having nothing but the pathetic explanation that Landau was Shemtov's asset, not his own, in response to Harari's merciless onslaught. And if Shemtov thought that he, Levy, could be jerked around one more time on the matter of Landau, he should think again. Levy would go directly to the Prime Minister within the next day if Harari wasn't given access to his client, traitor or no traitor. Levy didn't know what little game Shemtov was playing but he wasn't going to be put into the position of colluding with a power-hungry paranoid. And he never wanted Harari to come near him again; he hoped he was making himself clear. He'd had his hands full keeping them away from Harari's stringy chicken neck. Harari had an opinion of himself bigger than all Sinai. Trickier, too. Shemtov should at all costs keep Harari away from him.

Levy's ranting, punctuated by intermittent grumbles from his stomach, had persuaded Shemtov that he'd better see Harari. Elaborate arrangements had been made for them to meet secretly later in the day, shielded from the prying eyes of local and foreign reporters, inquisitive political hacks and assorted international spies, agents and operators. Neither Shemtov nor Harari was anxious to be observed in the other's company at this early stage of Landau's case, when the conclusions that might be drawn couldn't even be estimated. If Shemtov had known that the American would be at Yaron's funeral, he might have suggested they walk back to their cars together, murmuring quietly without attracting much attention. Ten to fifteen minutes was all he was going to let the old man have, anyway. He hadn't been put on earth to make it easy for the chairman of the Knesset Committee on Security to breathe down his neck and sniff his underwear while he defended the nation's security against its most bitter enemies. He would give Harari only enough time to get him off his back for a few days, neutralize him until he was sure that Gershom was safe.

Looking up again as the last amen was murmured and people started moving away from the grave, Shemtov was irritated to find that he'd lost sight of Harari, whose pale fishy stare no longer pierced him from across the coffin.

"I'm right behind you." Perhaps the clipped, highly cultivated voice or the words themselves were intended to be reassuring, but Shemtov didn't find them so as he swiveled around to find Isaac Harari planted securely at his back, a thin smile at the corners of his closed lips, an icy scrutiny of everyone standing nearby lending an inquisitor's hostility to his eyes.

"I thought," he said, as if he'd peered into Shemtov's mind and read it as easily as a Dick and Jane primer, "that we'd be better off trying to talk here than going through the rigmarole your office planned for us."

Shemtov immediately regretted attending the funeral. Agree-

181

ing to any arrangement proposed by Harari was intrinsically offensive. But his desire to be done with Harari prevailed. Nodding agreement, he moved toward the edge of the crowd and set off in the direction of his car at a moderate pace, Harari at his side.

"What's going on, Dan?" Harari asked neutrally, hands clasped behind his back, trousers bagging in the seat, curving around his hips in much the same way as loose skin drooped in half-moons around the outer edges of his eyes.

"What's going on? The Arabs come up with new ways to harass us every day. The Americans are pestering us to yield land for peace so the Saudis won't be so disappointed in them and the Iranians will lose momentum. Imagine. The Queen of England has a new grandchild. The P.M. is collecting opinions on using live ammunition against protesters in Jerusalem. What do you mean, what's going on?"

Harari didn't smile. He didn't even glance up from the rigid, irregular ground.

"I mean, what's going on with Landau, Dan?" he said evenly.

If he didn't know better from long and convincing experience, he wouldn't believe this man could cause anyone any trouble at all, Shemtov thought irritably.

"Landau met George Zaggad in a greenhouse near Philadelphia and gave him the name of a deep-cover agent of ours on their Invasion Committee. That's what's going on."

"Yes, I've heard that on the radio. I've read it in the papers. I understand from these public sources that Landau will be charged with treason, is that correct?"

"Oh, yes. Absolutely. Quite so."

"He has repeatedly asked to consult with me, but I was never informed. Not even once. Explain this to me, would you?"

"Landau is in Aron Levy's custody, naturally. I suppose he had his reasons for the delay."

"Dan, Aron Levy insists that although he is holding Landau at Ramleh, you are calling the shots, he's your asset, you are keeping very tight, personal control over the management of

Landau. Levy, in fact, is somewhat peeved at being excluded, as I understand it."

"Mm." Shemtov didn't even try to subdue his delighted smile, which sent rare curling lines upward from his eyes and lips. They vanished almost as soon as they appeared, however, because Shemtov felt his elbow sharply pinched in the wiry grip of Harari's long pale fingers.

"Dan," Harari persisted, "why have you prevented Aron Levy's office from contacting me? Landau keeps asking for me, you know that perfectly well. This is Israel, Dan. This isn't some steamy little jungle where self-appointed colonels swat mosquitoes and make the rules. It isn't a sheik's tent in the desert where some old man cuddling his dirty old goat decides who's guilty. This is Israel. People accused of crimes are entitled to the advice of a lawyer. Suspects have to be produced in court and accused of a crime and defended by a lawyer. Am I correct?"

Shemtov hesitated, while he mentally fingered alternative responses.

"Answer me. Explain to me. If there's been a change in the rules, I have not been notified."

"Isaac, of course you are correct. Of course. There's been no change in the rules. But the time wasn't ripe, Isaac. That's all there is to it." Shemtov stopped walking and turned to face Harari. Looking into his freezing eyes with the air of a man making a blunt, honest declaration, however difficult, he added, "This is a matter of national security, Isaac."

"Yes," Harari said grimly, removing his hand from Shemtov's elbow and wiping it carefully on the drooping fold of fabric beneath his left buttock. "It certainly is a matter of national security. We're not going to have much security if we feel free to ignore our own laws whenever the fancy takes us."

"Bullshit, and you know it." Shemtov walked smartly forward. "I'm not in the habit of ignoring the law on a whim. I'd be grateful if you'd acknowledge that. If you please. The time wasn't ripe to bring Landau into court. I needed some time. There's more at stake than you can possibly know."

"Let's remedy that. Right now. Ben Landau betrayed one of our operatives to Zaggad. Didn't he in fact do this on direct orders from you?"

"You've been talking to his American wife, of course?"

"Certainly I've been talking to Kate. Nothing wrong with that. They're retaining my services. Why shouldn't she talk to me? Now then. Wasn't he doing a job for you, Dan?"

"Yes, Isaac. At least I hoped he was. When you send an agent, even a very experienced one, to talk to a member of the High Command, you have to be aware that he may not say exactly what you intend. Sometimes one is regrettably compelled to employ damage control. Landau has known Zaggad well for many years. Are you aware of that?"

Harari started to speak, but abruptly swallowed his words and cleared his throat instead. He patted his lips firmly with two fingertips.

"What's this about turning one of Landau's first wife's murderers and sending him back to spy for us? Is that what you told him?"

Shemtov slowed slightly, then picked up his pace again. Staring straight ahead at the pink and mauve hills in the distance, he said, "Yes, Isaac. Yes. That's what I told him."

The skin of Harari's face creased and puckered into hundreds of tiny, intersecting ripples erupting across his face. He veered toward the left, in the direction of his parked maroon Audi, studying the ground in front of his sandaled feet as if searching for shards of ancient pottery. Moving away from the scrub toward the rough sandy parking ground, he found a tamarisk tree. He leaned against its trunk, until Shemtov joined him in its shade.

"But why, Dan? Why did you tell him that? Of all things, why that?"

"Think, Isaac, if you please. Think. It was the only way I could get him to go and talk to George Zaggad."

"It had to be Landau?"

"It had to be Landau. Trust me."

The cascade of ripples upon Harari's skin deepened noticeably, as if they curtsied to mock the notion of trusting Dan Shemtov.

"Why did you need someone to talk to Zaggad, Dan? Explain to me, why?"

"I cannot explain it."

"And why Landau? And why would he betray one of our people?"

"That, you'll have to ask him."

"What are you doing?" Harari lifted his right arm slowly to shoulder height and held it out, palm up, toward Shemtov. "You must have sent him with disinformation to Zaggad? Is that true?"

"It's possible." Shemtov's shrug was only just perceptible.

"And it had to be Landau because Zaggad would believe him because they're old acquaintances?"

"If you wish," said Shemtov. His shrug was high and protracted now.

"But you claim Landau told him something he shouldn't have? Not what you sent him to say? He told him what? The truth? Was it the truth?"

"Listen to me, Isaac, if you please. He told him the truth, yes. He betrayed the name of a secret agent of ours, a man we've had hidden in the center of their operations for years. That is treason, sir."

"Why would he do that?"

"Ask him. You ask him yourself."

"You must be protecting treasure more valuable than the Dead Sea Scrolls to have sent Benjamin Landau to George Zaggad. What a risk you took!"

Shemtov nodded at Harari's shivering stare.

"Exactly. I am protecting treasure beyond price."

"Will you tell me what it is?"

"I cannot. If I could, I would tell you."

"Do you think I would betray my country, Dan? Israel is my country as much as it is yours. Why can't you trust me with this secret? Why? I have the credentials, I have the clearances, I have the highest possible national security clearances, and you know it. Tell me what you're protecting. Tell me what you sent Landau to tell Zaggad."

"I cannot, sir."

"Not now or not in the future?" Harari demanded roughly.

"Not in the foreseeable future," Dan Shemtov said slowly, his face wiped clean of all expression.

"Who the hell do you think you are?" Harari hissed. "Who anointed you sole guardian of state security? What right do you have to manipulate Benjamin Landau and God knows who else for some convoluted operation you've dreamed up? What authority do you have?"

"The very highest, sir. I have the authority of the head of state. And that is all I need in this matter. As you are aware." Shemtov could be as icy as Harari when he chose.

"Ah, what happened to the dream?" Isaac Harari cried. "What happened to social justice and civil liberty, society founded on the highest ideals, man and his freedom the ultimate value, equality, diversity, a light unto the nations? What happened, I ask you?"

"Do you think there is no price? You're not a young man any more, Isaac Harari. Haven't you discovered that dreams don't come free? Not in the real world, they don't, I'll tell you that much. And there's no light unto the nations if you don't exist at all. Think about that. That's the priority. You have to survive. You have to live if you're going to shed any light at all." He didn't want to be overheard, but his voice had risen. People approaching their cars on all sides were watching them curiously, as they waved their hands at each other under the tamarisk tree.

"One more thing I'll tell you, Harari, and then I'm going back to Jerusalem to get on with the work so you and your kind can dream. Go and see Landau. Go to Ramleh, consult with the traitor, prepare to defend him. The first phase is coming to an end, I won't keep you from him any longer. We'll have him in court in a couple of days."

"I'm going straight to the P.M.," Harari said quietly. "I want to know what you instructed my client to tell Zaggad."

"You do that," Shemtov nodded. "And then, when he won't answer, but confirms that Israel's survival is at stake, you drive out to Ramleh. Ask your client, the traitor. On the way, look out on the sides of the road for the rusted tanks and the twisted metal and the smashed outdated weapons. Watch the memorials on the road from Jerusalem to Ramleh and remember 1948, sir. Remember the War of Liberation, when the Jews of Jerusalem were cut off under siege and the remnant of the Holocaust battled the Arabs on the slopes to get supplies through. Go out to Ramleh and put your head together with a traitor, Isaac Harari. I'll be seeing you."

And leaving Harari propped wearily against the trunk of the tamarisk, Shemtov strode off toward his car. Ignoring speculative stares, he roared away in a cloud of hillside dust, wondering if a message from Beirut might already be waiting for him.

TWENTY-THREE

Since she'd been forbidden to contact Harari until the evening, Kate Landau had time to drive across the country through Bet Shemesh and Ashkelon and south to Yad Mordechai to visit Avner. She certainly didn't want to see Benjamin again, at least not yet; she hadn't recovered from yesterday's appalling scene with him in Ramleh, when he'd made it clear that he didn't trust her, didn't care to talk to her and was fixated on seeing Harari.

She and Benjamin had no comfort to offer each other; that was obvious even to a halfwit chasing mountain goats with a stick and a song. Besides, she hoped that Harari had thrown his weight around enough to get permission to talk to Ben himself. She would only be in the way. She could achieve nothing at Ramleh Prison, but talking to Avner would be useful, she was certain. He might know who was stacking the chips of colored glass that constantly revolved and reassembled in segments in Ben's mind so that it resembled a kaleidoscope twirling out of control, but even if Avner didn't know, he would be able to find out.

Avner's connections, his *protectsia*, his membership in the Establishment were impeccable. He would be able to carry his credentials intact to his grave, Kate thought. They were of a quality which, once earned, was never lost. Kate shivered suddenly in the stifling little car, not because of any superstitious unease from thinking about Avner's grave but because of the memory, piercing more sharply than the heady lemon fragrance from the citrus groves, that she'd once believed that her husband possessed those credentials also.

Benjamin had believed it, too, of course, though he'd have expressed it differently. But he believed it; it had been woven into his air of authority, his habit of command, his reluctance—no, it was really his inability—to question the assumptions of his upbringing. But he must have been wrong all along, he had obviously been misinformed about this also, or he wouldn't be raging in Ramleh, more than halfway out of his mind. The image of her strong and confident husband reduced to slapping his hand miserably on a square metal table in a prison cell produced a hot rush of tears, which Kate blinked furiously away.

Nothing in Israel was the same anymore; nothing was what it had seemed.

Steering cautiously, trying to maintain a decent distance between herself and the pugnacious drivers who'd survived incessant war and therefore felt entitled to conclude that they were immortal, Kate reflected uneasily that she had no idea how Israelis were reacting to the cruel depiction in the media of Benjamin as a traitor. She'd made certain that she didn't know; she'd contrived to avoid conversation with all Israelis since her arrival. Except for Harari, of course, but he was part of her American life and didn't make judgments the way ordinary Israelis did.

Avoiding Israelis must have been the reason why she'd chosen to contact Becky Raskin as soon as she landed at Ben Gurion Airport. An American who'd grown up in Boston, Becky was a friend from the old, simple days when Kate was researching her doctoral thesis and living in Jerusalem, enmeshed in her agonizing affair with a married Israeli hero who insisted that his wife didn't understand him. At this moment in her life, her husband in prison and her children far away in Philadelphia, those months in Jerusalem almost fourteen years before reverberated as a long, open-ended stretch of tranquil days and joyful nights, a time without ambiguity. The time before she ever laid eyes or hands on Benjamin Landau. Becky, who taught courses in western civilization at Hebrew U, was married now to an archaeologist originally from Australia.

Just as Kate had hoped, Becky welcomed her warmly, insisting that she stay with her in her new, cunningly designed two-bedroom maisonette on a slope overlooking Yemin Moshe and the Montefiore Windmill, which basked, that autumn, in the embrace of flaming chrysanthemums and great mounds of burning pyrocanthus bushes. Roger was away on his annual military reserve duty, increased for everyone, even men of fifty like Roger, to an additional month ever since it became obvious that the disturbances weren't about to dissolve.

Heading south through Ashkelon, Kate watched the Mediterranean sparkle under its gauzy gold paving of sunlight, thinking of all the friends she hadn't called, all the neighbors and colleagues and relatives, including Ben's parents, that she'd bypassed. She'd selected Becky, because she knew that she could depend on her to be loyal and uncritical, or, at the very least, to avoid passing judgment about Benjamin's arrest. And Becky had obliged, of course; she'd built a career on that quality of indiscriminate acceptance, so different from Kate's own style of ironic engagement. Becky had always described herself as "objective."

Though hadn't there been something, just the tiniest shade of mild demurral when, in response to Kate's recklessly uncensored account of the events, she'd asked, "But, Kate, how can you be sure exactly what Benjamin said to that Arab in the hothouse?" And, a little later, "Frankly, Katie, I wonder if you should be telling me all this."

Kate shifted uneasily behind the sticky steering wheel of Roger's Volkswagen and assured herself, for the seventh or eighth time since she'd set out from Jersualem under a mother-of-pearl morning sky, that Avner would help. Her father had restored

Avner's life. Avner was virtually one of the family. He admired Benjamin. Once when Kate grumbled about Ben's long absences, Avner had hugged her and whispered, "Don't complain, dear, your man is a hero, we can't do without him," demonstrating to Kate that, unlike her parents, Avner knew perfectly well that Benjamin wasn't a purchasing agent. Avner would want to help, she was certain. Avner would know what to do. But Kate hadn't called the kibbutz in advance. She'd persuaded herself that a spontaneous, spur-of-the-moment arrival would be easier to handle.

She worried now that she had made the wrong decision, but as she toyed with stopping at a roadside cafe to make the call, a ruined water tower appeared just ahead. It was toppled awkwardly onto its side, rusty steel beams protruding upward like poisoned weapons. She had arrived; she was in the northern Negev, a few hundred yards away from the Gaza Strip. The gray mound of filthy, splintered concrete riddled by cannon shells was surrounded by a profusion of brilliant flower beds, flowering oleander trees and a small pool. Kate had always slowed in respect at the memorial entrance to Yad Mordechai; even now, although she urgently needed to get past her first minutes with Avner, she forced herself to brake and turn to stare at the huge bronze statue, looming above the treetops, of a man in his shirtsleeves clutching hand grenade, looking over the dunes to the ocean beyond. The rough statue represented Mordechai Anilewicz, twenty-two years old when he commanded the desperate revolt against the Nazis in the Warsaw ghetto in 1943.

Kate had seen the statue often before; she had told her children about the Holocaust more than once, adding greater detail as they got older. Now, for the first time, she was uncomfortable thinking of the resistance as a failure. Site of the final agony for an undefeated remnant of one of Europe's oldest, most vibrant communities, the ghetto was, in the end, savagely razed and destroyed. Its defenders were murdered. But they did not acquiesce for an instant in their own obliteration. They held their barren strips of ground, halting the advance of massive

German tanks into the walled, fetid slum with stones and pebbles and their own emaciated bodies; they fought with every shred of their ingenuity and self-assertion. And when Mordechai Anilewicz and his destitute, sick and starving band perished, they left behind a testament to human courage and dignity that would endure as long as people inhabited the planet and recorded their history.

You couldn't call that failure, Kate thought, distracted briefly from her preoccupation with Benjamin by what she perceived now as eternal inspiration. When she tapped her fists lightly on the steering wheel to jerk herself out of reflections she didn't have time to explore, her eyes lingered for a minute or two on Yad Mordechai's other memorial, the shattered water tower, which still lay where it had toppled on the second day of the Egyptian advance toward Tel Aviv in 1948. Advised by Haganah officers that the Egyptians would not invade, the eighty men and boys capable of fighting weren't expecting a battle. Yet, armed only with antiquated rifles, three-thousand rounds of ammunition, four-hundred hand grenades, two machine guns and two-inch mortars with fifty shells, the defenders of Yad Mordechai stalled an entire Egyptian brigade for six days, giving units farther north time to improvise a defense and halt the invasion. Children not much older than Kate's Roni and Ruben helped to slow the advance by arming themselves with homemade Molotov cocktails to attack armored vehicles.

When the images of her children superimposed themselves upon the rusted, useless water tower, Kate shifted herself and Roger's car back into gear. She wasn't doing Benjamin any good, brooding over recent harsh passages of history, no matter how triumphantly they were now celebrated. The price, the human cost, was so great that it was as utterly inconceivable as the concept of billions of dollars to a woman on welfare. Renewing her pledge to herself not to offer up her children to what she feared might be the interminable reiteration of life-or-death struggle, Kate drove on, past broad, shady lawns and neat small cottages set in groups around the central communal buildings.

From the wide driveway, she saw the transparent roofs and walls of the greenhouses where exquisite tea roses were cultivated for export by air to Europe. She knew the beehives were just beyond. She had visited the cotton and barley fields, the cowsheds and canning factory, because Avner had proudly shown her around, more than once. Breathing air drenched in piquant citrus, Kate realized that she didn't know where to find Avner; she thought he might be in the museum and didn't want to go there unless she had no alternative. She drove forward, instead, to the communal building, where someone in the office or the library might able to direct her.

In the office, an elderly woman with wispy pale hair, withered skin and brilliant green eyes sat perched behind a computer. In Hebrew still tinged with the husky sounds of her native Magyar, she told Kate that Avner was pruning his roses. He'd be back soon for lunch, if Kate would care to wait. Or she could call him on the phone. Who would she say was asking for him?

"Don't worry, thank you." Kate forestalled her quickly, trying not to stare at the faded numbers punched into the thin skin about her wrist. "I'll walk across and find him."

Did the woman look after her oddly? Advising herself irritably to stop imagining things, Kate walked around to the greenhouses. Even from a distance the radiant colors and perfectly molded shapes of the large tea roses made a flamboyant display. Avner had personally crossed strains to breed several entirely new roses, with color so subtly blended that they had won him international prizes. Not bad for a boy out of Dachau, he boasted, when he taught the secrets of his art to a younger generation of kibbutz cultivators.

Kate spotted Avner before he noticed her. He was reaching up to cut long stems from a deep purple rosebush with flowers as unique as his own face, with its broad, bulging forehead and sensuous mouth above a rounded chin. His head was thrown back to examine the curve of a petal at the tip of the bush, which was raised on a potting table in a large clay pot. Avner's shock of thick white hair flung out behind him. His dark absorption, the fiery glint dazzling off the surface of murky black eyes, combined to give him the appearance of a biblical prophet.

Only when Avner dropped his arms, tossed his shears on the table and stepped back to narrow his eyes for another view of his glorious purple creation did Kate remember his stature. No one ever thought of Avner as a very short man, though he stood barely five foot three inches high. But his forceful personality and quick intelligence, and especially his arresting looks, simply overcame his height. Avner always dominated everyone around him, exuding passionate charm.

Kate was sufficiently apprehensive about her welcome that she was tempted to linger there, watching him through the glass, but she forced herself to walk around to the entrance. By then he'd seen her coming and was waiting to let her in. He closed the door quickly behind her.

"How are you, Katie?" But there was no hug, no kisses on both cheeks, followed by the usual stream of extravagant compliments. Avner adored women; as he aged, he admired them more than ever. He'd not been joking all down the years when he'd announced his lust for the sleek smooth daughter of his friend and savior. He kept his lechery under control, at least as far as Kate was concerned, but he wasn't a frivolous man. He meant every word he uttered; he felt every gesture sincerely. This time there was no luxurious stroking of the curve of her shoulder or shining brown cap of hair. Kate felt the denial as an unexpected loss.

"How's Monty? Your mother? Here in Israel, too?"

Kate shook her head. She stood looking at him, arms folded tight across her body.

When did you arrive?"

"Two days ago." For some reason, she was breathless.

Avner nodded gravely. No beating around the bush for him, no deceptions, nothing false. He knew what she was doing in Israel; he wasn't about to pretend he didn't. He'd been extremely agitated weeks earlier when she'd called to announce her return to the States with the children. No matter how many times she tried to explain about the hardship of life in Israel with Benjamin in a French prison, Avner had not been sympathetic, although in the end he said he supposed he understood her need to take the children and go to her parents. He felt sure, he said then, that Ben would be released soon and everything would change again. But even in that exchange Kate had been given his old affectionate warmth, his eager spurts of inquiry, his energetic advice. On this day, the muggy hothouse air between them was laced with formality and constraint. Kate waited for him to speak, but he turned away, picking up his shears as if he had nothing at all to say to her. She felt tears well behind her eyes, blinked them away and moved a step closer to Avner.

"Avner, I've got a lot of trouble."

His nod was cursory. This information wasn't news to him.

"I'm here to try and get Benjamin out of jail. Avner, he's not a traitor, you know that."

"I? What do I know? These are not matters I have intimate knowledge about. I know what my government says. That's all I know."

Attacked by a fluttering sense of abandonment, Kate resisted the idea that Avner wasn't going to help her.

"Avner, there's something weird going on. Ben's no traitor. He was acting on orders from—"

"Enough." The sturdy, deep-chested survivor commanded. "I don't want to hear it. Don't tell me state secrets, you hear me?"

"Avner, I . . . we . . . really need your help. Your advice. My father told me to ask your advice. Let me tell you what really happened."

"No, you will not do it. You shouldn't even know these matters yourself."

"Avner, there's been a miscarriage of justice. Don't turn away from us. You know the country isn't perfect, the Service isn't perfect. There are sometimes mistakes. You know it happens." She hadn't realized that she was crying, but as the tears trickled down onto her lips she wiped at them with trembling fingers. It was hard to breathe in the clammy air.

"There have sometimes been mistakes, it's true. Not often, mind you. Sometimes. We Jews are human beings, after all. We never claim we're gods. But this time, there's no mistake."

"How do you know?" she sniffed hard, swallowed mucus. Her words sounded thick and low. Moisture crawled on her skin. Through the glass wall at her left she saw three men trudge up from the factory toward the communal dining room. "How can you know there's no mistake?"

"No mistake, I tell you. We don't capture one of our own—my God, a *sabra*, born and raised on a kibbutz—we don't capture him and fly him home and put him in Ramleh and charge him with treason by mistake. That we do not do. We don't do it, Kate Landau, and that's all there is to it. Listen, if a man is a spy, you must be very careful. He can turn around and spy for the other side any time. He can pull over your eyes the wool. You think I didn't see that, long ago, in Poland? Dear God, who could you trust? A spy? Never. We have a clever chief in the Service. He knows he must be on guard every day to make sure that one of ours isn't tempted by the other side. And he does watch, I promise you that. I guarantee it. He's the watchman of our freedom, Kate. Our watchman. I trust him."

"Avner," Kate said very quietly, "you know very well that all his adult life my husband served his country. Then it was just fine with you that he was a spy. All honor to the spy, right? Now, through some dreadful mistake, you just abandon us. How can you do that?"

"It's not a mistake. I'm telling you. Whatever it is, it's not a mistake. Don't keep saying that. And don't say I'm abandoning you. I will advise you, Kate Landau, because you are the daughter of Monty. If you are part of your husband's activities against Israel, don't try to see me again. Ever. And if you are not, go home. Go home to Monty and Iris and wait for the trial and let's see what he did and why he did it. There's nothing else for you or anyone to do. Justice will take its course in Israel."

Kate felt that she was choking. Patches of sweat were collecting under her arms and between her legs. The roots of her hair were damp, her nose was blocked, her eyes spilled over. People walking past the greenhouse looked in curiously but didn't stop. No one would casually invade Avner's territory.

"What's going to happen to him?"

"He'll be tried in court," Avner said brusquely. "Some lawyer will be provided to represent him. He'll have a chance to explain or argue or whatever he wants to do. Then, you should know, he'll go to jail for twenty, thirty years. For life, more likely."

"No."

"But yes. Listen, girl. If your husband gave George Zaggad the name of an Israeli agent living under cover with Arabs for twenty years, then he'll go free no more. And that's how it should be. You should get used to it. What kind of thing is that, I ask you? And listen. They would never make such an accusation if it weren't true. You should know that. Even an American should understand that. It must be true."

Avner nodded in emphasis. Then he finger-combed his straight white hair up and back from his head and turned away to poke small, agile fingers at a mound of tangled roots he'd excavated earlier from an overcrowded trough.

"Avner, please, just tell me," she was breathless again. "Do you *know* it's true? That Benjamin told Israeli secrets to Zaggad? Do you *know*?"

"I'm sure it's true," he snapped.

"How can you do this? How can you just—"

"How? I'm going to tell you how, Mrs. Landau." He turned and faced her full on, his passionate, intense face inflamed by rage, blood surging hot under his dark skin. "I've got no time for traitors. I've got no patience for anyone who betrays his own people. What kind of animal sells his own country to her enemies?"

"But he didn't. I'm sure he didn't, he—"

"Listen to me, will you? This is not some ordinary country; you should know." Avner hurled the mess of tangled roots and dirt across the rough table. "Do you know what it took to build this country? Your father's daughter ought to know. You're standing on sacred ground, Mrs. Landau, soaked in the blood of martyrs. Listen. A handful of pioneers escaped from Poland just before the war and came here to found Yad Mordechai. I came later in '47. Liberated from the Nazis and Dachau, stitched together by your father Monty, then stuck in a camp with barbed wire in Cyprus. I lost everything, you should try to understand. Everything was gone—my entire family, my dignity, my ambition, my hope, my health—everything except my determination to go to my homeland in Palestine and try to live. It was illegal. Even then, after all that, it was illegal. We had to run the stinking British blockade. We almost drowned like so many others. We crawled out of the sea at Nethanya in the middle of the night, under fire. Do you understand?"

Kate gulped, trying to speak, but Avner hurtled on, utterly immune to interruption, off on a flight of anguished memory that nothing would ever soften.

"So what do you think? I came here to try life instead of every variety of death, but before there was even time for my first seeds to sprout, before my first harvest, we were at war again. The Arabs were talking bloodbath; you should understand. We'd heard that stuff before. We'd watched it happen, some of us, waiting our turn. Now the Arabs were talking genocide. Again, you understand. We didn't expect it. We still had this dumb, Jewish optimism that they don't mean what they say. We didn't expect it at all, but the Egyptians took it in their heads to make for Tel Aviv and we were in the way. So. We held them off for six days, Mrs. Landau. Do you know they surrounded us and fired at us all the time? And from the air they bombed us also, a few dozen pathetic survivors, noses not yet even cleared of the stench of the camps, not healed from the whips and bullets and scars of the German swine. Never healed. Never a chance. Twenty-four were killed. What the Nazis couldn't manage, the Egyptians finished off. Thirty were wounded."

"Avner," Kate whispered through a screen of tears.

"No, wait," he shouted, impatiently swatting tears off his own grooved cheeks. "Wait, I'll finish; you should understand. We couldn't hold out, our last gun was useless, our little patch of earth was burning, the obscene smell of rotting corpses filled the bunkers. Some wanted Masada again, the Warsaw ghetto again, they wanted to resist, fight until the last man fell. Others chose life, even though it meant retreat. I was one of them. We found a way to get out between the Egyptian lines, out and up to Gvar Am, you know it? A few miles north. Gvar Am. Afterward, at Negba, our *chaverim* stopped the Egyptians." He held his palm up in front of Kate to silence her while he drew a deep shuddering breath and dried his eyes. "They were pushed back to Gaza and their own frontier. And then we came back, Mrs. Landau. We recaptured Yad Mordechai. Rebuilt it from rubble. We left the water tower right there to remind us all. And to remind you. And your husband. Do you understand what we've been through to make ourselves a home in this place? It's the same all over Israel. Do you think we'll allow some kind of a traitor to take it from us? Give us over to the hands of our enemy?"

Kate, who was too choked up to speak and wasn't sure she wanted to anyway, turned to leave. But Avner caught her arm and swung her around again to face him, his eyes smoldering.

"I can't get over it," he shouted. "I can't get it straight in my mind." He seemed to turn it upon himself, as if forcing his voice down, and went on more quietly. "A member of Monty's own family? How could it be? Since I was seventeen years old and desperate, nearly dead, one hundred percent totally alone, Monty's been my hero, my uncle, my family. How did a serpent get inside Monty's family? I can't understand it. Tell me, Kate, did you know what he's been doing? How could you have been so deceived? I know, God help me, I know you're not an idiot. Did you know something, all along, did you know or guess or even maybe suspect a little something about your husband, the spy?" He spat the words at her.

Kate turned away again and opened the greenhouse door. This

time Avner didn't try to stop her. He called out after her, "If you know nothing, turn around and go home to Monty, Kate. And don't come and see me for a time, please. I'm getting too old for all this. I can't take it."

TWENTY-FOUR

In the cracked mirror opposite the revolving door of the Commodore Hotel Gershom saw a lean, narrow man, Mediterranean bronze, with thrusting bones, a triangular chin and wavy black hair streaked with gray—a serious, self-contained, elegant man, who sauntered into the lobby as if his only concern was obtaining refreshment and the relief of a circulating ceiling fan.

It was a few seconds before Gershom recognized himself, reassured that his facade of poise and self-sufficiency was intact. Evidently no one would be able to discern that the nonchalance reflected in the mirror was a precarious mask held in place by habit, training and self-protection. And by terror.

Gershom would have avoided meeting George Zaggad if doing so was safe, but ignoring Zaggad's summons would have signaled guilt as loudly as an admission to an American television reporter. Only Gershom knew that the reason Zaggad had flown into Damascus from New York and driven down to Beirut was to investigate Benjamin Landau's charge that the Invasion Committee was penetrated by an Israeli spy. The others believed what they'd been told: that Zaggad was there to investigate leaks of information to the Israelis.

When Gershom heard about the evening meeting his first instinct was to make straight for the southern border, crossing the "good fence" to Kiryat Sh'mona. Then he thought of heading north to Junieh to board a boat going anywhere, as long as it was away. But Tewfik Mahmoud asserted himself, drawing on his prolonged experience of duplicity to piece together another shot at survival.

He had dawdled and delayed so as to arrive after the others. He didn't want to be the one to tell George Zaggad about Kamal Hussein's disappearance. He thought it likely that Kamal's antics would turn out to be nothing but a distracting nuisance, though they might create suspicion. Gershom didn't want to point a finger at Razan's father.

What name had Landau given Zaggad? Gershom was afraid that Landau's accusation would be contradicted by Kamal's flight or by the decoding of his own message. He wished Shemtov had not added this convoluted mystery to his terror of exposure; surely he'd be in a stronger position if he knew whom Zaggad suspected?

Sniffing and circling the specks of information like a cat roaming a bombed-out crater, Gershom strolled across the lobby toward the dimly lit lounge with its dusty potted palms and hard-drinking newsmen swapping scandals as relief from violent news stories. For the hundredth time he recalculated the number of days since Akman hung his messenger from a tree. The message must have been decoded, though Akman had not said a word about it and Gershom compelled Tewfik not to inquire.

He spotted Zaggad as soon as he crossed the wide entrance into the lounge. Even settled sturdily in a green brocade armchair at a round table with his back to the flocked velvet wall, even seated in shirtsleeves in artificial twilight in the bustling crowd, made noisier by the intermittent shrieks of the Commodore's famous parrot, Zaggad projected an air of absolute authority. Full lips pursed under a bushy mustache, with more salt than pepper in the thick hair sweeping his broad, lined forehead, Zaggad listened intently to Ahmed Khalidi, whose hands were clasped tightly over his protruding abdomen as if holding it in place.

Just as Gershom noticed that Walid Toucan wasn't there, Akman looked up and waved and beckoned.

Zaggad greeted Gershom gravely. There was no indication that he knew he was shaking hands with a spy. He might have been receiving a supplicant from Nablus with a proposal for outwitting the occupying Israelis or a fawning representative of an opposition faction or a graduate student in Logan Hall on the campus of the University of Pennsylvania.

Gershom pulled an empty chair over from an adjacent table. Sweat trickled from his armpits, down his sides, it bubbled in his groin, it lay like drops from the waterfalls at Rosh Hanikra across his upper lip. But he murmured a polite apology. The clotted traffic on the Avenue de Gaulle had made him late; he bowed his head respectfully toward the representative of the High Command, and settled down on the glittering brocade, pressing a long brown forefinger against the vein in his forehead that might reveal his hammering pulse to a perceptive observer.

Old Ahmed Khalidi had been telling Zaggad about Kamal Hussein's sudden disappearance. Gershom watched Zaggad as Ahmed ponderously explained that Razan refused to share her father's message, insisting that his note contained only his bank account access code and greetings. Zaggad stared with such absorption at Ahmed that he might have been hard of hearing, having to help himself out by lip-reading. Gershom, aching to know what name Landau had given Zaggad, reminded himself that Tewfik knew nothing of that encounter. Like everyone else, however, Tewfik did know about the big clumsy Israeli, bewildered and stumbling on the tarmac at Ben Gurion Airport, the agent whom the Israelis had caught, imprisoned and were that day denouncing as a traitor. Anyone who read the papers or watched television had seen the pictures of Landau, though the accompanying news stories had not mentioned the name of the Palestinian Landau had met, let alone the name of the comrade he had betrayed.

When Ahmed at last fell silent, his face slumping into several matched rolls of chins, Zaggad leaned back and sighed. His square-tipped fingers tapped out a rhythm on the scarred surface of the table. He nodded thoughtfully as if he'd arrived at a conclusion.

"Where is Kamal? We must find him at once." He forgot to mute his full, commanding voice at first, then, looking around the lounge, crowded with raucous drinkers, he lowered his tone. "Any ideas? Where has he gone? Why?"

But no one knew. Akman shifted in his chair, jerking his head back negatively; Khalidi shrugged, double chins echoing the gesture; Tewfik stretched his long fingers wide, palms up on the moist, ringed table. Zaggad studied each of them in turn, smoothing his mustache with square, immaculate fingertips.

"Where is Walid Toucan?" he asked quietly, somehow making the question reverberate again and again. But all three made their ignorance clear. Zaggad sighed, drummed his fingers rather rapidly and sat up a little straighter, evidently having arrived at a decision.

"Our officers have successfully decoded the message Akman captured near Sidon," he announced evenly, looking from Akman to Gershom and back again, a curious flicker at the side of his left eye, which Gershom would normally have identified as a nervous tic. Since he was convinced that Zaggad possessed no nerves, he couldn't explain the flicker. He only knew he didn't like it.

Khalidi launched into a commentary on Akman's irregular procedure; the information belonged to the Invasion Committee and should have been transmitted immediately.

"I got the decoding only today," said Akman firmly. "It shows—"

"It shows," Zaggad interrupted smoothly, "that there is a traitor among you. That is what it shows."

"What does it say?" asked Tewfik, not hiding his concern at this threatening news.

Zaggad turned toward him, lips curved in a smile under his streaked mustache.

"But you've known for some time there were leaks, haven't you, Tewfik?"

"Of course. But not that—"

"Yes. So. The message was that Tewfik Mahmoud and Walid Toucan were going to Rome to meet an American. Contact to be made directly from Rome. No names."

Tewfik, appalled as he absorbed the implications of the message, leaned his forehead on the palm of his right hand, propped an elbow on the table and closed his eyes briefly.

"The assignation in Rome was a matter of the greatest carefully guarded secrecy." Ahmed Khalidi was at his most pompous.

"Quite so," Zaggad agreed. "The only people who knew about the meeting with the American were the five of you. The members of your sacred Invasion Committee. One of you must have written that message. Knowing, I need hardly add, that it would be delivered to Israel. To the Service, I take it."

"May I ask, how did you know about the American?" Tewfik cleared his throat nervously.

"I did not know until Akman told me an hour ago when he gave me the decoded message. I knew there were leaks. I knew Akman had been assigned to find the courier and had trapped him with a coded message. I knew two of you were going to Rome. Several of us on the High Command knew of these things as a matter of routine. I did not know and neither did anyone else about an American."

"Who informed you about the courier and the message?" rumbled Khalidi suspiciously.

"Kamal Hussein, naturally,," said Zaggad, eyebrows arched high, gesturing dismissively. "He's your contact with the High Command, after all. You don't work in a vacuum, you're part of a large organization, virtually a government in exile. And now Kamal is gone, it seems. Why?" He didn't appear to expect an answer.

Akman leaned urgently across the table.

"So, someone is talking, leaking, spewing out our secrets." He was careful to keep his voice down. "We can't just sit here. What happens next? We have to take control. You're here to find the squealer, yes?"

"You might put it that way." Zaggad sighed. He brushed hair away from his forehead. "Right now we have to find Walid and Kamal. That's the priority; that's essential. We must find them without any more delay. What suggestions? Could they be together?"

"Phone for Tewfik Mahmoud," the bartender called across the room. "Mahmoud. Phone. Are you here?"

Gershom jumped up and pushed his way through the lounge to the bar, eyed inquisitively the late-afternoon drinkers, almost all of them reporters on the alert for a story, or even the nuances of yesterday's story.

The phone rested on the polished oak surface of the bar. An argumentative group of European correspondents sat on stools around it. Gershom reached over to pick up the receiver.

"Yes?"

"You remember the rooftop behind the An Nahar Building?" asked a breathless Walid Toucan.

"Yes."

"Meet us there as soon as you can. No more than twenty minutes, okay?"

"Us? Our missing man?"

"No, no. The friend we met in Rome has information about Kamal. He won't say a word till you get here. He says he must tell us together."

There was a click. Walid was gone from whatever booth he'd used.

"Thank you for letting me know. Keep well," said Tewfik for the eavesdroppers at the bar.

Although he was tempted to leave immediately, he forced himself to walk calmly back to Zaggad's table.

"That was Walid," he told them. "He needs me urgently. I have to leave right now. Excuse me."

"Wait a minute," said Akman. "Why isn't he here? What's he doing?"

"Did he explain his absence?" asked Zaggad.

"I think he's with the American. He has information about Kamal. I'd better go. I'll be in touch as soon as I can."

He had always enjoyed the ability to leave a room quickly, never more so than at that second when he put distance between himself and George Zaggad.

He strode the few blocks north toward the newspaper building, past half-rebuilt buildings edged by mounds of rubble and barbed wire, past restored chic boutiques and cafes on Hamra, past iron spiked fences, destroyed embassies, sandbags and shattered glass, ignoring the constant rattle of gunfire, the acrid odor, the smoke lying on the air, suffocating as clinging plastic wrap. He avoided the filthy encampment in the public gardens, making for the rooftop on the abandoned, damaged building behind the *An Nahar* newspaper offices, where he and Walid had transacted business with suppliers more than once in recent months. After years in West Beirut, a man learned when and where he could safely move about. If there were snipers on any of the roofs above, they ignored him.

Approaching the crumpled building from the back, Gershom swung himself up to a window ledge and inside, finding the disintegrating remains of the staircase. He climbed it carefully. Any dusty stair might collapse under a single step. He heard swift pattering, knew it was a cat, sneaking about ready to pounce, eyes glittering, back horribly arched; he thought there might be more than one occupying the shell of the building. The light was too dim to see the marks Walid's rubber-soled shoes must have left. Gershom concentrated on testing each step. His first fear that this might be a trap came at the second he stuck his head up through the scarred opening to the rooftop, most of it caved in. But Walid was waiting for him, leaning down to grab his wrist firmly and haul him up onto the narrow ledge at the rim of the roof that they knew from experience was stable enough to bear their weight.

Rich, the talkative American, stood just beyond Walid. Although the light was fading fast, it was not too dark to observe the familiar moist glaze upon Rich's lank lacquered hair and rat-colored skin.

"Ah, Tewfik, good to see you." Rich held out a puffy hand, which Gershom found damp also.

"Rich asked for a meeting but he didn't want to talk until you arrived," Walid began. Rich interrupted at once. "Two's better than one, let me tell you."

"I've been telling him we do want the toxins but we're busy now. We can't close the deal until we finish some current business. Then we'll take delivery," Walid told Tewfik.

All five members of the Invasion Committee had recommended that the High Command buy the new chemical weapon and allow Rich to train their guerrillas to use it on the army bases controlling the West Bank occupation. They all wanted to wait until Zaggad left Beirut and the leaks were firmly plugged. They'd been concerned that this might annoy the American, but Tewfik saw immediately that Rich hadn't come to the mangled rooftop to discuss toxins.

"Listen," said Rich conspiratorially, "we're buddies, aren't we? You scratch my back and so on. All that. I'm delighted, absolutely delighted, to know you're taking the toxins. I know they'll do it for you people." He waved his arms about as if embracing all dispossessed Palestinians. "But I'm not here for that right now. I got something else in mind."

Tewfik and Walid looked from the gabbling American to each other. It was impossible to guess what the merchant wanted.

"I know you guys have your balls pointed in another direction at this point in time."

"What do you mean?" Walid didn't even try to sound polite.

"Kamal Hussein." The American smiled. "Vanished, yes? Gone?"

"How in hell—?" Walid started, but Tewfik coughed loudly.

"What are you saying, Rich?"

"Look, man," said Rich. "Kamal Hussein disappeared during the early hours this A.M., right? Let me tell you, the word's shooting through town like rockets. I've just come from our embassy, taking a meet with a couple old buddies. You can imagine what they're getting into in this cesspool. Even Saigon had nothin' on it."

Walid Toucan hammered his right fist into his left palm. Then he loosened a notch on the studded belt holding up his skintight Levi's.

"What have you heard about Kamal, Rich?" Tewfik was known for his gentle manner and reliable courtesy. It made a startling contrast with Walid's barely suppressed violence.

"It seems that your Kamal has been running a little business on the side," he confided. "Didn't know that, did you?"

Tewfik tapped his foot, nudging Walid's ankle boot.

"Tell us, please," he urged. "We'd appreciate you help."

"Making plenty, let me tell you," Rich said. "Pockets full of piastres. Trading, y'know. Big-time."

"Trading? Trading what?"

"Three Ds, man. Dope, diamonds and dirt. Shorthand for dirty little secrets, know what I'm saying?"

"Who's he selling to, Rich?"

"Foreigners. Enemies." Rich licked his lips as if they were coated in cognac. "And when he heard George Zaggad was coming here to look things over, he figured he'd better get lost. His trading partners are lending a hand. Well, they would, wouldn't they?"

Walid and Tewfik glanced at each other, then turned back to Rich.

"Kamal is in the U.S. embassy?" Walid was incredulous.

"No, no." Rich shook his damp head vigorously. "Absolutely no. Wrong track, man."

"Do you know where he is?" Tewfik demanded, thinking that

he'd rather use the knife nestled in his sock than stand by while Walid blew Rich away.

"Yeah, I know where he's tucked away right now. And I know where he's going."

"Will you give us the address?"

"Of course," said Rich. "Sure I will. That's why I'm up here with you on this excuse for a roof. He's in a safe house. Hiding place for a foreign operation."

"The address?" Tewfik asked pleasantly.

Rich announced it as if it were the equation for a pernicious new chemical killer. "He'll be out of there in early A.M.," he added. "They're taking him out by boat in a few hours. I'm warning you, better get with it."

"May I ask," said Tewfik, "why you are being so kind as to share this information with us?" He had a vivid recollection of entering a House of Horrors in Berlin. It was supposed to be fun. Perhaps it was designed for people who had no terror in their everyday lives.

"I'm helping you guys, aren't I?" Rich explained. "Doing business; that's what I'm doing. I want to sell you my toxins. It's called building goodwill. You people know all about that, don't you?"

They gazed at him in wonderment.

"There is another reason." He smoothed his hands over the sides of his head with the mistaken notion that his strands of hair needed straightening. "I'm interested in see you people liberate the West Bank and whatever other bits of real estate you can grab. I can be very helpful to the new government there, let me tell you. I'm interested in becoming a supplier. Advisor, too, maybe."

TWENTY-FIVE

Benjamin Landau and Isaac Harari strode in step up and down the length of a fenced exercise yard behind the hospital wing at Ramleh Prison. Benjamin set the pace, keeping it measured, not so much from respect for Harari's age or the flaming heat of the autumn afternoon, but in a conscious effort to force a steady rhythm upon his agitated body and jangled, disjointed thoughts. He was struggling to believe that Harari had been allowed, at last, to see him.

The suspicious rage lodged in Benjamin since his arrest in Paris had established control as tenaciously as an occupation army, taking nourishment by devouring his reserves of reason. However, using what meager judgment remained, he had refused to talk to Harari in the whitewashed interview room, where light bounded off the walls and trapped heat burned the air. The room was certainly bugged, no doubt of that. And there was probably a one-way mirror somewhere, perhaps in the puny central light fixture, dangling from the ceiling like a scorched sunflower. Benjamin made such a fuss that Harari was compelled to bang upon the door and insist that the guard take him to the warden, where he negotiated permission to talk to Benjamin outside by bartering insider gossip about the effort of one chief rabbi to eliminate the other by pressing temptation, in the form of small pretty boys, upon him.

Although they were alone in the bare, scraggly yard, they were aware of curious eyes beyond the small windows spotting the white cement wall that formed one long side of the yard. The other was a six-foot-high chain-link fence, topped by barbed wire. Benjamin and Harari gravitated automatically to that side and walked parallel to the fence. Benjamin knew they might be using distance mikes to pick up their conversation, so he kept his head bent low and turned away from the building.

Harari apologized for not visiting earlier. He'd only learned of Ben's request for his counsel for the first time from Kate the previous day.

Benjamin swung wildly into the fence, blinking rapidly, banging his clenched fists again and again into the knots of wire. Harari made no attempt to stop him, mindful, perhaps, of the power of Benjamin's large, violent frame. He waited for the rage to subside, as Benjamin stared at the pinpricks of blood that grazed his already abrased knuckles as if they were droppings from Syrian tanks.

"It doesn't make any sense," he erupted in English. "Whatever they do contradicts everything else. Is it Shemtov? What's he doing?"

Harari nudged his elbow, urging him to walk steadily forward, murmuring sympathy, reviewing his discussion with Kate, assuring Ben that he would find the truth and expose it. Like a freak breeze at midday in the Wilderness of Paran in the Negev Desert, Harari's automatic assumption of Benjamin's innocence delivered an unexpected draught of relief, and a reminder that there was at last someone willing to listen, equipped to evaluate, able to help. And a damned astute someone at that. Isaac Harari couldn't just be dismissed, not by anyone in Israel, not even by Dan Shemtov. That was obvious. And it was freshly demonstrated because Shemtov had not been able to keep Harari away from him, though he had evidently tried.

Benjamin didn't press the great man for details of his confrontation with Shemtov. He was consumed by a drive more singleminded than voracious hunger to tell Harari exactly what had happened to him. He had to make absolutely certain that Harari knew how unfair it was that he was accused of treason. Treason had never entered his mind. It was unjust. It was outrageous. Nothing was as important as explaining this to Harari.

He began with Uri's commanding him to go to Philadelphia with a message for George Zaggad. Harari interrupted at once. Benjamin started to object, but was cowed by Harari's frosted blue gaze, piercing the air between them. Benjamin should begin at the beginning, he said crisply, with the assignment to Paris, which had cost him six months in prison before Shemtov traded him for the terrorists. Was Benjamin aware that Shemtov had rejected a proposal for the trade, insisting that the terrorists should go to trial, and then a week or ten days later agreed to free them in exchange for Benjamin's release?

Benjamin jerked forward, then halted abruptly. He half-turned to face Harari, a mottled mulberry flush staining his cheeks. Here was confirmation of the official savage indifference to his suffering in Paris. His recent obsession with his kidnapping in Philadelphia by Israelis had driven from his mind the sour conviction that he'd been set up by his own Service. And he would be crazy, really, finally out of his mind, not to wonder what Harari knew. What sources did he have? Whose breast pocket was he tucked into? Who controlled Harari anyway?

"Kate told me about Paris," Harari remarked calmly, walking on and talking as if Benjamin had asked his questions aloud. "And I sit on the Knesset Security Committee, remember that. I knew about the spare parts for Iraq and the hijack operation. And I knew about your trial, naturally. Who didn't?"

Harari's matter-of-fact reference to the Security Committee stroked Benjamin with reassurance. Besides, Harari was obviously correct. The mission to Philadelphia, so crucial that Shemtov himself had followed him home to insist that he undertake it, must have been connected somehow with the Paris operation. He'd been exposed as a spy, branded incompetent, sentenced and jailed; somehow that had given Shemtov the means to manipulate him.

Benjamin recognized that his own reasoning ability was warped by his isolation and his fury; Harari had demonstrated that without even raising his voice. Though the great lawyer's face was as lined as if an amateur Japanese calligrapher had practiced upon it, though his pale bald head trembled from time to time, and his bare, bony knees threatened to buckle, his mind was obviously as acute as ever. You didn't own the reputation of the toughest legal mind in a nation of argumentative scholars and self-styled authorities for nothing. Benjamin succumbed to the security of Harari's authority and reputation with the relief of a boy awakened from a nightmare and soothed by an omniscient father.

As if in gratitude for the release from terror, he poured his story out to Harari. He began with his suspicions in Paris, his encounters with Uri and Shemtov, his visit to his parents' kibbutz and his terrible discovery of Natan's death in battle on the Heights. When he heard that Kate had gone back to the States with the children, he felt as if his whole life was destroyed. He'd been pretty vulnerable when Shemtov made his extraordinary appearance at his apartment. Shemtov wanted him to go to Philadelphia with a message for Zaggad. He hadn't wanted to go. He was through with the Service, anyway. And even then he grasped that there was something weird about Shemtov pressing so hard. But he certainly needed to see Kate. He needed to see his children; he knew how they suffered during the long separation from him. Shemtov guaranteed it would be his last mission. Still, he would not have gone if it hadn't been for the message Shemtov wanted him to deliver. That was Shemtov's ultimate argument; Benjamin could not resist giving Zaggad the message.

Harari had heard from Kate about her lunch with Zaggad, and he appeared to be less interested in Ben's meeting with him than in his capture in the parking lot at Longwood Gardens. The great man's blue gaze whitened, hardened and settled into a menacing glare. Lips pursed, hands clasped tightly together behind him, he paced grimly on.

Benjamin, who had talked more in the past hour than in days, didn't want to stop. He launched into speculation. A power play, possibly? A bureaucratic struggle between Shemtov and Aron Levy, chief of the rival Internal Security? Exploiting Benjamin to demonstrate Levy's corruption somehow? But how? He had a number of theories but...

Harari tried to speak. Benjamin spurted on, forgetting to turn away from the distance mikes. Harari produced from his pocket a large purple-striped handkerchief, which he waved about in front of Ben's face.

"Listen to me, now," instructed Harari, with a final flutter of purple handkerchief before stuffing it back into his pocket. "My turn."

"Sorry."

"Shemtov told you to tell Zaggad that Kamal Hussein is an Israeli spy. Is that correct?"

"Yes."

"He told you he couldn't trust him anymore, right? That's exactly what he said to you?"

"Yes, I told you."

Harari pursed his lips and looked off into the distance. Then, evenly, he inquired, "Did he say why he stopped trusting Hussein?"

"I don't think he did. No. He said I must betray him to his own people so they would take him out."

"But he didn't explain what Hussein had done that made him untrustworthy. Suddenly? After...what, twenty years?"

Benjamin shook his head. These questions hadn't occurred to him. After all, he'd been obeying Shemtov for a very long time.

"And you didn't inquire?"

Benjamin felt foolish, a big man tripping over his own feet.

"I told you before, I was terribly shocked. Shemtov said

Hussein was one of my wife's killers. My first wife, Miriam. I never even knew they'd caught him. I was appalled. I was horrified to learn they'd permitted the bastard to live. That's all I was thinking about. I wanted to end it."

"End what?" Shemtov pressed.

"Oh, all of it, every filthy, rotten part of it. He killed Miriam; he should have been gunned down at once with the other two. I wanted to punish him. But there was something else in my mind." He paused and rubbed his eyes with his fingertips. The backs of his hands swarmed with red spots and scabs where blood had dried.

"I only went into the damned Service after Miriam was killed. I joined to fight the enemy, spend my life making her death worth something. That's how I felt when I began. But when I got back after Paris, my life was wrecked, blown apart. My wife and children had gone, I had no common ground, nothing at all left with my parents. Dear Natan was dead in the same endless war. I wanted out, out of it all. Shemtov promised if I'd do one more mission, I'd be finished. I could try and make a different life for whatever time I have left. That's what I was thinking about. That—and fingering Miriam's murderer."

His pain and rage stirred the air. Then they heard the distant shouts of ordinary prisoners playing Frisbee on a field.

"Benjamin," said Isaac Harari, in the tone of a man who has made a difficult decision, "I have something important to tell you. You should pay attention. Put everything out of your mind and listen to me now."

There was a steely authority in Harari's voice that made Benjamin swing around to stare at him. But Harari strode steadily on, waiting for Ben to fall back into step beside him before continuing.

"I don't know what Shemtov has been up to, but I do have information that might help you work it out. There is a very important fact missing from your account." Harari ignored Benjamin's jerk of irritation. "It is not your fault. It is a fact you cannot possibly know. For some reason you are not supposed to know it. I, however, am in possession of this fact and it alters everything."

"What is it?" Benjamin sounded like a man craving water.

"The man Kamal Hussein was not your wife's murderer."

Benjamin gasped, stopped walking and grabbed Harari tightly by the elbow.

"Wait," he said. "What are you saying? How do you—?"

"Release my arm," Harari snapped. "Release it at once. Thank you. Don't get excited, Benjamin. I suggest we continue our walk. Perhaps we are being observed, hm?"

Blinking rapidly, shoving his fists into his pockets, Benjamin obeyed.

"You are not aware of this, though your chief certainly is," Harari went on, as smoothly as if there'd been no reaction from Ben. "I was in the picture at the time of Miriam's murder, Benjamin. I knew you, or, rather, knew about you, long before you married my best friend's daughter. I approved the plan to recruit you. I had followed your effort to recover after Miriam's murder. I admired your commitment, Benjamin, and I admired your skills. Still do."

No amount of blinking halted the sudden flood of tears. Benjamin didn't take his hands out of his pockets to wipe them away. "I don't understand all this," he muttered tiredly, his shaggy head drooping.

"I was...high up in army intelligence at the time," Harari explained. "I was on a task force and several committees with Dan Shemtov. I had some responsibility for internal security. Naturally, I cannot supply the details. But you may be sure I am familiar with the tragedy. I know all about it. I have always known."

He hesitated, perhaps to mark the moment when, for the first time, he revealed state secrets, perhaps to give Benjamin time to compose himself. But it would take more than a minute or two for Benjamin to absorb and find a way to handle the fresh revelations of Miriam's death and Shemtov's deceit.

"Your wife's third killer was caught near Metulla, Ben. Later that same night. You've forgotten—maybe you never knew—the kibbutz sent out a patrol immediately. They knew they'd only killed two of them. The army sent out a unit also. No one could tolerate the chance that the murderer might escape. It was the army unit that caught up with him. He tried to run, but he tripped and fell; as they closed in, he fired a shot. They killed him. His gun was one of those used on Miriam. His red scarf was hidden under his khaki shirt. He carried a crude map of the Huleh Valley and a matchbook from a bar in Beirut. No one turned him and sent him back, Benjamin. He's been dead for twenty years. Shemtov fingered Hussein for a different reason."

Benjamin swayed. Harari reached out to steady him, but withdrew his hand almost immediately, brushing it surreptitiously against his safari jacket. Benjamin's face bubbled with sweat. The graying hair in the V neck of his navy prison shirt glistened wet. His hands, crusty with pinpricks of dried blood, came away wet when he rubbed the back of his neck.

"Why did he lie to me? Why? Tell me that?"

"It seems to me that he had to find a way to make you take the message to Zaggad. It had to be you. No one else would do. I assume he used what he could to force you to go. For some reason, he wanted to destroy Hussein."

"But why? What's it all about? What's it for, I'm asking you?"

"I'm not sure, Ben." Harari surprised himself by his uncharacteristic gentleness. "Perhaps he thought Zaggad would believe you because you knew each other in Philadelphia years go."

"No." Benjamin was vehement. "Shemtov knows better. He knows Zaggad wouldn't trust me because he knew me before."

"Well, I can only guess. He did succeed in persuading you to go and tell Zaggad that Kamal Hussein is a traitor, didn't he?"

"Yes. He succeeded."

"Why did he want Zaggad to know that, Benjamin? What's he got against Hussein? It must have been very important."

Benjamin increased his pace, clenching and unclenching his raw hands inside the pockets of the navy prison uniform.

"Hussein is on their Invasion Committee," he ventured. "That's the charming little gang that sets up the connections for their fucking takeover in the territories."

"Correct." Harari pursed his lips and cast his icy blue eyes up toward the sky, as if in gratitude, not only for what Benjamin said, but also for the way he said it.

"Who are the others?" Benjamin asked curtly. "Remind me." He was struggling to push past his rage and his sense of loss so that he could concentrate at last.

"The others are Ahmed Khalidi, Walid Toucan, Tewfik Mahmoud and Akman Salawi."

Benjamin nodded, frowning. He was quiet for several minutes. Harari waited.

"We may be getting somewhere," Benjamin said slowly.

"Perhaps I've given you something to think about," Harari said. "I'm going to leave now, but I'll be back in the morning, Benjamin. By then you may have figured out why Shemtov's been working you over."

They were standing side by side in front of the steel door when he added, "One other thing. They're charging you with treason tomorrow afternoon. We'll plead not guilty, of course." Harari held up a palm to silence Benjamin. "No more talking now, okay? I'll see you in the morning."

TWENTY-SIX

One of Walid's teenage fighters lifted his head and raised th
gleaming barrel of his Kalashnikov an inch or two above th
parapet on the roof to signal that he was in place. And ready.

Two others were covering the only back entrance of the wor
two-story building. One more manned the narrow centr
hallway, which had doors to the two ground-floor apartment
and a single flight of stairs to the second floor.

The dimly lit side street in front of the building was deserte
except for Walid and Tewfik, sitting across the road in Walid's o
black Mercedes, the vehicle of choice for anonymity and speed i
Beirut. Walid had kept it intact for a lifespan three or four time
as long as most by a gimmicky lock system and a diligent sear
for bombs.

Behind them, squatting illegally on the narrow cobble
sidewalk, was the vegetable truck that had brought the fighte
from the training camp at Shatilla, just north of the airport.

It had taken almost four hours to work out a plan to captu
Kamal Hussein from his hiding place in the safe house, summo
the boys, collect the vehicles and equipment and decide what t
do about George Zaggad. Walid had persuaded Tewfik not t
return to the Commodore Hotel to consult the representative o

he High Command. It would, he declared, be an admission of failure. The Invasion Committee didn't need Zaggad's approval. And did Tewfik realize how many men craved the prestige and security of a place on the Committee? Kamal's flight was their own filthy droppings. They'd better clean it up. Tewfik eventually agreed, but was able to persuade Walid to leave a message for Zaggad at the hotel that they'd been called away to an emergency and would meet him the next day.

No longer able to avoid the likelihood that Kamal Hussein's disappearance was somehow part of Shemtov's plan to save him from discovery, Gershom waited quietly for Walid to signal the boy on the roof. The small drab building was located on a seedy street only a few blocks from the steam shovels and bulldozers that would start up at first light, digging new foundations for the mutilated grand hotels and restaurants near the once glamorous beachfront. On the other side, the address that Rich had offered so ebulliently wasn't more than a block or two away from the Green Line, the turbulent bullet-riddled dividing line between Moslem and Christian Beirut. And it was very close to the port. The apartment building was so strategically situated that it was an ideal location for a safe house.

Well-chosen, Gershom thought, shifting his shoulders in a light shrug, trying to bypass his annoyance that Shemtov ran a safe house on his territory without his knowledge.

Walid was studying the lights in the apartments. One appeared to be unoccupied. It had been in darkness for over an hour already and no shadows moved behind its uncurtained windows. The other lower apartment was definitely occupied; two little girls with long black braids had come out onto the small railed porch, giggling and snacking from a large bowl. Since they'd been called in, all lights but one deep inside had clicked out.

Both apartments on the second floor were lit behind heavy drapes. Kamal Hussein was probably in the one on the right that had the name "Tanouri" scrawled in pencil on a bit of tape stuck over its mailbox in the lower hall; the apartment on the upper left

had "Ribak Family" neatly printed in raised, scrolled lettering o
its mailbox.

They couldn't afford to wait much longer. If Kamal was reall
planning to escape by sea, they should move in on him fas
They'd have a much better shot at grabbing him and keepin
him alive here than on the docks, where control swung brutall
between fierce, unstable gangs for whom even the anarchy
West Beirut demanded too much law and order.

Chilled by an eerily accurate physical recollection of Razan
breath in his ear, Tewfik shivered suddenly. He had to take h
father alive. As he turned to say they must begin, he was startle
by Walid's rough whisper jumping out of the dark like an agitate
rat.

"Tewfik. Listen, I was thinking it's not possible Kamal ha
been reporting on us to the Israeli sonsabitches. I can't belie
that. Not Kamal. But it has to be one of us; we are certain of tha
isn't it so? There is no other way; we have agreed, haven't we
So. He ran here. Why? You know it must be him. Kamal
selling us to our fathers' killers. May his flesh burn forever an
his descendants rot. Animals should gnaw their bones."

He cleared his throat raspingly and spat from his ope
window. Tewfik, distressed by the curse Walid laid on Razan
tempted by loyalty to her father, was on the point of suggestin
they should wait and see if there was a legitimate explanation f
Kamal's behavior, but he remembered, just in time, that if th
traitor wasn't one of his brothers, it would be him. He pressed
palm to his lips and swallowed hard enough to gurgle.

Shemtov had made it harder for him with his mysteries an
maneuvers, he thought angrily. Was it possible that Razan
father was really a traitor? Had he sold information to th
enemy? Or had Shemtov concocted it from thin air and secr
ingredients? The idea that Kamal might have betrayed them a
lay like a hefty weight on a scale in his mind, balancing th
weight of terror that he would be exposed as a traitor himsel
Gershom folded his arms tight around his chest, holding Tewf

and Eliahu deep within, as far from each other as he could manage. He had to remember who he was; he had to be certain.

The last light blinked out in the Tanouri apartment.

"We can't wait for the Ribak family to go to bed," Walid whispered. "It's almost midnight. Are you ready? Watch those porches, Tewf."

Tewfik nodded. They agreed to take Kamal alive. He had to watch more than the possible escape route by the porches.

Walid stretched his arm out of the window away from the car. He fired two shots in quick succession at the sky. While the explosive outburst still echoed and smoke clustered densely in front of the building, the aerial on the rooftop was ripped from its base and hurled over the parapet. If it had been used for sending messages abroad, this would show its operator who was in charge. A youthful, cracking voice screamed, "Fire! Fire on the roof!" as flames flickered brightly just above the parapet.

Walid and Tewfik flung themselves from the car. Crouching at its side, guns ready, they watched orange and purple flames spurt higher. The young man with the scratchy voice went on screaming, "Fire," as he disappeared from the roof, lowering himself through the trapdoor into the upstairs hall of the building.

There was no movement, no sign of life at all in one downstairs apartment. But lights blinked on in the other, a man in long yellow underpants stumbled onto the porch, looked directly at Tewfik and his weapon and ran back inside, banging the door so hard that the glass shattered, its edges catching ribbons of light from the flames above. The man wasn't Kamal Hussein; Tewfik glanced at Walid to make certain he didn't plan to shoot, as the man rushed out of the front entrance pushing two little girls in front of him. A bewildered, wailing young woman in chartreuse baby-doll pajamas trailed after them. "Not involved, nothing to do with me, not involved at all," the man yelled. Arriving at the sidewalk, he moved his gaze from Tewfik for an instant to look up at the roof. What he saw there made him shriek, high and horrible. He grabbed both his daughters and ran, his wife losing speed and a piece of chartreuse nylon as she struggled to keep up with him.

No one even came out onto the balcony from the upper apartment on the right, but the downstairs family was followed immediately by a short, flabby man, covered by hair from the waist up and by a striped blanket from the waist down. One hand holding the blanket in place, he rushed quickly out of the building, looking wildly about, ignoring the two nubile girls who followed, pulling flimsy nightgowns over parts of their bodies. One carried a broad leather belt, the only object anyone had so far attempted to save from the fire.

Tewfik was relieved that Walid's boys were following orders. They hadn't interfered with the residents at all, not even going behind them to loot. If there were any valuables in the mean little rooms inside, they would burn with the building. But, Tewfik knew, someone could still get killed. It mustn't be Kamal Hussein.

The fire had spread rapidly across the entire surface of the roof and had nowhere to go but down. It began biting into the frame behind the whitewashed brick of the upper floor, some of its long fangs reaching down to tip the windows. Walid hurled himself across the road and ran inside, shouting for the boy who'd started the fire on the roof to shoot out the lock on the Ribak apartment and then get downstairs before he was burned alive.

Tewfik, gun trained patiently on the railed porch, watched for Kamal. This was the kind of operation where Walid naturally took command, which suited Tewfik. He preferred strategy to combat, though he'd had plenty of experience in battle.

"Don't move." Walid's roar sliced through the din. "Stand still there."

No one appeared on the porch. But above the furious rushing crackle of the fire, the cheers and obscenities from the adolescent fighters and the retreating sobs and screams of the residents, Tewfik caught the sound of a high, thin wail of agony.

A body fell heavily out of the front door. Legs bent out sideways, blood spurted in a three-headed fountain from the back. Tewfik raced across the street.

It was not the body of Razan's father. It was a young, slender man, whose revolver had fallen from his hand when Walid shot him on the threshold of the burning house as he tried to escape. He must have been Kamal's companion. Or his guard. He wouldn't be able to answer any questions or sell any secrets to the highest bidder anymore.

Crouched on one knee, Tewfik looked up to watch Walid push Kamal out of the house in front of him. It could have been me, it might still happen to me, he thought, and his own insides lurched and weakened as he imagined his bones breaking. Kamal's handsome, narrow head was lowered. Under his luxurious mustache his lips were twisted in a bitter sneer.

"You also, Tewfik? Even you?"

But Walid's gun pressed between his drooping shoulders. Kamal walked on, all the way across the road and into the truck, watched contemptuously by the young fighters who had already gathered there, away from the burning heat and gritty smoke.

They all turned to watch the house burn from the top down, its inside collapsing with a deep spastic rumble, its shell irradiated by the light of the flames. Belching black smoke, the building blazed. Tewfik stopped the boys from cheering. That might bring the authorities, though it was hard to imagine that the fire and shooting hadn't already been reported. In Beirut the authorities weren't only slow. Often they didn't even exist.

While Walid gave the boys their instructions, Tewfik watched Razan's father, whose hands were bound behind his back with thick, scratchy rope. Walid ordered the boys to hold him in the house in the demolished neighborhood overlooking the sea. Kamal didn't say a word. He knew that Walid's gangsters were violence addicts. But he didn't protest at all.

Did that mean he was guilty of treason? Why had he run rather than face George Zaggad? Even if it was his name that Landau had given Zaggad, Kamal couldn't know it.

Walid nudged Tewfik back into the car.

"A good night's work." He was complacent. "What is called a surgical strike, yes?" He started the car. "Only the Lebanese babysitter dead, no other property burning, no residents hurt. Damn fine job, I say."

They'd captured their own brother and prevented his escape from Beirut but they both knew that it was up to George Zaggad to interrogate Kamal. That's why Zaggad had come to Beirut after all; he couldn't be excluded now. In the morning, they agreed, they'd have to report the capture and wait for Zaggad to decide what to do.

Walid drove the Mercedes directly to his apartment, where they would spend the few remaining hours of the night. Gershom closed his eyes and saw, instead of the torn and filthy streets, his own hands bound, his eyes masked, his mouth gagged, hunched naked in a corner in the house over the ocean, waiting for them to come and interrogate him, waiting for them to come and teach him the consequences of treason. He jerked forward, racked by a spasm deep inside his body. It sliced into him as he grasped that Kamal Hussein might be tortured and murdered so that he could live.

Though Shemtov would call this good news, Gershom could not halt the spasm invading his system. And he could not erase the vision of himself, helpless, humiliated and despised, losing his fingers and toes one by one, then his eyes, his feet, his . . . who knew where they'd cut next?

TWENTY-SEVEN

"I want you to take a message to Shemtov," Benjamin said as soon as the steel door crashed closed behind the guard who'd brought Harari to the yard to meet him.

Holding out his hand to shake Harari's, Benjamin's big frame, silhouetted against the sleek morning sky, towered over the stooping, elderly attorney.

"Sure," Harari shook hands cursorily, peering uneasily at the mottled spots on Ben's palms. "But first, tell me what you think he's up to."

"I can't do that, I'm afraid."

"Excuse me?" Haughty incredulity.

"I have an idea. If it's correct, it would be treason for me to tell it to you. I have to ask Shemtov first."

"Surely you understand that this is outrageous? I am your defense attorney; everything between us is confidential, protected by law."

"Yes, yes, I know all that. But I must see Shemtov now. It's the only way I can do it."

Isaac Harari placed his hands on his sagging hips and took a few steps away from his client. With his back curved away from Benjamin, he stood reviewing his options. It didn't take long.

"You have an idea what's going on and you won't tell me in case it's a matter of national security, right?"

"That's about it, yes."

"I'm not obliged to manage your case, you know, Benjamin."

"I understand that."

"You have acquired some of the more irritating qualities of your chief," Harari muttered. "He's always had grandiose ideas, you know."

Benjamin was silent. Head tilted back to look up at the sky, he enjoyed the sun on his battered skin. Under bushy raised brows, heavy lids dropped over his eyes. He had become inscrutable.

"Look here," Harari ordered abruptly. Benjamin fixed dark eyes upon him. "There are some principles here that are important to me. I despise the way this matter has been handled. I believe you are innocent. I believe you've been caught in a web of Shemtov's deceit, taken advantage of, jerked around like a puppet, accused of treason for the wrong reasons. I don't approve of the way your damned Service does business. Don't approve at all. Never have, really. But it's much worse these days."

Benjamin nodded. It made perfect sense that Harari had his own agenda. He'd learned that this was inevitable. Anything else would have been surprising.

"This is not the way it's supposed to be. This is not what I've worked for all my life. We had ideas about justice, liberty, the ultimate value of human life. Can you understand that?"

"Oh, yes."

"Then I'm going to defend you, dammit. Now. You'll plead innocent this afternoon, of course."

"I can't plead today."

"What?" Harari's eyes were pale astonished crystals.

"I told you, I must send a message to Shemtov."

"What is it, then?" Harari was exasperated.

"Tell him I must see him."

"He's had that message a dozen times, hasn't he, Benjamin?

From Aron Levy, every day, morning and night. It hasn't brought him here, has it?"

"No. But it will now."

"Why?"

"Because this time you'll add one thing more. Tell him that I must see him because I don't know how to plead until I talk with him."

Harari stared up at Benjamin, lips pursed, pale eyes narrowed to frigid slits.

"That'll bring him, I promise you," said Benjamin. "Shemtov will understand."

He strode across the gritty yard to bang on the steel door so the guard could take him to his cell and Harari could go and deliver his message to Dan Shemtov.

TWENTY-EIGHT

George Zaggad didn't say much at first. But even in silence, energy vibrated from his sturdy body, seated beside Tewfik Mahmoud in Walid's old black Mercedes. They were heading south down the coastal road, toward the little house above the ocean where, not long ago, Tewfik had waited for Akman to return from hanging his messenger from a cedar tree. Walid's toughs were holding Kamal Hussein prisoner in that house now, until Zaggad should decide what to do about him.

Gershom tried to keep his eyes on the road, a patched, ragged seam between the ocean and the slopes, but every so often he glanced at Zaggad. Discreetly, because he didn't want to invite his attention. Zaggad's forearm rested on the frame of the open window. Dense dark hair, silky straight along his arm, coarsely curled in the open neck of his American sport shirt, rose in the breeze and flew backward in a feathery spray. Silver-glazed black hair tumbled in a wave thick enough to mask the deep grooves in his forehead, though nothing hid the frown lines carved between his eyebrows like permanent exclamations, always there even when he was in repose, even when he smiled. Zaggad's eyes, his full, upward curving lips, even his hands clasped on his lap seemed gathered in concentrated intensity.

Zaggad's preoccupied silence aggravated Gershom's already churning anxiety, although he had plenty to think about himself. He supposed that Zaggad was preparing his questions for Kamal Hussein. As soon as he heard about Kamal's capture the night before, Zaggad had explained that it was his duty to make absolutely certain that Kamal was guilty. While his flight to the Israeli safe house didn't look good, Zaggad would make no judgment until he'd conducted a fair and thorough examination. One, he reasoned as if in a seminar, he had to ensure that justice was done, their great cause deserved no less; and two, if Kamal was innocent, he must still hunt down the traitor. They didn't want an Israeli operative to go free, did they? He had stared solemnly at each of them in the dim lounge of the Commodore, drab and deserted on a working weekday morning. They had to be certain, didn't they? Naturally, they all agreed.

Zaggad wasn't the only one with questions, it appeared. Ahmed Khalidi wasn't convinced they could be certain that the apartment was an Israeli hideout. Perhaps Kamal had something different going. Why not? The American, Rich, hadn't identified Kamal's trading partners, had he? Walid assured him that Rich had not. Ahmed Khalidi insisted that they couldn't be sure that Kamal Hussein was spying for Israel.

"You're right, of course. We can't be sure. But it does hang together." George Zaggad tapped his fingers on the pitted table as if privately checking off the evidence. "The best explanation is usually the one where all the pieces fit."

If you know all the pieces, Gershom thought. But then, who ever did? Perhaps only Shemtov, perhaps not even him.

No member of the committee had the nerve to ask and Zaggad didn't share all the pieces; he never mentioned Benjamin Landau. Only Gershom suspected that Landau had told him Kamal was an Israeli agent. That might be one of the pieces in Zaggad's mind; another was the American wire story on the front page of *An Nahar* that morning.

Tewfik and Walid had read about Landau's indictment for treason while they sipped Turkish coffee and ate dates and figs, exchanging conjectures about why Landau's attorney had asked the court to postpone hearing his client's plea. When they arrived at the Commodore, Zaggad was reading the same front-page report. Though he didn't mention it at all, Gershom felt sure that he believed that Landau had told him the truth and was being punished for it.

Gershom didn't understand how Shemtov could have organized Kamal's flight. He reasoned that it didn't really matter. It all hung together, the pieces fit, it was convincing. Then why did his nerves jump, why did his bones seem to shrink within his skin, his organs shrivel, his chest tightly swirl as if submerged under a stormy wave?

Driving out of the city, approaching the turnoff to Bourg al-Barajneh where his neglected café waited, locked and shuttered, for him to return to normal life, if that were ever possible again, Gershom used Zaggad's silence to grapple with Eliahu, who was making his presence felt more insistently than he had done in years. Not since the Israelis besieged Beirut had Eli's instincts and tendencies, no doubt genetic, surfaced so tenaciously. Eli yearned to meet Landau face-to-face, to thank him and congratulate and bless him. Eli marveled at Landau's self-sacrifice, admired his courage, anguished over his future. Eli's sympathy for Kamal Hussein was emerging also, mined dangerously with guilt.

Gershom, balancing between his twin selves, silently, carefully, ardently as if in prayer, recited the litany of his Palestinian identity.

He had not chosen to be alone with Zaggad for the ride to the house on the hill. He never took risks if he could avoid them. It had been the vast protuberances of Khalidi's swollen belly and bottom that had led them to take two cars rather than squash into one. The others followed Gershom in Akman's car. They were all going to the safe house overlooking the ocean, although they were not all going to question Kamal. Zaggad's preference that he interview him alone had been swept aside by the committee. Zaggad might be from the High Command, but this was their territory. This was their trouble. It would be very dangerous for Zaggad to be alone with an Israeli spy, if that's what Kamal really was. Which was more than likely, because if he wasn't, then one of them was a traitor, which was out of the question. Then, too, Kamal was their brother, a limb of their tree. They needed to hear it for themselves.

When Zaggad argued that their presence would inhibit Kamal and prevent him from discovering the truth, they'd compromised. One, but only one, would accompany Zaggad. The others would wait outside.

Tewfik was chosen unanimously. With his natural sensitivity and insight nourished by years of subtle deception, he thought the others were concerned for him because of his intimacy with the traitor's daughter. Perhaps they understood intuitively that Kamal's betrayal was harder for Tewfik to endure than for themselves, grieved though they were. Bewildered and bitterly enraged as they certainly were and had every right to be. Perhaps they judged that Tewfik should have the opportunity to discuss his personal affairs privately with Zaggad. Was it possible, Allah should forgive the thought, that Tewfik had a conflict of interest? In any case, once he was the companion for Zaggad's interrogation, he was the obvious chauffeur. There'd been none of the customary debate. With shrugs, murmurs, a clap on the back and averted eyes, it was agreed.

They were all subdued anyway. The implications of Kamal's betrayal were like the skins of a monstrous onion. As each layer was painfully peeled away, dozens more were exposed. This was an onion whose center was so deeply buried it might never be revealed.

The others might have had Razan in mind when the arrangements were made. Tewfik, however, had something to discuss with Zaggad before they arrived and it was not Razan, about whom he was determined to postpone all thought.

They were not far from the path leading up to the oddly intact little house when Tewfik slowed slightly and glanced at his passenger.

"A very sad business," he said with his languid charm.

"It certainly is," Zaggad agreed robustly. "Looks like Hussein has really fucked us over." Tewfik was astonished by his use of the expression, the touch of an intrusive American accent and the ripeness of a rage he had not previously observed in the distinguished professor. If this was how he felt about Kamal, what if he knew the truth?

Suppressing the question before it was fully formed, Tewfik demonstrated his judiciousness. "If I may suggest, could there perhaps be some other explanation for Kamal's presence in that house?"

"About as likely as I'm Sadat, reincarnated," Zaggad answered quickly. Tewfik was aware of Zaggad's eyes burning into the side of his face. He couldn't control the blood that surged under his skin, but he took his hand off the steering wheel and rubbed his cheek over and over, as if soothing a sudden toothache.

"Or don't you think Kamal is the traitor?"

Each word was a stab.

"I suppose... I don't really know," Tewfik said lamely. He was anxious there should be no doubt about his decent concern for Kamal, his desire for justice, his urge toward the truth. To buttress these claims, he said, "We aren't even sure it was an Israeli house, are we?"

Zaggad stared at him solemnly and Tewfik guessed he was remembering that he shared a bed with Hussein's voluptuous daughter. He shifted a little under Zaggad's hot gaze, rubbing his cheek again.

"Who can it be, if not Hussein? Tell me that," Zaggad said almost boisterously. He delivered a little jab to Tewfik's upper arm, a trainer urging endurance upon his athlete.

"Kamal Hussein is the one who disappeared the night before you arrived to investigate the leaks; there's no getting around that." But Tewfik did not expect George Zaggad to be diverted that simply.

"Let me tell you about another complication." Zaggad didn't take his eyes off Tewfik. Like a big, confident cat waiting to jump, he held out a hand toward him, then withdrew it. As if curved claws threatened to rip his skin, Tewfik cringed. He did not trust himself to speak.

"There is a man from Junieh," Zaggad went on. "Name of Raymond. Raymond Mansour. Do you know him? Ever met him?"

Tewfik shook his head. The heat began to drain from his skin but he still could not speak.

"He runs a restaurant in Georgetown these days. Just outside Washington, that is. It's a cover. He's a Company man. CIA." Tewfik felt challenged and didn't know why.

"I've not met him," he murmured.

"I saw him last night. Had dinner, while you were hunting Kamal Hussein, as a matter of fact. Raymond was returning to Washington today, so he dropped by for a visit."

Zaggad was watching him openly again. Tewfik tried to handle it by looking back at him, but returned to the road immediately. Eye contact with Zaggad was like walking naked into the lobby of the St. George's Hotel. If he insisted on staring, so be it. Tewfik concentrated on making certain there was nothing to see, no matter what reactions he had to Zaggad's provocation.

"He's been in Israel. He saw the spy chief there, Shemtov, isn't it?"

Tewfik repressed a shudder, rubbed his cheek, stared stoically at the road.

"The Israeli officer in this morning's paper? You read about it?"

"Yes." Faint, but he could speak. He thought he sounded almost normal.

"Well, Raymond already knew. He said last night that Shemtov told him Landau is a traitor."

"I see," said Tewfik slowly, thoughtfully. He pushed his back hard against the cushion and took a deep breath.

"But I don't understand, not really. What does that Landau business have to do with Kamal?"

235

"It has everything to do with him," Zaggad declared. "I am the unnamed Palestinian Landau visited in Philadelphia. I knew him there long ago, when he was in a secret satellite program."

Slowing the car to a crawl, it was Tewfik's turn to stare.

"Landau felt betrayed by his Service, so he betrayed it to me. He told me that Kamal Hussein is an Israeli informer. That's why they're charging him with treason, according to Raymond."

Tewfik's eyes widened. He sat straighter behind the wheel of the Mercedes, shaking his head in admiration.

"So you see, it all hangs together, doesn't it?"

"It looks that way," Tewfik admitted, wondering why he wasn't bathed gently in a soothing shower of relief, why his chest still choked congestively, and his nerves flinched and twitched. He supposed it was because George Zaggad was staring intently at him again.

"No," Zaggad said, "it fits together too well. If Kamal hadn't run away like that, I'd have had no doubt. No doubt at all. But now...I have to say that it looks as if someone wants me to believe that Kamal Hussein is a traitor. I've certainly been getting a lot of messages to that effect, haven't I, Tewfik?"

"We have to talk to Kamal," Tewfik murmured, drying his forehead with the back of one hand, while with the other he parked the Mercedes carefully on the wildflowers blooming brilliantly beside the coastal road.

TWENTY-NINE

"You're protecting someone else."

Benjamin hurled the accusation at Shemtov, but only after Aron Levy, who had personally ushered his rival into the exercise yard, had mournfully removed himself, demonstrating resentment by a clanging uproar from the steel door.

"Isn't it so? You're protecting someone? Yes?"

"Yes, Benjamin."

Shemtov turned away from the prison building on the assumption that Levy was using distance microphones to eavesdrop. His petulant distress at his exclusion from the Landau affair had become more of a nuisance than a petty triumph. He'd made the headlines that morning and had appeared on a popular talk show, discussing the conflicts between democracy and national security, with scathing references to certain autocrats acting independently. The P.M. had actually noticed and was annoyed. Shemtov was too busy to deal with Levy; he would retaliate later.

"You have someone on the Invasion Committee? One of the five?"

Benjamin had spent much of the night on his back on the narrow cot in his cell, trying to reconstruct the links in the chain that trapped him in Ramleh, publicly disgraced. He'd worked it out, he thought, but he needed to test it on Shemtov. And he had to know if Kate was right that his reason had been destroyed along with so much else.

"An agent on the committee?" he pressed.

"Yes, you are right." As if Benjamin was a conscientious student. "I have a man in place there."

"For how long?"

"Almost twenty years, Benjamin." Shemtov easily summoned the image of the boy he'd molded so audaciously, the boy who'd grown up into Gershom. Treasure beyond price, as he'd told Harari.

"Why did you have to protect him? Suddenly, after twenty years?"

"Don't raise your voice, if you please," Shemtov said. "And turn away from the building, Benjamin. Surely you know they may be listening."

Benjamin obeyed immediately. Shemtov thought that he looked older, more worn, more used than he would have if he'd spent his life farming and raising a family, but considerably stronger and infinitely more sane and rational than Levy's rantings and Harari's protests had implied.

"He was in danger of exposure. They caught his messenger. needed a diversion." Shemtov explained.

"You had to distract the Fatah, so you fingered Kamal Hussein?"

"Exactly. Precisely."

"It could have been any of them?"

"Well, not quite. Anyway, the important thing was that it shouldn't be my agent."

Score one hundred percent for his reconstruction so far Benjamin thought bitterly. At the mercy all his adult life of master manipulator, he'd finally learned how his mind worked

"Why me? Hadn't I had enough? More than my share?"

"That is precisely why. You were the perfect messenger Benjamin. It had to be someone who could make Zaggad believe he was bitter enough to betray his comrade. And it didn't hurt

238

that you happened to know George Zaggad." He reached into the breast pocket of his immaculate khaki shirt and pulled out a package of little white mints.

"Don't expect me to believe you sacrificed me to the French six months earlier so I'd be the perfect messenger."

"Of course not. Paris was just a useful coincidence."

"A useful coincidence! Damn you to hell!" Benjamin stamped in fury, stirring up a cloud of gritty red dust.

"Benjamin, I use whatever is available. I have to. Your arrest in Paris made our hijacking possible. Of course, I didn't want you to go to jail, but it couldn't be helped. It was a balancing act, well worthwhile. Later, I used your anger to make you credible to the Palestinians. I use whatever there is. I always have. That's what I do."

"You'll say anything, won't you?"

"Have a mint."

Benjamin knocked the mints from his hand and trampled on them.

"You lied to me about Miriam's killer. You lied about catching him and sending him back, didn't you?"

"Listen, if you please. When Uri told you to go to Philadelphia, you refused, remember? I had to find a way to make you go. I didn't think you'd refuse to betray the terrorist who killed Miriam. I was right, wasn't I?"

"Oh, you were right. Are you ever wrong?"

"Not if I can help it. Look, Benjamin—"

"You put my wife's murder and my pain to work for you. You used me like a whore."

"Yes. But I was very economical."

"What?"

Shemtov's whimsical little shrug infuriated Benjamin as much as his words.

"My lie about Miriam served two purposes. It made you go. And it made you credible. Think, if you please. It made Zaggad believe you."

"Did he believe me? Did you pull it off?"

"I hope so. I can't tell yet."

"What the hell do you mean, you can't tell?" Benjamin was sick and tired of Shemtov's pedantic precision, impatient to be done with his intrigues. "Did they take Kamal Hussein out? Is he alive or dead, man?"

"I believe he's alive. It seems he's...er...in their hands."

"Poor bastard," Benjamin said glumly. "You know what they'll do to an informer. I know you don't give a shit—he's only an Arab, it's them or us—but I feel sorry for him."

"Rather him than my man." Shemtov was decisive.

"What I've been through for an Arab collaborator and you don't even know if it's worked."

"Ben, my man on the Invasion Committee is an Israeli."

Benjamin stared at Shemtov. Suddenly he covered his face with his scaly hands, hunched forward in horror.

"It's impossible." It came out muffled. He took his hands away from his face, returned them to his navy pajama pockets, kept his head bent. "He can't be an Israeli."

"He is, Benjamin. He is one of us. I trained him myself and sent him in almost twenty years ago. He's lived among them like a trapeze artist without a net for twenty years. My God, if any man could walk on water, it would be Gershom."

"Gershom?"

" 'I have been a stranger in a foreign land.' Gershom is the name of the operation as well as his code name. Thousands of lives, Benjamin. Victories in war, triumphs in peace. If they ever find out..."

Benjamin understood. He felt more trapped than when he first stumbled into his cell without a hint of the cause of his isolation.

"You made a big display out of kidnapping me in Philadelphia and bringing me back to a media reception at the airport and shoving me into solitary and charging me publicly with treason to make sure George Zaggad believes me, isn't that so? Isn't it?" He didn't care if Aron Levy, his long-distance mikes, and all the prisoners in Ramleh heard his roar. It escaped from his lungs like howling bereavement.

"Yes, it is true," admitted Shemtov, popping into his dry mouth a stray mint that had escaped destruction in the seam of his pocket.

"And now," Benjamin said grimly, clenching his itching fists rather than lay them on his chief, "now you want me to go into court and plead guilty. To make doubly sure. Again. Right?"

"Wrong," said Shemtov. "Wrong. It doesn't matter how you plead. It's up to Gershom now. If you plead guilty and Zaggad is suspicious, it won't help. If you plead not guilty, no one will believe any different from what they believe already."

"So why did you come here then? I thought my message brought you. You wouldn't come before. Why now?"

Shemtov raised his chin and looked up at Benjamin, the lines in his forehead disappearing all the way up into his thinning hairline.

"I know your message meant you understood what I have done, Benjamin. I thought you deserved to know about Gershom. And I wanted to thank you. You've done your country a great service."

Stunned, Benjamin wasn't sure whether Shemtov was serious. He was afraid he'd lose control and punch him, so he strode quickly to the metal door. Unconcerned, Shemtov followed. "Benjamin," he said, "there is a great deal to discuss about the future, but that'll have to come later. Afterward, I'll be back to talk some more. Thank you."

Benjamin kicked the metal door as hard as he could. When it opened, he returned inside the prison without a word.

THIRTY

"I was never in the house of Israelis," Kamal Hussein insisted.

For half an hour or more, he'd been denying everything. Seated awkwardly on a small folding chair tipped against a wall, resolutely avoiding Tewfik's melancholy gaze, shaking his narrow, handsome head at George Zaggad, he hadn't hesitated. Not once.

He was deeply offended by the questions. He didn't understand at all why he was placed in such a position. How was it possible, a man of his history, descendant of mukhtars, a man always yearning for his beloved land, laboring faithfully in the struggle to return? He was falsely accused, falsely betrayed by his four brothers, among whom the real traitor was unquestionably harbored.

Kamal rejected every proposition suggested by Zaggad. He dismissed every hypothesis firmly and clearly, unhampered by the bruises around his jaw and neck or the raw cuts on his arms or the rips in his clothing, all of which were apparently inexplicable and mysterious to Walid's toughs, whom Tewfik had commanded to wait outside, some distance down the slope.

Patiently, meticulously, Zaggad took Kamal through the accusations, repeating the questions several times from different angles. No, Kamal answered him, he had certainly not been operating for Israel for twenty years, hidden like a slow-growing tumor amongst his brothers, selling them out for filthy Jewish shekels. Certainly not, the idea was laughable. No, he had not crossed the border long ago, he had not even been in Lebanon at that time, he had not crossed to blow up a thriving settlement and kill a pregnant Jewess who screamed a warning to the settlers, he was not the third fighter, one who escaped, he was not turned and returned to spy for the enemy. No, it was nothing but a fairy story, a bedtime tale for wide-eyed babies, inspiration for future guerrillas. By the way, Kamal was nearly certain that the attack was one in a long series by patriots of Fatah, in the early days when they first discovered that there was glory in martyrdom. Did any fighter come back from that attack? This could be checked, surely? It seemed to Kamal nothing but a waste of the liberation struggle's precious time, hardly worthy of denial.

As for the other accusations, they were bullshit also. He hadn't fled to an Israeli safe house, he should be forgiven for mentioning it, but only a crazy man would suggest such a thing. Why would he place himself in the deadly grip of his bitter enemy?

"Do you know what happens to collaborators?" Zaggad interrupted the free-flowing fountain of Kamal's denials. Perched on the windowsill, he rested his broad back against the shutters, open just enough to permit a haze of sunshine to embrace his head and shoulders.

Watching from where he slouched against the closed door, revolver held loosely in his right hand, Tewfik could not measure how Zaggad, shielded by his nimbus of light, was judging Kamal Hussein. But he could see his old friend quite clearly, unimpeded by the illusion of a golden halo or the mystique of Zaggad's prestige. He could see Kamal Hussein as clearly as he always had, and he knew that he was lying. Which was very strange, since Tewfik knew for a certainty that Kamal was also telling the truth. He was not the traitor whose messenger to Israel Akman had murdered.

"I am not a collaborator. Never." Hussein's voice rose and trembled for the first time. "How do you dare to name me that? I am one whose father dropped mutilated and dead in front of Israeli guns in Jenin in '65. And my brother Salim fell under their bombs at Ain-el-Hilwa. I am one whose mother moved with her babies from one poor relative to another in Jordan, until Black September, when the little king chased them out from there to Sidon, running from one shack to another tent until I lost my mother to an Uzi bullet. I am one with a wife whose nerves were long ago destroyed by wars. She had to run also; that one ran to America. I have remained. Through it all, I have remained to struggle. How do you call me a collaborator?"

He raised himself stiffly from the hard plastic chair and moved away. Tewfik thought he was going after Zaggad and raised his gun, tightening his fingers, but Kamal ignored them both, stepping down the length of the little room. His ripped clothes hung limply about him, flopping in echoing, agitated denial. Watching him, pity for his friend opening like a wound within him, Tewfik tightened his nerves as he had tightened his fingers on the trigger. He knew that pity was weighted with danger. On that sad, memory-laden route lay the menace of exposure, the end of his service to his country as well as his way of life. The end of life.

Zaggad persisted, pounding at Kamal again and again, but Kamal never wavered. He didn't seem intimidated by Zaggad, the way Tewfik was himself. He had an answer for everything. Why did he run to an Israeli safe house? Israeli? Nonsense, it was the house of the Rafik family, old friends of his. Why leave a note for his daughter, if he was only visiting? Just a note, surely he was fully entitled? How long had Kamal been an informer? Never, it was a damnable lie, Kamal insisted, drawing himself up with dignity, as if a piece of the right side of his formerly luxurious, manicured mustache were not missing. Perhaps he wasn't aware that he looked ridiculous, Tewfik thought painfully. He didn't want to watch Kamal's humiliation so closely and turned again to look at Zaggad, dragging from his depths the questions that he hoped would lever the truth from Kamal, force a crack in the obdurate stone of his denials.

It occurred to Tewfik that there were measures that a professor in an American university might have forgotten how to use, if indeed he had ever known them. Tewfik had heard many times how George Zaggad dealt with questions he was asked in America about Palestinian terrorism. He drew a sharp distinction between terror and freedom fighting and he never denounced Palestinian tactics, making the point that a people pushed beyond endurance were entitled to whatever means were available. That's what he always said, but Tewfik also knew that George Zaggad never dirtied his hands, so he never had to rinse them in water.

The fact was that the professor's questions weren't making so much as a dent in Kamal's defenses. If a street fighter took a turn, there might be some progress, and Tewfik could demonstrate good faith. He walked over to Zaggad at the window. Standing with his back to Kamal, he murmured in Zaggad's ear.

"Shall I perhaps make some inquiries?"

Zaggad nodded thoughtfully. Tewfik made a fist, tapped his own chin.

"Can I exert a little extra persuasion?"

Zaggad shrugged.

"If you must," he said uncomfortably.

Tewfik walked back to the door and leaned against it. He saw Razan's high cheekbones on her father's bruised face and used his pain to stir up a feverish anger.

"It's not Israeli, the apartment we burned? Hm? Not an Israeli hideout at all?"

Kamal ignored him, angling himself disdainfully in the opposite direction.

"You will answer Tewfik Mahmoud," Zaggad commanded.

"I told you before, many times, not Israeli at all," Kamal hissed.

"You're lying, pig. Who is the owner?"

Kamal turned and retreated to the plastic chair, folding himself stiffly onto it, wrapping his long arms around his shoulders.

"Answer." Zaggad boomed so loudly that Tewfik was afraid he'd alarm the others and bring them running from the ruins of the village that had once occupied the slope, where they waited to learn the verdict on their brother.

"The Rafik family, my friends, Lebanese, ordinary people, not at all Israelis, I have been telling you already—"

"Who was the man Walid shot running out of there?"

"Saeb Rafik. I was visiting him, there was no need to—"

"Where was his wife? His children?"

"I told you. They were gone."

"Who else was in that apartment?"

That question had not been asked before. Tewfik recognized a thread of terror that stretched across the dusty room between himself and Kamal Hussein. It was a thread he had to vibrate. He knew his life might depend upon it.

"There was someone else there, yes?"

Kamal Hussein could not disguise the tremor that shook his body.

"Who was it?"

Kamal looked wildly around the dusty room as if the answer crouched in its shadowy corners. Tewfik, frantically whipping up the temperature of his rage at his old friend's betrayal, knew that his moment to display his allegiance had arrived. He crossed the room in a leap, yelling, "I'm sick of your lies, you sewer rat," and cracked his gun across the side of Kamal's head. He tried, though he thought that it was probably pointless, to avoid his eye and he succeeded; a long, swollen, purplish bruise rose immediately above it, blood seeping in a thin line down Kamal's cheek.

"Speak up! Tell the truth for once, you pig!" Tewfik shouted.

Kamal was mopping blood from his face and didn't answer, so Tewfik had to whip him again. The connection between gun and skull made an ugly thud, and Kamal fell, crumpled on the floor.

Geoge Zaggad walked over, helped him up and propped him back on the folding chair. He sniffed loudly, rubbing his nose. A rank, fetid odor invaded the room, settling on its plaster and chipped tiles. Zaggad dismissed Tewfik with a gesture, precisely judging the appropriate instant for his re-entry.

"It will go easier for you if you tell me the truth, Kamal," he urged sympathetically. "Talk to me. If you tell me everything, I might be able to protect you."

Tewfik was disgusted by this display of treachery; he hated to be part of it, yet there was nothing at all that he could do to warn Kamal without risking his own exposure.

Breathing deeply, Kamal expelled air in shuddering sobs. He jerked his battered head in Tewfik's direction.

"That scum is my daughter's lover," he cried. "Ask him—"

But Tewfik didn't want to hear Kamal's question. Above all, he didn't want George Zaggad to hear it. With a furious roar, he smashed his gun across Kamal's right shoulder, tipping him sideways, releasing a shrill scream.

"Who else was in that house?" Zaggad demanded sternly, ignoring the banging on the door.

Kamal whimpered. A bone from his shoulder stuck out of a tear in his shirt like a stick of driftwood. He didn't look like the popular Don Juan of West Beirut, much in demand by the city's most prominent society matrons, whom he serviced regularly with special flair.

"Was there an Israeli spy in that house? Your controller, yes?" shouted Tewfik suddenly. Kamal, a pathetic huddle on the floor, was sobbing. He may not have understood the question. Tewfik slammed the butt of his Beretta on his kneecap. He heard the brittle snap that followed, but slammed into it again anyway to be certain. Kamal's scream sliced the air again and again, each scream higher than the one before until the sounds died like a bird thudding to earth after a final cry.

"Don't let him touch me again. Keep him away from me. I'm going to tell you everything, everything true, but keep him off me," Kamal begged.

Zaggad made a stop sign with his square, immaculate hand, holding it up, palm toward Tewfik, until he backed off, breathing heavily, to lean against the door.

Zaggad retreated toward the windowsill, without ever taking his eyes off his prisoner.

"It was an American house that burned," said Hussein in a soft, moist singsong, dabbing at his wounds with a rag from his torn shirt. "Not Israel, never that." An astonishing trace of pride laced through the pain in his voice. "I've done nothing terrible. I'm no murderer, like Tewfik and Walid." A sudden sob, a long gasping breath. "There was an American who burned to death in there last night, yes. They are responsible for that, not me. He was not a controller, something more like a case officer, they call it. Listen to me, you'll see I'm not the informer."

He mopped his face with his left hand. The crack in his shoulder had immobilized the right one. Every motion brought him excruciating pain; it clutched and clawed at his face as he tried to speak.

He'd stumbled, he told them, through his silk and leather business, into a European who offered morphine for diamonds. At the same time, three or four years ago, by an extraordinary coincidence, some would call it a stroke of good fortune, he was approached by certain Americans who offered to pay almost anything for morphine and more than that for information. Kamal muttered unintelligibly for a minute or two, then said that he had desired very much to save his beautiful daughter from her crazy mother and bring her, a poet and a patriot, from Detroit to join the struggle. She was his only child, after all. He rested, panting for a minute or two, before continuing. His fingertips brushed his smashed knee and he groaned, closing his eyes. They waited silently while he made the effort to talk again.

The silk and leather business had virtually collapsed in the aftermath of endless civil war and invasions from Syria in the north and Israel in the south every year or two. He needed money. He needed money to carry on his work for the struggle. Truth to tell, he needed money just to survive. And there it was, available easily if he could only work out the trading in the proper sequences. That's all he'd done, only that. His words half swallowed in sobs and gasps of pain, he insisted that it wasn't too bad, many had done far worse, taking advantage of the devastation and the disease and starvation and confusion of war, isn't it so? He'd never killed anyone in the course of his little business, what harm had he done, after all? He shrugged and tried to smile again, mopping up bubbles of blood, wincing and squeaking as he did so. Color had drained from his skin, which resembled spotty clay.

What information had he given the Americans? Oh, nothing much, nothing important, certainly nothing they couldn't get from a dozen other sources. Which Americans? He sniffed. The CIA, that's all. He'd been nothing but a stringer for them. They always said they were grooming him for the real thing, but he knew they were just using him for his supplies of dope. He was nothing important, he was really like a reporter, just like a stringer for the Associated Press. That's the kind of feeble information he provided. He pressed his battered head against the wall. With his jaw clenched and his eyes almost closed he looked as if he was about to pass out.

Unable to look any longer at Razan's father, Tewfik turned to watch George Zaggad, whose face and body had assumed a solemnity normally associated with religious ceremonies. If Zaggad had sincerely doubted Kamal's guilt when they'd talked in the car, what did he think now? Did he still think he had to search for an Israeli agent?

For an instant Tewfik judged himself to be safe. Before the thought was fully formed, he was convinced that he was on the point of exposure, and then he veered one way and then swung in the opposite direction again. Only one thing was certain at that moment. Zaggad did not look confused. Not at all.

Kamal babbled on, repeating his reassurances, saliva trailing from the corner of his smashed mouth, fingers frantically tracing the outlines of his wounds.

"Tell me for the last time," Zaggad said slowly, "why did you run away to the American safe house?"

"It was you, as I was saying." Kamal whispered as if he wanted to avoid disturbing Zaggad. "We knew why you were coming. The Israelis were catching our boys every time they infiltrated; someone was warning them. Akman caught the messenger and the message, so we were making sure there was an informer. You were coming to catch him. I was afraid it would come out that I was fooling with the Americans, I was afraid you would find me out while you were investigating. I was afraid of that."

"Yes, I imagine you would be," Zaggad murmured, but Twefik could see that he was thinking of something else.

"But it was never me, talking to Israel, you must be sure of that," Kamal said hoarsely, unable to control his spittle. "You must find the collaborator. He is still free; you must find him, whatever you do. It isn't me." He swayed sideways, pulled himself upright, swayed again.

Zaggad didn't even look at him. Moving toward the door, he told Tewfik to put the boys on guard again.

"We're driving back to Beirut," he said. "We'll discuss everything at my hotel, while I get ready. I have to leave for Washington."

Tewfik stared at him.

"I'll let you all know what I've decided when we get back to the Commodore," he said. And then, to Tewfik's horror, he added, "Akman can drive me back. You go with the others."

THIRTY-ONE

There weren't any cats stalking the grass squares between the university residences on Mt. Scopus, but that didn't fool Shemtov. He kept a sharp eye open for them. You never knew when they'd jump out from a perfectly ordinary hibiscus bush or an innocent-seeming drainpipe, claws scraping viciously, indiscriminate venom searching for an object. He didn't like surprises, so he remained alert.

Shemtov, who had experienced vicariously every plausible outcome of Zaggad's visit to Beirut and had even endured some implausible ones, urged himself to take a measured pace. He ambled along the paving stones between sunny lawns, looking at students hurrying from one building to another, late for classes.

The bells that summoned them had faded into silence and the grounds were nearly deserted by the time he permitted himself to walk about the side of the administration building to the pavilion overlooking the domed city. The smoke that signaled disturbances smeared the sky in at least six different locations. Leaning against the stone wall at the perimeter of the terrace, a narrow, well-dressed man waited, his dark chocolate eyes widening in welcome at Shemtov approached.

" 'I saw this morning morning's minion,'" mused Peter Bennington's emissary.

"'Kingdom of daylight's dauphin, dapple-dawn-drawn Falcon,'" Shemtov responded with a lilt, not bothering to hide his anticipation.

"Good afternoon, sir," said Raymond Mansour. "A pleasure. But first, may I ask who that is?"

"Who what is?" Shemtov turned a startled glance over his shoulder.

"No, no, I mean the 'daylight's dauphin,'" Raymond assured him.

"Oh, that." Shemtov pulled out a box of mints. "Hopkins was alluding to the Son of God. Dauphin, you understand." He had judged the Lebanese accurately, he saw, as Raymond's Catholic childhood briefly brushed his face, leaving a rosy glow of tranquil recollection.

"Thank you," said Raymond. "For the explanation as well as the mint."

"Shall we walk?" Shemtov suggested. "It's windy today."

"I've just flown in," Raymond said. "I was in Beirut this morning. Beirut to Athens, Athens to Israel. Very roundabout. Tedious."

"Aggravating," Shemtov agreed. "Consider how close, if you'd been able to fly direct from Beirut. However..." He'd exceeded his ration of small talk for the day. He was impatient to hear about Gershom.

"Yes. Well. I have news for you, several items. First, I had dinner last night with my old friend George Zaggad. I happened to confide that you'd mentioned to me that Landau is a traitor, you're very bitter and you're going to make an example of him." He smiled gently.

"Thank you," Shemtov murmured.

"I also thought it would be useful to tell him in complete confidence that the Company had provided some support for your capture of Landau, so you'd felt free to discuss the matter with me." Raymond waited anxiously for Shemtov's approval; his creamy mocha face softened when he received it.

"I suppose you are aware that Kamal Hussein tried to escape from Beirut and was caught by his comrades. While we were dining last night, as it happens," Raymond went on.

"Where is Hussein now?" Shemtov sounded abstracted. He wondered why Hussein had tried to flee. It fell right in with his own operation, it was quite consistent with his intentions; he couldn't have organized it better if he'd planned it. Still, it was disconcerting. Had Zaggad told Hussein that Landau had betrayed him? Shemtov doubted it.

"I don't know exactly where they're holding Hussein," Raymond said. "But I heard before I left that Zaggad was going to question him. I am sure that is happening now, somewhere in Lebanon. This interests you?"

"Very much. Thank you. What about . . . the others?"

"The others?"

"On the Invasion Committee?"

"Anyone in particular?" Raymond inquired nonchalantly.

"No, no," Shemtov smiled and patted Raymond's arm. "Just generally."

"I believe they are all with George Zaggad, I don't—"

There was a sudden scurry, a squabbling, hissing uproar somewhere off to their right. They both stopped walking to search for the cause, both with hands suddenly thrust into pockets. Two bony, emaciated cats, tails curling in the air like hanging rope, sparse dull hair upright, pointing like thorns, tumbled out of a bank of oleanders, consumed by a quarrel, ripping at each others eyes with cracked amber claws.

Disgusted, Shemtov nudged Raymond's elbow. They set off briskly in the opposite direction. There'd been cats like this in the rubble of postwar Europe, when Shemtov and Bendington had roamed the wasted cities, learning who to hunt. And how.

"They're in Beirut, too, the cats," Raymond observed. "Starving and crazy. You should see them in the public gardens, near our embassy. Many refugees camp there; they have nowhere left to go. It's filthy and crowded; even the water is unclean. Some people try to catch the cats. For food. They're also desperate, you see."

Shemtov thought he'd spent as much time with Raymond as he needed to and began the essential ornate routine of thanks and farewell. But Raymond wasn't quite finished.

"I have other news that will interest you," he interrupted. "It will also interest your old friend in his greenhouse."

"Yes?"

"You asked him about an American called Rich. I made the inquiries. I remember telling you he'd retired from the Company several years ago."

"Is he in Beirut?" Shemtov was alarmed. He'd had no time to mount an operation to hijack the chemical weapons. He hadn't considered that there was any urgency yet.

"He was in Beirut. Until yesterday. Since then he's been on a boat, under arrest, with his merchandise padlocked and guarded in the hold, going home to be used as evidence." Raymond's satisfaction rose like the fragrance of an orchard in bloom.

"What happened?" Shemtov asked eagerly.

"Your inquiry alerted us. It gave us a lead we've been searching for. I'm sure you know there's a warehouse near Washington full of poison; its a gigantic supermarket for all kinds of chemical weapons. And biological weapons." He shrugged mournfully. "Very nasty. It's supposed to be dumped when someone can find a safe place to get rid of it. The toxins are outlawed and we stopped making them fifteen years ago, but it's tough to dispose of that stuff and, well, I guess not everyone was in a big rush to do it. Our people see other nations using nerve gas and mustard gas and all kinds of new cheap poisons that can be fitted on missiles and dumped on thousands of people with one shot."

Shemtov nodded grimly. "More than a few of our neighbors have been using poison gas," he said. "It's got no odor, you can't see it, it lingers for days, it causes burning, convulsions and paralysis. Slow death. We've got enough problems in Israel without chemical weapons."

"I believe I spared you some immediate new problems when I picked up Richard Dorman. I've been looking into this for a while now, because supplies from our warehouse have been disappearing. My superiors—the official ones, of course—suspected a rogue operation to market the junk; it keeps popping up in southern Africa, for example. We thought the Fatah might be trying to get their hands on it, and then you asked your friend about Rich. So the Company sent me out here, which coincidentally satisfied Mr. Bendington's curiosity also."

"And you found Rich in Beirut with the Pentagon's poisonous chemicals?"

"I called in at our embassy, naturally, and heard he'd been hanging about, fraternizing with old buddies, trying to get some support out of them for his scheme with the Fatah. He wanted gas masks and someone to train the Palestinian kids. He was very disappointed when they wouldn't play." Raymond smiled at Shemtov. "He's a vindictive son a bitch, so he told Tewfik Mahmoud that Hussein was giving the United States information. Actually, Hussein was dealing dope more than intelligence, but he did drop a scrap in their dishes occasionally. Rich took his revenge for being treated like an outsider. He stopped their drug supply. He betrayed Kamal to Mahmoud and the others."

Shemtov stalked forward, moving the elements of the operation around in his mind as if they were counters on a backgammon board. At last, sniffing the sky as the smoke blew nearer, he turned to Bendington's man.

"I congratulate you," he said. "How did you catch him?"

"I invited him to an old boys' party at the docks," Raymond explained. "We had a ship nearby. I was able to bring in it. I've had a very busy few days, not a vacation at all. When Rich arrived at the docks, he found a lot of former Company colleagues partying on an American vessel, several embassy people, that sort of thing. We even had a little music. He came on board, got a welcome fit for a well-connected insider, had a few drinks. I had a couple of Lebanese agents, part of the old Gemayel gang, searching his hotel room while all this was going on and they turned up a sturdy steel strongbox along with his Gucci luggage. They brought the strongbox to me on the ship."

Shemtov offered Raymond one of his rare, delighted smiles. He even clapped him lightly on the back.

"Do go on," he murmured.

"We had him trapped, obviously. He was surrounded by U.S. officers of one kind or another. I made him open the strongbox. It contained samples, protectively wrapped. I promised him he'd get a shorter sentence if he cooperated. He accused us of kidnapping him. I asked a few questions, mainly to find out where he's got his supplies stored. Didn't get very far, but I'm pretty sure it's Angola. By the time he gets to a U.S. port they'll have dragged it out of him, I hope."

"The best way to thank you is with a message for Bendington," Shemtov said. "Tell him I owe him a big one. Tell him he knows how to choose a good man." He hesitated and then, with proper respect for Raymond Mansour's very professional skills, he added, "How fortunate that our interests have coincided so neatly this time. Hussein had to go. No way we could trust him anymore. It's a shame, but he was finished as soon as Landau met Zaggad in that greenhouse."

THIRTY-TWO

In West Beirut, Tewfik and his brothers sat grimly around a table against the wall in the back of the Commodore's lounge. No one wanted to be the first to speak after George Zaggad left, driving to Damascus in a rented car, his final instructions lingering like mustard gas in the air.

"Execute Hussein," he'd repeated. "There's no choice. A traitor's death by gunshot, quick and certain. Execute him."

When he'd first told the committee his verdict, no one had questioned it, certainly not Tewfik, whose return journey to Beirut had been an ordeal of terror from which he had still not recovered. By the time he arrived at the Commodore it became obvious that Zaggad's choice of an alternate driving companion was nothing but a reflection of his democratic instincts; Tewfik was still chilled and shaken by the fear that somehow Zaggad had peered under his mask. He wasn't taking any risks, sticking his neck out by asking any questions. He ached with yearning for Zaggad to fly out of the Middle East.

But old Ahmed Khalidi, who had appeared to be dozing after his long outing, had no such reservations; he had asked Zaggad how he knew that Kamal was lying. Perhaps, after all, he had been trading only with the Americans? Then the informer who put his toes in Jewish slime was still among them? He glanced around at his brothers, chuckled deep in his chins, winked broadly at Zaggad.

The professor, however, had evidently made up his mind during a silent drive back with Walid. Hussein had admitted to spying for the Americans, Zaggad explained, only to take some heat off himself, only to distract. The fact was, he had confessed to taking money from the Americans in return for information. It was inconceivable that there was more than one traitor hidden among the five respected leaders of the Invasion Committee, brave freedom fighters who had worked together so well for so long, too long for him or anyone else even to try and trace the beginning of their mutual efforts. It was hard enough to accept there was one traitor among them; two were out of the question.

Logic and reason convinced him that Kamal Hussein was the traitor. Execute him, he commanded, and departed to his books and papers and students and meetings and votes in America.

The men he left behind at the Commodore, sheltered from eavesdroppers by the high pitch of the crowds of late-evening drinkers, each had his own preoccupations. Kamal Hussein's betrayal inflicted grief on all of them, and rage for some. Guilt in Tewfik, who eased his burden only slightly by reminding himself that Kamal had betrayed his cause to the CIA. He wasn't innocent. At least he wasn't innocent.

After a very long silence, one of them, it must have been Akman, murmured that someone would have to do the job, perform the execution. For once, he displayed no zeal. No one else volunteered either. But after another long pause, Walid waved a hand to draw them closer and said quietly that it was not so simple as the professor thought. They could not simply execute Kamal.

"We must obey Zaggad," Khalidi said sleepily. "There's no alternative."

"Ultimately, of course. He cannot live. But first, he has precious jewels for us," Walid said. Kamal Hussein had Israeli contacts, he had codes and plans, he knew about other safe houses. More especially, he could identify other operatives.

"We don't just execute," Walid said. "It's wasteful. Before he dies, he will have to teach us what he knows; we shall use this information."

Tewfik, looking around at his brothers, saw that they were persuaded; they were nodding agreement. He had no choice but to do the same. Chilled again, the spasm tearing deep inside him, he did suggest that Kamal would not yield the information, not even if they told him he could trade it for mercy. He would know they had to execute him. He probably knew it already.

Walid laughed unpleasantly.

"There's no deal, no mercy, no nothing with Kamal. He'll talk, because he won't be able to bear the pain if he doesn't. That's all. We'll go back there tomorrow." He rubbed his hands against each other to loosen their joints.

Tewfik sank back in the lumpy chair.

"There is one other matter," said Akman slowly. "I'm sorry about this, Tewfik, but you'll understand, you'll see I'm right. We must question Razan. Who knows what Kamal told her? I think you must bring her with you in the morning. We'll have to deal with her also, I think."

Walid and old Khalidi were watching Tewfik as Akman spoke and must have observed the color rush to his skin, the sweat ooze on his hairline. He couldn't control it, but it would seem natural to them. He felt entitled to protest. "I'm certain she knows nothing," he said feebly.

"We'll find out. I hope you're right" said Walid stretching, bending, flexing his fingers.

Razan was asleep in their large bed when Tewfik arrived at her apartment. She lay flat on her back, arms flung wide, ankles neatly crossed. Her face was framed by rippling black hair, shining in the pale moonlight, which also lit the high arched bones of her cheeks, the satin curves of her breasts, her long, rounded thighs.

Tewfik had not seen her for two days, since her father disappeared from his well-appointed flat. It seemed longer than that; it seemed that he had done nothing but crave her hands soft on his neck and thighs, her tongue in his mouth, her legs twisted around his back; it seemed that he had yearned forever to escape his divided self, abandon his disguises and all his rituals and lose himself deep inside Razan's generous body. Seeing her sleeping, innocently open to him, he was certain that she was the best thing that had happened to him in all his life, the only person he had ever truly loved. Then, terrified, he wished to withdraw the sentence he had just pronounced upon Eliahu Golan. When he could not, he wept again, watching Razan all the time, feasting upon her with his eyes in case he had to make the enchanted vision last for the remainder of his time on earth.

On his way from the Commodore Hotel to the apartment, a long, roundabout walk with many detours to allow him time to plan, Tewfik had decided that he had no choice. To be credible he had no alternative but to do as they demanded and take Razan with him to the little house above the ocean, the house they reserved for important meetings, prisoners and murders. But when he stood in the doorway of the bedroom where they had joined so joyfully so many times, he knew he could not take her to them there.

Tewfik pulled off his shoes. Weeping, he stepped out of his jeans, flung away his shirt. He knelt on the thick white rug next to the bed. He waited until he could halt the flow of tears. Then, with the tip of his finger, he traced the line of her, from the inverted V of the hairline at the top of her forehead, down, over her nose and lips and neck, down between her breasts and over the tight skin of her stomach and lower, down to her center and along the line where her thighs touched. And back again. And saw her smile lazily, with her eyes still closed. One hand lifted to caress his cheek. When she opened her eyes, still dazed with sleep, gleaming in the moonlight, he knew he could not lie with her and make love, as he had planned. Every minute mattered.

"Razan," he kissed her mouth, her eyes, the tip of her nose, her cheeks, her neck, her mouth again. "Listen, it's urgent."

He pulled her upright. He sat beside her on the edge of the bed and told her that her father was a prisoner in the little house above the water on the road to Sidon; he was accused of treason, Tewfik told her; he'd been sentenced to death. Before he got that far, the back of her hand was jammed hard against her own mouth to stop herself from screaming. The other hand had caught the sheet and clutched it over her nakedness. Even in the pale light from the moon, he could see that her eyes were wider, darker than ever, shadowed by painful denial, furious grief. She shook her head, back and forth, biting her lower lip while he talked.

It was Zaggad's verdict, Tewfik told her. They had no choice. But Zaggad had left the city already, the others intended to question Kamal before they . . . well. Before. She cried out then, and shook uncontrollably in the effort to contain her sobs. She understood what he was not telling her; she, a leader of the struggle, knew what happened to collaborators. Tewfik held her close, trying to comfort and calm her before continuing.

"My father is no traitor," she snapped, jerking away from him. "It's a lie; someone is setting him up."

"He's confessed, Razan," Tewfik said sorrowfully.

"I don't believe it. It's not possible. He would never go near an Israeli. If he confessed, he must have been—"

"No, no one has touched him," Tewfik said, quite forgetting how he had beaten Kamal with his own gun. He was thinking only that the torture had not yet begun and that when it did, Razan must be far away.

"He confessed to selling information to the Americans, Razan. That's where he got all the money he's been spending. And giving you. Selling dope, too."

She retreated farther from him; she cringed against the brass

261

rails behind the bed, as if she had suspected it, as if she feared that these were betrayals she could not deny.

"The Israelis have been getting information from someone. It must be Kamal." Tewfik tried to smooth her hair, but she brushed his hand away impatiently.

"Never," she said. "He's been set up. He'd never deal with the Israelis. Someone else is spying for Israel. It's not him. It's one of the others."

Tewfik didn't flinch. He stared at her resolutely.

"Whatever you think, Zaggad is certain. The brothers are certain. Listen, I have to get you out of here."

Razan lifted her head and looked at him as if he was deranged.

"I can't leave now. Why should I leave?"

He told her they wanted to question her. He explained that they suspected she might have information about her father's activities. About his supplies, his sources, his diamonds, dope and secrets. About his money. They wanted to interrogate Razan and they'd demanded that he take her with him to the house. He couldn't answer for what might happen there. It would be very dangerous. He wouldn't be able to protect her. There were too many, they were too angry, no one knew what would happen. He had a plan.

Razan listened quietly. With a magical talent he had seen only hints of in the past, she seemed to be detaching herself from him, moving farther and farther away, though she was in fact motionless. Even her eyes, which had been fixed on Tewfik, seemed to drift abstractedly away into the distance.

He explained his plan for her escape. She must drive to Damascus. At once. She would get on a plane, the first plane out, to anywhere, anywhere on earth that wasn't Lebanon. And then she would go to her mother in Detroit. Or wait for him somewhere. As soon as he could, he would come for her. But she must leave at once, before it occurred to the brothers that they couldn't trust him to deliver her. She must leave immediately.

Razan didn't answer for several minutes.

"Razan," he said urgently, but she raised two fingers of her right hand in a tiny gesture. He waited. He was surprised when she said, "All right," quite briskly. He had been braced for a long, spirited fight.

She went to the cabinet where she kept her clothes and pulled out underwear, trousers, shirt. "My makeup," she muttered and found it in the purse in her big shoulder bag. She gathered it all and went into the bathroom.

"I'll be as quick as I can," she called out, as she slammed the door. He heard the water running in the shower stall and started to get dressed himself. He straightened the bed and went out to the kitchen to find something cold to drink. It occurred to him to pack some fruit for the long ride; he threw oranges and figs and bananas into a basket, washed apples, tossed in a can of tomato juice for Razan. He heard the water still running in the shower and walked back to bang on the door to tell her to hurry.

He couldn't bang on the door because it was open. Steam billowed from the bathroom, where hot water poured relentlessly onto the tiles in the empty stall. The steam didn't linger in the bedroom, however, because the door to the little railed porch was wide open. The fresh night breeze blew right in.

Tewfik called her name a couple of times as he looked again into the bathroom and crossed to the porch, but even as he shouted for Razan he knew it was pointless. She'd often said that one of the best things about the apartment was that you could escape from the porch if you had to get out of there quickly. Tewfik stood at the second-story railing. On the porch beneath it, a clay pot with a monstrous cactus had fallen onto its side when Razan dropped onto it. In the moonlight, he saw specks of soil scattered across the porch. It was not a long drop from there to the street below, where Razan's little red convertible was usually parked.

Worrying how to chase her without a car, Tewfik thought of Kamal's Porsche, which probably still sat in the place of honor in the alley behind his apartment building. Tewfik was fairly certain that he knew where she'd gone. If the Porsche was still there, he could catch her, he thought, rummaging through a bag of tools, shoving them in his pockets as he tore out of the building, his Kalashnikov over his shoulder. Running to Kamal's apartment, he stumbled and paused to adjust his knife against his calf.

He was going to catch her and get her on a plane out of the Middle East, whatever she thought.

After that, he'd decide what he had to do before joining her, faraway.

It didn't take long to find the Porsche in the alley and get it started. He drove as fast as he dared, grateful for the moonlight, focused entirely on catching Razan before someone else did. He put everything else out of his mind, concentrating on the almost deserted road. He saw lights winking from ships out at sea; he noticed boats bobbing near the shoreline and wondered if that would make a safer escape than a plane out of Damascus. Once a sleek Italian limo, doing well over a hundred, overtook him on the narrow road, rocketing ahead out of sight, and three times cars sped by toward Beirut.

Razan must have driven like a Phalangist commander escaping from the Islamic Jihad, because Tewfik didn't see the little red convertible on the road ahead of him all the twenty-odd miles along the coastal road. Unless he'd guessed wrong and she had gone somewhere else. But Tewfik didn't think so; he knew Razan.

He watched for Razan's long black hair tumbling out behind her shoulders in the convertible, but he didn't see it. He didn't see the little red Mercedes until he was almost on top of it, parked at a crazy angle near the bottom of the path leading to the house the Fatah had commandeered years earlier when the once prosperous Druze neighborhood with its old stone villas was bombed too badly to save.

He parked just beyond Razan's car. A few yards ahead he saw the truck that Walid's tough young men had used. No other vehicles, he noticed gratefully, and started up the slope, trying to remember how many boys Walid had used to hold Kamal Hussein prisoner.

Tewfik climbed as fast as he could without making a noise. Listening intently, he heard rustles, a crunchy sound he couldn't identify and then the sound of voices. A pace or two higher he caught the words "...visiting her father." He couldn't hear anything but murmurs after that, until he reached the top of the slope not far behind two boys who were sitting there, apparently on guard.

"It's no problem. She can't do anything. We're surrounding the place," one freedom fighter assured the other.

He could take them out quite easily, Tewfik knew. The other two or three must be behind the house. But if he killed them, he'd become an instant suspect. He might blow everything.

So, with his gun pointing steadily at their heads, he snapped, "Stand up and turn around with your hands on your heads."

They recognized Tewfik at once as the brother who'd interrogated the prisoner with the great Zaggad hours earlier.

They scrambled up, awkward, shamefaced. Tewfik blasted them for their negligence. He could, he pointed out, even have been an Israeli coming up behind them; he could have killed them; what kind of guards were they? They cringed, mumbled, apologized.

And where was the prisoner's daughter? Tewfik demanded. Yes, yes, it was all right to permit her to talk to him. He had followed her to listen to the conversation, see what he could learn. And where were their comrades? Three others, yes?

No, it turned out, there were two others, and they were sleeping in the shelter of what had once been the sitting room of an old family house. They were taking it in turns to guard in twos, quite safe, because there was absolutely no one anywhere around on this destroyed old hill. As for the woman, they'd let her into the room where they held her father because she'd persuaded them she had permission to visit. They knew who she was, of course, a courageous woman; they'd heard her speak at their camp. And gorgeous, too. One of them made motions with his hands to mimic voluptuous shapes and winked obscenely.

"Wait here," Tewfik instructed them firmly. "Don't disturb the others. I'm going to observe what happens. I want to hear what he tells her." He walked ahead a few steps. "Remain on guard," he commanded sternly.

He walked very quickly around to the back of the house. His rubber-soled shoes made no noise on the sandy ground. He didn't want to alarm Razan, but if she thought she could help Kamal escape, she was wrong. He couldn't permit it; there was far too much at stake. If he allowed himself to dwell on everything that depended upon him now, he would be too late to save anything at all. He stepped up to the shutters of the front room and listened.

He heard muffled sobs; they were not Razan's. There was no other sound for a long time. He was afraid the boys would come. He thought he would have to go in and get her. Then he heard her.

"Is it true you traded with the Americans?" she asked evenly. "Look at me. You must answer me. I have to know."

Tewfik couldn't hear Kamal, but perhaps he answered, because Razan breathed out in a long groan.

"Is it also true that you spied for Israel?"

"No. No. A thousand times no. It's a lie."

"They are convinced you did it," she told him.

"Razan, I swear by the Koran, you must believe me, I swear, Allah should strike me dead if I lie, I did not spy for the vermin."

"I believe you," she said. "But they don't. They're going to torture you to make you talk."

He wailed, a high, haunted cry torn from deep within his battered body. Tewfik edged as close as he could to the window and peered between the cracks in the shutters. He couldn't see anything at first. Then, eyes narrowed, he focused on a single crack between two slats. He couldn't see Kamal at all. But opposite Tewfik, her back to the window that overlooked the Mediterranean, Razan seemed to be gazing straight at him.

She wasn't, of course. There was no way she could see him through the chinks in the shutters, with the lamp in the room. But he could see her, or rather, he could twist himself against the warped and splintered wood of the shutter, peer through a space between two slats and just manage a glimpse of the side of her face. It looked steady, reflective and still. Her lips were closed. While he watched, her gaze shifted slightly; she seemed to focus sorrowfully, unwavering and unblinking on a single spot on the floor. Tewfik assumed it was her father.

Was she imagining what the brothers would do to him? Tewfik worried. Was she staring at him, thinking of the slow ripping away of the flesh of his fingers and his toes, his ears, his testicles, his eyes? Razan knew the formula for the interrogation of traitors. Did she see the stumps of bleeding tissue raw on his body as it faltered, withered and finally failed? Or was she trying to work out how to get him away from there with his broken bones and desperate pain?

"How many boys are guarding you here?" she asked.

The only response was a whimper.

Razan moved forward a step or two. Tewfik could see her face more clearly, but nothing below her neck showed through the chink. He couldn't even see her hands.

"You must tell me, Papa. Talk to me. How many? The two I found when I came and how many more? Tell me." Her voice rose sharply. She jerked back suddenly toward the shuttered window behind her, apparently in response to a rasping groan from her father on the floor in front of her.

Tewfik, terrified that the loud exchange would alert the sleeping guards, watched as her lips ground tight against each other. Her lovely face squeezed inward toward its center. Her eyes narrowed. Tewfik heard rustling, a sound like a cat stalking some small creature in high weed grass. Razan must have heard it too, because she swiveled around to the window behind her.

Then she raised her right hand with a gun in it. This was the first time the gun had been high enough for Tewfik to see; he had no idea where it came from.

Alarmed, he left his watching post and ran around the little building. But he was late, far too late. The boys behind her, frightened by Kamal's high hoarse cry of pain, had rushed to the window to check up on their prisoner. When they saw Razan's gun, they fired, a booming rattle in synchrony from two submachine guns, to prevent her from shooting first, whether at them or at the prisoner they were charged with guarding.

Tewfik arrived just as the other fighters, wakened by the scream and frightened by the shooting, raced across from the remains of the house where they'd been sleeping.

"Wait," Tewfik yelled, as he rounded the house, shooting his own Kalashnikov into the air. "I order you to wait. Hold your fire."

He saw torn strips of shutters and chunks of plaster falling into the room, spattering Razan's head and shoulders.

"Wait, Razan," he shouted. "Do not shoot."

But nothing would stop her now. She'd turned full on to face the teenage guerrillas after the first round of fire. She saw them joined by their comrades, she saw the long-barreled submachine guns, she heard her father sob on the floor beyond and she raised her gun. She took aim, just the way she had been taught.

And a second storm of bullets ripped into the room.

Screaming "Papa," Razan fell below Tewfik's range of vision.

His own barrage of bullets, falling onto barren, rubble-strewn earth on the desolate hilltop, was nothing but a wasted, lifeless echo.

THIRTY-THREE

Benjamin Landau refused to meet his wife in the prison interview room, so they brought Kate out to join him in the yard.

He was standing near the chain-link fence at the end, half-turned away from the building, hands in the pockets of his navy prison pajamas. He pulled one hand out to wave when he saw her standing near the steel door. Kate walked quickly across the reddish sand, noticing, as she drew closer, that his hand was almost healed. The raw, scaly blisters had disappeared, along with the rapid blinking and the jerking shoulders. He kept his head down and his voice low when he greeted her, though that didn't surprise her as much as the quick kiss he bent to drop on her cheek.

Benjamin had refused to see her, ever since she'd first consulted Harari. She'd had no choice but to follow developments through Harari's reports and had seen Benjamin only from a distance, when he'd been charged in open court. He was more stable generally, though, Harari had told her, his lips pursed disapprovingly. The great man had explained awkwardly that her husband didn't want her to visit for a few days. He needed to be alone to think things through. Kate had tried to be patient. But after more than a week, she called Isaac Harari and told him that her children needed her. She didn't tell him that she couldn't bear the anxiety she heard in their voices when she talked to them on the phone at her parents' house. She didn't mention the pain they didn't know how to express in their brief letters. She just insisted that she had to see her husband and make some decisions about the children.

Harari had reported back to her after a few hours. Benjamin was willing to see her. He was ready to talk.

Now that she was with him, Kate didn't quite know what to say. The bewildered rage that still gripped her didn't seem to match his frame of mind, which she couldn't quite measure. As it turned out, however, she didn't need to make conversation with her imprisoned husband.

"Kate," he began, "I'm glad you came. Thank you."

She started explaining why she couldn't wait any longer to see him, until, glancing at his tolerant expression, she realized that she'd missed the point. He'd been referring to her coming to Israel when he was arrested. She bit her lip. They'd often talked at cross-purposes, she remembered; she'd always thought it was part of being an American married to an Israeli.

"You've been such a help, getting to Harari, persuading him to help me, all that. And I know Avner gave you a terrible time. Harari told me. I'm sorry. I wish I could have been better for you, Kate."

"Why didn't you plead not guilty the other day in court, Ben?"

"I hadn't decided then," he said.

"What do you mean? Decided what?"

He didn't seem to hear, so she asked sharply, "Is Isaac Harari going to defend you, Benjamin?"

"He's taken my case, yes."

"I don't understand. What's happening?" Her voice faded as she watched him. Something in his expression terrified her. He saw it, and reached his arm around her shoulders, nudging her into a slow stroll.

"Kate, go home to America. To th·· children. I'm going to be here for a long time. Too long for you to have to wait."

"What are you talking about?"

"I'm going to plead guilty, Katie."

"What?" she shouted. "Why? You know you aren't guilty. What's wrong with you?"

"Shh," he said gently. "They may be listening." He jerked his head toward the prison windows. "They have mikes in there. I don't want them to hear us."

Kate jerked away from his side to look at him suspiciously, but he didn't seem crazy. He seemed quite rational.

"It's very complicated," he said softly, pulling her back close to him, bending his big, shaggy head to rest his cheek against her brown cap of hair for a second or two. "I can't really explain all of it. But listen, Kate. A long time ago, long before I knew you, years and years before the children came along, I made a promise to my memory of Miriam and our life together. This is part of that. I have to go on with that."

He nuzzled her hair again.

"That's all, dear. I wish it wasn't so rough for you. And for Ruben and Roni. But it's who I am. I'm going to plead guilty and stay in prison. For a time. I don't know how long, of course."

"Why?"

"Kate, you don't know what I told George Zaggad at Longwood Gardens, do you?"

"No. But I know damn well you didn't betray an Israeli agent to him."

"Thank you. You'll teach the children that for their sakes as well as ours, won't you, Katie?"

"Why must you do this?" She stamped her foot, crying, banging her hands against his chest.

"It's part of my job," he said. "And it's what I believe."

For a second, Kate thought she understood.

"But your Service betrayed you," she cried. "Your goddamned chief sold you down the river. He doesn't care about you or anyone else. With him the grand design comes first, second, third and every other place."

"I know that," said Benjamin. "And I don't like it. I don't even agree with it. But it's not the Service, you see. I want the same things he does, the same result. I was born to that and I'm stuck with it."

"And me?" Kate wept. "And your children? We all have to be stuck with it, too?"

"Go on with your lives without me, Kate," he said. "I told you long ago in Philadelphia that I'm not a family man. I can't be. This time listen to me. Go back to America and the children and go on with your lives. I'm here for a reason that's good enough for me. It wasn't easy to come to this, but there it is. *Ein breira*. No alternative."

After she'd gone, raging, and returned, to kiss and hug him and whisper painfully that she'd write, she'd visit in a few months, and was gone again—after he was certain she was gone, Benjamin Landau paced the yard awhile longer, while the clear autumn light drained from the sky and gathered at the horizon, spectacular as an explosion. Shemtov hadn't been prepared to lay out his proposals for the future yet; they couldn't make any plans until the upheaval in Beirut following the killing of Kamal Hussein and his daughter faded entirely away.

Shemtov had reason to believe that Gershom remained entrenched in the heart of the Palestinian struggle, his position enhanced by recent events. When—if—they could be certain that he continued securely in place, when the new methods of intelligence transmission were operating safely, then Shemtov would be willing to discuss Ben's future.

Until that day, Benjamin would be Israel's most famous and most visible traitor. He would go to trial and be sentenced, certainly. Where he would live in Israel, what features might be surgically altered, what identity he would take, what work he would do—these were all questions for the distant future. Who knew, really, how long Gershom would go on? Or how long he would be permitted to live the life he had so carefully constructed and grafted onto himself?

Before the last light faded entirely, Benjamin reached into his breast pocket and drew out a postcard. It had been delivered personally by Shemtov, in care of whose private post office box it had been addressed.

It was an Italian postcard, mailed from Rome. On one side was a reproduction of Michaelangelo's *David*. On the other, a message.

"Never die," it said. "Deep regards from Gershom."

AUTHOR'S NOTE

I am grateful to my friend and agent, Ray Lincoln, for her constant enthusiasm and support; to Yechiel Ben Yishai, Janet and Shmuel Levy, Sivia Elgart, Barbara Karafin and Barbara Lorry, for valuable comments and help; to a senior officer of the Israel Defence Forces, who prefers not to be identified, and to two Lebanese informants with the same preference. My special thanks to Gilla, Charles and David for their encouragement, advice and caring. And to Joe, for everything.

This is a work of fiction. The characters and incidents are the product of the author's imagination and any resemblance to any persons, living or dead, or to actual events is simply a reflection of the intricacy and deception in human affairs.